# <EDIT>

ISBN (paperback): 978-0-578-29243-4
ISBN (eBook): 978-0-578-29249-6

# <EDIT>

A NOVEL

L.C. PENN

# FEBRUARY 9, 2025

Good Evening Doc.

I can call him *Doc*, right?

Shit, that's what I'm calling him. Made up my mind right this moment as I'm scratching my ass, thinking of the next thing to type, tapping my forehead with this fork I was using to eat day-old Thai. What can I tell ya, it makes sense. 'Cause if you think about it, they're doing me right, making me whole again, fixing me like they fix so many others, the way a surgeon takes away a tumor, the way a dentist fills a cavity, the way an ophthalmologist operates back vision to look at things.

< 1 >

And these guys? Well, they're gonna help me see.

It's evening now, and real late. My wife is asleep. We were watching some crap on Netflix or what have you and she sorta passed out on the couch an hour or so ago. I walked her half-asleep ass back to our bed and she hung onto me like an old mannequin the entire way.

The lights are still on in the kitchen. They buzz so damn loud. In New York, it's a luxury to live in a place without noise. Every building is old enough to talk, and boy, do they have stuff to say. I swear, I sometimes wake up happy my nose isn't plastered in the fiber-glass that makes up my ceiling. The pipes clog once a week, and some nights we order Happy Dragon 'cause we're afraid the fuckin' stove is gonna blow. That's our favorite Chinese restaurant. I don't know where you are, but if you're in the area you should try it. It's a hundred years old and still kickin'. Something must've worked.

Also, I can't sleep. It's been months, but I'm so festered with guilt, and all I could do is wait for her to fall asleep before walking out to Gilligan's or Southies or Jackie's or some other crappy pub kept lit with flickering neon

< 2 >

tubes and dangling light bulbs and filled with everybody on the block with problems. I've even gotten to know some of these guys, but they aren't much help.

"Not your fault," they'd tell me. "You're a good guy for caring." Or my favorite, "look, you're lucky to have one another." Deep down inside, they probably think I'm a shit.

Okay, first question from this website, looks like I'm supposed to introduce myself.

*I'm Jay.*

Jason Valentino by birth, but everyone calls me Jay.

I live in upper Manhattan, just north of Central Park. Grew up just a few blocks from here, and if my parents were still alive, they'd be within walking distance. God rest their souls, it was their inheritance that paid the principal for the place after all, so who knows where I'd be if they didn't die. It costs a hit job to buy a place in Manhattan nowadays, probably one on the fuckin' mayor to afford the down payment.

Anyways, to pay the mortgage, I run my own freight business dealing in ethnic produce. I can tell ya I'm doing well. Started small with a single storage area and now I've got warehouses up and down Jersey City, Bronx, Queens, parts of Chinatown, Newark, you name it. No need to worry about me financing or nothing. If you know of anyone in the food business here in New York who's looking to start a Chinese restaurant or pho place or whatever, check out my website, www.jaybigsimports.com. Rated A+ by the Better Business Bureau for over five years. We've got everything, promise.

Okay, I guess this is the part I gotta start talking, and it's 11:30 already.

Oh hell, I don't sleep anyways.

*   *   *

So what am I looking for? What kind of question is that? I don't know what I'm looking for, that's what these schmucks are for, right?

Oh, wait a second, it looks like there's more. I'm to explain what events or circumstances in my life drew me to this thing.

Well okay, I will sum it up with the shittiest word in the English language I know. Love. I don't know how else to put it, but it's because I love my wife. I love our marriage. I love the idea of spending the rest of my life with her and I'll do anything, go anywhere, to make it happen.

Love. The most undefined, illogical concept in the human dictionary. With any other word like that, we'd usually ignore, but for this one, we'd challenge reality.

I met her in grad school, the summer between her junior and senior year of undergrad. I was struggling to finish my master's degree in mechanical engineering and working double shifts as an inventory specialist at the campus library, and she worked as a barista in the coffee shop a block down.

The story is pretty straightforward. You know, guy meets girl he likes, keeps tabs on when she works (morning shifts from Monday to Wednesdays and evenings on Fridays), walks in to say hi on the regular, you know, nudge his way into her universe bit by bit, girl not ready 'cause of a bad breakup from three or four years prior. I'm not gonna bore you with a romance novel.

Eight years ago, we started dating. Then three years ago we married. Every year a new journey, every year a new hurdle. Every year I'd find a new way to make her fuck me dead on

Valentine's day, every year I'd find a new way to make her fuck me up for the other three six-ty-four. I exaggerate, but I'll be honest, I haven't always been there in the marriage. Work was busy, business grew. For many years she made more than me working in accounting so I could only don a mask of masculinity for the first two years. Jealousies over old friends, resentment over not moving out of New York like I promised her, or her not convincing her father to like me and stuff like that. That guy still thinks I'm the reason his daughter couldn't be everything he wanted her to be; an astro-naut or a senator or a movie star, though I am sure she's content as a fucking accountant head at *Sazera Inc,* some high-end boutique clothing store in the Garment District.

And things were just starting to look up. This last year, we didn't have one major fight. Sure, little skirmishes, but overall everything was going full steam. A trip to Marco Island, an overdue honeymoon that I had finally saved up for, an outing with the father in law, where although we didn't patch anything up it made her happy all the least. She got a new job, found community with her new colleagues, and though I know, somewhere deep down, she still wants to get out of the city one day, she hasn't bitched about it since our second anniversary.

Look, I know by how I complain it doesn't sound like I love her much, but sometimes the most obvious things are the hardest to recall. Memory is like looking in a mirror, my ma once told me. A pimple just a millimeter in diameter could hide a thing of unimaginable beauty.

And boy oh boy, are we talking about a thing of beauty.

I could've photoshopped her face onto any magazine and people would've sworn they saw her in some musical or movie or Estée Lauder catalog. My goodness, what a goddess, I'm looking at a photo of her right now. It's from last Christmas, and she's wearing that red sweater that fits her figure so well, sitting on the rooftop overlooking the city, unaware that I had just snapped her into eternity with a tap of my finger. Once again, I find myself subconsciously touching every part of her face; running my index finger across her perfectly trimmed dark brows that look like paint strokes above her eyes, simmering jade crystal balls that hypnotizes me every time, my future and present and past on full display before me. I'd rub her hair, her short boyish bob that hangs just behind the bottom crevasse of her skull, colored in glimmering dark brown, her delicious bangs just flying over the top of her left brow.

Shucks, I'm losing my steady just a bit, so I'm gonna move on.

My mother had always told me that true love gives you super vision, eyes like x-rays that can peer into the person beyond the canvas of mascara and perfume and eyebrow graphite. If the body ceases to matter, then all that's left is two people unclothed without skin or flesh, free to collide and form something new.

My mother always tried to be deep like that; she was a writer after all. A failed one, but that didn't stop her, as she bored me pretentiously every waking hour of my adolescence with every new chick I met with another lecture on love or life or some hippie shit like that.

God. What I'd give for one more, just one more.

■    ■    ■

I remember it like what I had for lunch today.

Snowy night of January 15, our day of infamy.

< 8 >

That evening, I was working from home. I do that from time to time, the warehouse is disgusting. She had taken the all wheeler to work earlier that day 'cause it flies through the January snow like it were concrete. She was visiting some other store in Long Island, and I remember asking her to pick up some *Fu Run* from Flushings. They always have that stir-fried lobster dish I love so much, and I guess I wanted a treat.

A treat.

Just a fucking treat was all I wanted for three days of non-stop paperwork and staring at my monitor working through this new cloud software I hate and endless calls and client dick-sucking and missed shipments and audits with the Feds. All I fucking wanted.

It was seven p.m. but she said she'd be back by six. She'd told me she'd try to leave by three 'cause it takes an hour just to get past the fucking Queensboro during rush, especially coming from Flushing. I remember looking out and seeing over the streets below just a blanket of white, not on the ground, but in all directions. It must've been a blizzard and I figured traffic would've been moving worse than the clusterfuck that was usual.

Eight p.m. A gas station had exploded in Murray Hill. I saw it on my phone just as I was getting out of the shower. That story was developing.

Nine p.m. She still wasn't home. I've called her once at six, once at seven, once at eight, and by now it was beyond counting. Just as many times it took for her, or someone, to pick up.

"Hi, it's Judy, leave a message."

Such a sweet voice. I might have been conditioned to hate it right then. It wasn't like her to ignore my calls or texts.

Ten p.m. came, and I had swallowed half a fifth of Mezcal to think straight. I hate to admit it, but it's my go-to in such times. You wouldn't judge me if you'd seen everything it got me through.

Though maybe by then I had a little too much. I had already called her probably two dozen times in an hour. My voicemails were going through stages of their own; anxiety, panic, flipping-out panic, pissed-off panic, worried panic, crying-like-a-bitch panic, drunk blabbering. I listen to some of those voicemails now, you know, and I'm unrecognizable, saying shit that makes me wanna choke myself to death standing.

I wonder if she ever got to hear those. Maybe she'd be touched that I cared.

I was ready to get in the other car to look for her, but the snow was relentless, and it was a fucking smart car. It'd tip passing the first snowplow. I was checking the incident report online, but nothing was updating. The internet must've gone out around the block.

So fuck me.

You ever been caught in such a situation? Where suddenly you're out of control, and every horrible thought that never fully materializes into coherency becomes one feeling in your gut, and you want to act but are afraid of everything you'd do? When only one thing suddenly matters and everything else, the living room, the world, existence becomes a blur in the background that gets in the way? I don't even know if I was worried, or concerned. It was something I could never pair a word to.

Well, maybe drunk.

Eleven p.m. rolled around and by now I was passed out. Fucking useless. I know I could've, should've, done more. Called a cab or the police or a friend or one of her friends or coworkers or anyone, and had I pieced myself together rather than drown the agony away with booze, maybe I would've.

It was then that I got the call.

I woke up in delirium, head throbbing, inhibitions still on autopilot. But I may have only felt the booze for a minute or two, as by the time I hit "answer," all my faculties were running full shift.

A nun. It was a fucking nun. Sister who-gives-a-fuck was calling me. Not a doctor, not the police, not a nurse, a fucking nun. See, to my knowledge at the time, if it's anyone from the clergy calling you about a relative, it was worse than bad news. I nearly broke down bawling like a little bitch had she not told me to shut the fuck up and listen. Exact words. Probably, 'cause I was bawling. Like a little bitch.

"Sir, listen to me, sir please, sir, shut the fuck up and listen! Your wife is alive."

What kind of nun talks like that?

. . .

It was probably half past midnight, and I was sitting in the waiting room of the emergency department of some Catholic hospital network, St. Mary's near Murray Hill, still unable to understand the situation before me. I was sitting and waiting while my senses refused to believe I was really there, or that any of what I was just told was true.

Remember what I was just telling you about that gas station explosion? Apparently, it happened between 6:00 and 7:00 that evening. From the looks of it, everything was destroyed; the convenience store, the pumps, all the cars parked in it, including ours. Five were dead, three were critically injured, and Judy was one of the lucky trio.

She was taken to the nearest medical center, and there a nun called me; common for Catholic hospitals I was told. The Sister had told me she was in critical condition, and that she was only conscious enough to mutter my name. I guess it didn't take a lot of police work to find me. She keeps everything in her purse; ruffled bank papers, receipts, bills, credit cards, IDs, and, relevant to this case, both of our contact numbers in case she loses it.

What I did next was a blur; barely putting on shoes as I barreled out of the condo, running up every block looking for a working cab. Took me fifteen minutes to find one, couldn't even figure out where the sidewalk ended and the road started.

So there I was. Sitting and waiting with a

half dozen or so of other schmucks with their own emergencies in life. I was told she'd be in surgery, that she was in critical condition, and that she'd suffered first-degree burns from her torso to her face.

"To her face?" I remember blurting out loud.

It wasn't my proudest moment. The young Asian surgeon looked up at me in disgust. Like my wife was fine, lucky as a cricket to be alive, three and a half footsteps away from being gone forever, and all I seemed concerned about was how her face looked.

And mind you, I was counting my lucky crickets that she was okay.

But shit, I don't know why it mattered right then. I mean, I knew that no matter what, I'd love her to pieces, but my mind was racing. What if she came out looking like somebody else? How would I react? What if she looked like a man? An animal?

But again, mind you, I was fucking glad as shit that she was okay. Although it's creepy that I felt the need to repeat this twice.

She needed some replacing done to the burnt tissue around her cheeks. The surgery would go until early morning. I wondered how her face would look if everyone working to fix it were sleep-deprived.

So I sat in the waiting room, trying to read a copy of the police report that included the details of what happened, an interview with Judy before going under, miscellaneous incoherent scribbles above lines above lines above lines against a pink slip of paper. The details were brief; she was walking into the store for a bottle of water. Then a blast from her right, and that was it.

I passed out between two and three, four and four-thirty, probably another minute at five, then probably five-thirty and on. The television was playing old *Dancing with the Stars* re-runs, and the waiting room felt like the dead waiting for their train to whichever direction it would go. In and out of consciousness I went, awakened by the soft tapping sound of passing clinicians and PA announcements paging staff to go somewhere wherever. People were probably being carted in around this period of the morning, most with gunshot wounds, or for overdosing on some compound in need of a stomach pump. A bunch of tragedies must've passed before my half-dead lucid self as I half dreamt of myself, hands holding the collars of some unrecognizable somebody, asking, begging.

*Would she be able to get plastic surgery? Would she hate it if I asked? What'll this do to her mental state? What am I gonna have to put up with?*

*Did she pick up the Fu Run before getting blown up?*

It was six a.m. before the little Asian doctor woke me up to deliver the news. The surgery was a success, in that she was still alive, and everything went according to procedure.

Then she led me toward her room. Before I went in, I felt her rest a hand against my chest, and she urged me, for Judy's sake, to remain calm when seeing her.

And I remained calm. Against every screaming, pounding, agonizing screech of horror tearing through my skull, I remained calm.

. . .

She refused to remove the bandages, not even after the pieces of replacement skin had completely merged with the rest of her face. I guess at first it didn't matter; the skin they put over wasn't much different from the bandages covering the damaged area after all.

I told her as much while she lay in bed at home a day after she got back. I told her that she didn't have to take them off until she was ready. I thought I said the right thing, for crying out loud, but next thing I knew, she stopped talking to me altogether.

"What'd I say?"

I might have asked that once every five minutes for half a day 'cause by the end of it I was walking around the house repeating it over and over.

"What'd I say? What'd I say? What'd I say?"

I tried telling her how happy I was that she was alive. I told her how beautiful she looked. I told her how I loved her. I told her how she would always be gorgeous to me no matter what the fire did to her unless if she looked like my cousin in law Lanie.

I told and I told. She glared, and she glared. I tell ya, I've never felt sicker than that day, not for any reason other than the way she glared, right through the gaps between her bandages, unable to give me anything more 'cause it hurt to express. Maybe it was empathy, where I felt her pain and wished it all away.

Maybe it was guilt. Not over me asking

her to get take-out, 'cause hell, I got stuff for her all the damn time, and when I asked, she sounded pretty damn chirpy at the idea.

No, guilt over something else, something I couldn't put into words then or now, but something that overshadowed everything. Something that made me sick over the way I am.

Anyways, a few weeks went by and one morning she goes, "Jay, could we talk?"

She apologized. You believe that? She never apologizes, never!

We were at breakfast, and I was nibbling on some stale bread bowl from two days back. We were half our original selves, with the stress eating away at our appetites, stress from pain for her and unresolved guilt for me.

She told me how good I've been to her. Yeah, no shit. I should've gotten husband of the year 'cause you should've seen me! Cleaning the house, cooking her breakfast, lunch, and dinner, tucking her in, helping her shit and piss, all the while putting up with her wall of silence. I guess I figured she'd come through if I stuck to my guns, find out that I was true.

She told me about the pain she's been in. Like I couldn't tell, and I knew it wasn't the physical kind either. She told me how she felt dead, held up by societal expectations rather than her own will, a corpse of her original self, going through the motions so that I could do so as well.

She told me how she believed she was ready to take off her bandages.

And for the love of God, I forgot she had them on.

*     *     *

Why can't I have more control of myself? Why can't I tell my mind what to think? Why can't I look at her scorched face and tell her she's beautiful? Aren't I in love? Does it mean I'm not? Has the backbone of our marriage been held up by a sham? A superficial attraction to how smoothly her skin covered her face over how she covered her skin? What of all those schmucks who tell their wives that they love them for who they are even as the skin dries and the hair thins and the body shrivels up and all that's left is a prune waiting to decay back into the earth? Was I ever ready for that? Did I ever deserve to love? Was I ever able to?

"You look beautiful, honey!" I had tried to say after the cloth and medical tape dropped to the floor. "I'm supposed to tell you you're beautiful," she must've heard.

Those fucking doctors. Did they patch her up blindfolded? Did they not have a picture of her? A frame of reference from the other half? Did they not see how perfectly her cheeks ran along her jaw, how they blended into shades, how they fitted and never stretched, how they complemented her eyes, her nose, her lips, her brows? Does all a face really need is some skin?

"Look at me, Jay," she was telling me.

I was looking at her. Well, sort of. My eyes would dart back up and down once every second, eating it in chunks. Half her head was bald, well, not half, a quarter, like the right side of her forehead all the way to the top of her skull.

"Look at my face, Jay," she whispered.

Her eyebrow, gone; a tubular lump taking its place. Her left eye, squeezed shut; a line running through a bulge.

"Look at my face, please."

Her entire mouth, more or less the same. All the rest of what I could make out was a clump of skin that hung off her cheek that sagged towards where her jawline used to be, the line between her neck and face blurred, her nostril now just a hole, her ear looking like it'd just started growing out of the side of her head with the bottom part still submerged under the skin.

And my eyes would move back down.

"Jay, please, look at it," she begged in her deliciously tender voice.

"What do you want me to look at, babe, I'm staring right at ya," I replied.

"Your pupils. They keep moving."

"That's just how I stare, babe."

"You think I'm hideous, don't you?"

I tried to respond, but fuck, I was too slow!

"I get it," she whispered angrily. "I get it, I get it, I get it, I get it," she went on and on and on.

My balls showed up. Finally I could speak.

"Honey, you're not ugly. You're beautiful! Babe, look at yourself!" I shouted while turning her around. God, I must've exhausted all the prayers I had left in the day to keep myself from wincing. It was the greatest feat of acting I could do. There I stood, holding her in front of me, staring into her one and a half blue eyes, and all I could do was visualize, imagine her face as it once was, superimpose the left half on the right just so I could convince the disgusting little charlatan that I am to carry out something I've done every waking day of my married life.

Kiss her.

Fucking kiss her, you misogynistic waste of a human life.

Kiss her.

.   .   .

So, three weeks went by after the bandages came off.

I had spent the first of 'em shopping around for reconstructive surgeons, searching up and down the coast, looking for someone covered by our insurance, and let me tell ya, these guys are some bastards. They wouldn't pay for anything past looking good enough to get by, eat normally, see straight, most of which her last clusterfuck of a surgery already covered. Anything more we'd have to pay out of pocket, and after talking with a few about the cost of a full restoration, let me just tell you this, I'd have to sell my whole company and foreclose on the house. Naturally, it was out of the question.

"Babe, I wanna do this for you too, but it's half a million dollars we're talking about!"

We went in circles for nearly the entire weekend.

"Yes, I know, half a million dollars," she

replied with that attitude like half a million were just some convenient excuse.

"Yes, half a million dollars, that's a five with five zeros. That's our fucking net worth!"

"Yes, I know," she replied in the same way. You know, where she agrees with you in a way to tell you she doesn't agree with you? Like somehow she's helpless 'cause she's stuck with some broke fuck who doesn't have half a million stuffed in some offshore account? Like somehow I don't give a shit? You know what I'm talking about? It's like we could take a bullet for 'em and they'd just be annoyed at us for being dead.

"Good," I responded, "glad you know."

"You try anywhere else?"

"Babe, I looked up everything in the network, I've called ten doctors in ten states, I've looked this stuff up online. Half a million is the going rate!"

"Right, going rate, I know."

On second thought, not sure if she was actually blaming me. Maybe she was blaming herself, or the insurance company, or fate. Or maybe she was more or less accepting than blaming, convincing herself that this was the new normal.

"Judy, babe, you can't be blaming me for this, right?"

"No, of course not. I don't want you selling your dreams for me."

"What the hell does that mean?" I didn't even know whether to say "thank you" or "fuck you."

Then, out of the blue came Monday. Everything stopped, like someone hit the pause button between us. I guess both of us must've run out of steam and neither wanted to admit we were fresh outta ideas.

So the next two weeks were spent in avoidance, meandering around the place when we were home together looking for anything to distract ourselves from each other, avoiding any moment of nothing so that the dreaded something flowing in the undercurrent between us would wake, choosing to masquerade behind these cheap masks we fished out of the shallowest regions of our mental inventories.

At least we weren't fighting. We wouldn't survive one. The tension was so thick that it wouldn't have been but a spark to set off the fuse, so we put up with each other the way nuclear nations keep their peace; mutually assured destruction.

"Could you pick up your sock?" she would say.

"Yes, honey," I'd reply.

"How was your day?" I'd ask.

"Ugly," she'd reply.

I was once standing on the balcony smoking and she didn't say a word. She hated smoking, and I could only remember the hell I'd face if she ever caught me with a stick in my mouth. Right then she only looked and turned away. I haven't smoked again.

If it killed me to live for myself, I figured peace would only come if I lived for her.

So for the next weeks after the first, I threw my weight into cooking and cleaning, catering to her every need. Heck, I even attended her book club for her on this one Saturday evening over going to a Knick's game with some high school friends, and they work for the league, so they get second to front row seats!

Every night I would stroke her hair, give her a back massage, kiss her forehead, kiss her cheek, the good one, try to make her laugh, husband of the year shit and so forth and so on. Every day I'd work from home, sitting on the bed next to her in case she needed something.

Why was I being so class? I still don't know to be honest. Maybe it kept me busy, 'cause there isn't nothing a troubled mind hates more than shit to do and nothing repressed words love more than a moment of pause. A moment of nothing.

Forgive me, but that's all I can recall from this stint of time. Memory demands honest moments, I suppose. But by week two or three, I swear, I could see her mood getting better. Heck, I coulda sworn I saw a smile once, maybe even a chuckle. Maybe things were looking up for her finally. Maybe we could find a new normal for ourselves. Maybe.

Then this Saturday night happened.

"Jay!" she was calling me in a peculiar voice one night.

"Jay!" she sang.

"Jay!" it echoed through the halls, bouncing off the walls, the kind of stuff that happens when a clarinetist plays a tune at perfect pitch, or when Jimmy Page rips a high A-flat and lets it ride through the stadium.

"Jay!" that fucking siren, luring me with her sweet tune for the trap.

"Jay!"

She was dressed in a nightgown, twirling

her curled hair with her index finger, sprawled out on the bed with her bare toes pointed and her left arm supporting the stallion of a body she had. Shit, I'd rub one off thinking about it until I remember her face.

"Jay, look at me."

Oh, fuck me.

I tried my best, I swear. You're talking about someone who could go three or four times in an hour, someone who coulda populated upper Manhattan if it weren't for all the fucking gloves. I focused on everything else; her basketball breasts, her torso so slender she could swim with dolphins, her meaty calves, her tight round ass, the lavender smell of her hair, that perfume that covered her face.

Her face.

Oh, but her face! It wasn't like I could keep my head down in her pussy forever! She wanted me to kiss her face!

No matter how hard I tried to override reality, picture her body with a face dragged out from storage and superimposed over, I couldn't do it. I just couldn't. Like all I could see, even with my eyes squeezed shut, was the massive lump of skin running down her right side from her forehead to her lips, the slits, the flap of skin that outlined her jawbone and cheek, and God, I will tell you she's beautiful, she's beautiful. I told myself this a million times, she's beautiful!

So there we lay, side by side, my hands covering my face, and her staring at herself through her phone camera, and she didn't stop staring at it all fucking night.

.  .  .

So there it is. My sob story. It's one in the morning now, and if I don't go to sleep soon, I'm gonna be writing this thing in Klingon.

Between Judy and I, neither of us has spoken about it since, with every day being like the days before. Fake, cruising on autopilot, like you're living with someone but you're living alone. Like I see her and we acknowledge, care for, eat with, and sleep next to each other, but still, it feels like going at it alone.

I want her back. I don't want nobody else in this life but her, and I will jump on a fucking knife for that statement. I don't care if her face never changes. It ain't her who needs fixing.

It's me.

A week ago, I was ready to take a torch to my face.

Really, if you look around on the net, there are professionals who'll do it for you, birthday gifts for masochists or other kooks in need of getting out of something dishonest. It wasn't cheap, but I figured it'd be worth it in the end if she finally understood how I felt.

That if we were both monsters, we could face the world together, knowing that beyond the comfort of home there's nothing but shame.

That maybe, just maybe, the horror that would be both our faces would neutralize each other, leaving only ourselves, our beautiful fucking selves.

That maybe, just maybe, we could at least fuck again.

I told a guy at Micky's as much Friday evening; someone I've gotten to know, although I only remember him by face. Obviously, he called me nuts, chuckling and taking a swig of his beer as if I were pulling his leg.

He then asked me something.

"What if you could?"

I asked him, "What, take a torch to my face? Of course I could!"

"No, listen," he said, closing in to where I could see his nose hairs and smell 'em too. "I'm talking about what if you could see her beautiful self without having to desecrate your own?"

"Yeah, if only," I scoffed, throwing back my Woodford Rye and sticking my finger up for another glass.

He pulled up his sleeve. A prosthetic arm. I almost spat out my drink.

He explained to me how a mortar had taken it off while he was in Afghanistan years ago serving as a marine. He talked of how he'd spent months in rehab, learning how to adjust to the thing, from eating with a fork to wiping his ass.

"I'd shake with this hand, but these piggies have touched so much shit," he said, twirling his fingers, although I'm pretty fuckin', sure I saw him eating his fries with 'em.

The problem?

"This ain't my hand," he said. "Fucking look at it, will ya? Does this look normal to ya?"

I told him no, but it's better than not having a right arm. He nodded in return.

"Yeah," he responded with a shrug, "sure, but ya know what? How about having a real arm?"

"Howya gonna do that?" I asked, by then

feeling a bit out of sorts as I was on my third glass.

"Look here," he pulled out some glasses. After messing with it a bit, he held it in front of my face. "Ya see what I see?"

I tell ya, I couldn't fuckin' believe it. As soon as I put 'em on, I was staring at his fleshy, flakey-ass white arm, tattooed and hairy, complete with a big fucking hand stained with callouses and a lifeline running down the diagonal like he accidentally grabbed a kitchen knife by the blade. I swear to God, it looked exactly like the other hand. It was sorcery to me.

"Crazy stuff. What's the deal?" I asked.

"This is what my arm looks like."

"Well."

"This is what I see," he said waving his good hand around the screen and pointing its two fingers at his eyes. "Would you believe it?"

"Wait," I stammered, "no kidding?"

"If you can see 'em through those glasses, why the fuck not?"

Those glasses. I started taking 'em off and putting 'em back on, then off, then on. Night and day, perfect vision and more perfect vision.

"Now wait," I asked, "does it feel real?"

"Sure does," he responded with a smile. "Real itchy and flakey, just as I left it."

He pointed to his head. "I've got some work done up here." He paused. "Well, how do I put it in simplistic terms. Okay. There are some implants that read what I'm perceiving, sends the data to a supercomputer somewhere as well as other facets of my consciousness. It then comes up with some data and sends it back to the noggin, and those glasses, may I add. See, I know it's a robotic arm. But most of the time, your mind runs on auto-drive, and as long as you see something and feel something, you subconsciously end up believing it."

He picked up a pen that the bar-keep left and started twirling it with his fake fingers. "I could do this all day, 'cause you know, as crazy as it sounds, my brain still thinks my right arm is there. State of the art stuff, I tell ya."

"Holy shit," I said, "but that sounds fucking painful man."

"Didn't feel a thing," he replied twirling his finger around his temple, "crazy anesthesia, knocks you out for thirty minutes."

"Thirty minutes?"

"All it takes, and you'll wake up without feeling a thing. Look, trust me when I say it

< 32 >

happens quick, and other than some dots on your skull, you wouldn't have noticed a day's difference."

He began reaching for his wallet. "Ya know, maybe this could help you and your wife, you know, with her face and all."

He pulled out a card and handed it to me. "I work for a company called *Wondervision Inc.* Ever heard of it?"

I took a glance. It was cold to the touch, made of sheet metal. I could almost feel its weight against the palm of my hand.

On the front of it, the company slogan was inscribed in silver. *Wondervision. Your better reality.*

To its side was this weird-looking symbol; a swirl of lines converging into a beige circle, each one a different color.

"Nope, never heard of it."

"Well, maybe you've heard of our parent company, *AISys Inc.*"

I snickered. "Of course I have, big-ass company like that."

Who hasn't heard of *AISys*? I swear, it's grown into something like the mafia, what with a logo on every high rise in midtown, financing every charity, owning every piece of

< 33 >

our information, the sole distributor of every-one's cell phones to computers to hardware to software that runs the globe. Even Judy works underneath one of 'em.

"No shit? Which one?" He asked.

"The one above *Sazera*."

Hell, I used to joke to people that she indirectly works for AISys, providing all their C-suite folks with the C-suite gear, some almost coming in once a week for the latest ten thousand dollar getup. That was up until two years back. Better store, better deal? Beats me.

"So, um, I'm guessing your company made that?" I asked, twirling my finger at his head.

He smiled, "Yes. See, let me give you a bit of context. It's called *The Interface*, and the entire service that we provide is called *Interface Therapy*. Basically, it's a procedure where we edit your reality just enough to where you can live a normal life, or whatever you define as *normal*. Of course, *just enough* meaning to where it's safe. Like this arm, for example."

Then with a pause and a sip. "So look, here's the deal. Like you were telling me, if you can't afford to fix your wife's face, then you might as well make it work with your marriage, am I right?"

< 34 >

Asshole, but a sharp one.

"Hold up, hold up," I countered, "how much will it cost me?"

"What's your pain threshold?" he asked back.

I told him, spilling all of my financials, my company, the forty grand I've got in my savings account.

He sniggered.

"You may need to stretch a little, but you'll be fine," he said while taking another sip. "Details will follow, definitely a shit ton more affordable than a face transplant."

He stopped and took a drag of the cigarette that was resting on the ashtray in front of him. Then he continued with a chuckle, "and a lot less painless than lighting your face on fire."

"See, contrary to what you're thinking, it ain't open-brain surgery, and the process is smooth. When you're done, you'll see."

"See what? A hallucination?"

"Sure," he shrugged. "Isn't that what all reality is?"

"The hell do you mean by that?"

He answered with a chuckle and a shake of his head. "I've gotta run, but we could talk more if you're interested. You've got my email."

He then put out his cig, got his shit, and vanished before I could say another word.

.　　.　　.

Oh, that's right. His name was Gary.

I remember now 'cause I remember emailing him a day later. He gave me the steps, I
applied, and in a week, I was instructed to send
an email explaining my sob story. These guys
sure run a tight ship, I'll tell ya that much.

So, a Josh Rikkard, relationship manager,
probably a pro at dealing with schmucks like
myself day in and day out, and it looks like I'm
supposed to tell him what I need now.

What I need.

I need to see my wife's beautiful face again
and, I'll tell you this, it ain't 'cause it's what I
care about. I can't make that clear enough. Just
like I would love to shrug off an insult hurled
at my dead mother or drink without getting
a hangover the next day or fall asleep to the
ring of a bell and wake up like I'm doped on
crack, I would love to be able to fuck my wife
with half her face missing.

But as much as I try, it ain't me calling the
shots, but someone I just can't describe.

Something, another me with all the levers
in its reach, running underneath my conscious
mind, below my rights and my wrongs, beyond

< 36 >

my control, who I wish I could pull out from under and fucking beat into submission.

But shit, sometimes it feels like I'm shouting into the wind, a little man who thinks he could steer the will of God if he's loud enough.

The world will call me a horrible person, and believe me, I'm not gonna disagree. But I stand firm that I would never leave her side, that I would take care of her as I have been till the day I die, and that I can jerk off for the rest of my life and impregnate her through invitro for all I care.

This is all about Judy, a wonderful woman with a dirtbag husband who, aside from not having half a million, thinks she's too hideous to fuck, as if living without half a face wasn't bad enough.

Whoever I'm trying to convince, that something sharing half of the space between my ears, I've gotta get it to see the thing of beauty that I see, 'cause honestly, I'm not sure what she might do if I don't. Maybe it won't beat reconstructive surgery, but it's something. Good sex is always something in a marriage, especially when it's in crisis, and the only way forward is to convince her at the very least that nothing has changed between *us*.

Maybe it'll give her *something* to latch onto.

Maybe when we're together, she'd forget about her face.

Maybe that'll give her a recovery a fresh start, and we could tell everyone in the world to fuck off.

Or maybe, I don't know, maybe I'm just justifying my own selfishness, like all I really want is to see my wife the way I want. But really, if I were truly selfish, I would've left her and found someone else, right?

And if I don't got the money to fix her face, and if we continue down the path we're on, me not being able to see her the same, touch her the same, fuck her the same, her spiraling further into depression because of it, where will everything go? If she can't be at peace out in the world, at least she could be so at home.

Maybe this will be the best we can do.

So that's what I need, to see her beautiful face everywhere I go so I could pin her like there's no tomorrow, like this was all just shock, like she's still as gorgeous as she always was and that no number of exploding gas stations could change a damn thing.

< 38 >

Whatever it takes, I'll pay it. I've got a growing personal savings account for this Benz I've always wanted. Yeah, see what I'm giving up for her? Again, whatever it takes.

Okay, I can't think straight, it's 1:30 a.m. and I've been knocking myself out with some cheap lager for about a couple of hours now. It's getting cold and in a few hours I'm gonna hear the cleaning crew starting their morning shift. Heck, I can't even read what I'm writing. I'm just gonna close this out with a big fucking thank you and hope they get back with some good news.

Wow, I feel better already. Maybe I'll sleep tonight even, just maybe.

< 33 >

Good Morning, Jay!

Thank you for that introductory email. After an extensive background check in addition to reviewing your statement, we believe you may be a perfect candidate for our program.

First off, I would like to share my condolences in relation to what happened with Judy.

I cannot imagine the pain she must have gone through and the tenacity it must've taken for her to press on after such a tragic event. Also, from what you've told me, I can only see a caring husband who's willing to go to whatever lengths necessary for his wife. There are many reasons people use our services, but it's always honest and passionate folks like you who make my job worthwhile.

Secondly, I would like to introduce myself.

My name is Josh Rikkard. I've been with this company for well over five years now and have worked with numerous individuals such as

< 40 >

yourself, taking trying situations of equal if not greater complexity as yours and flipping them for the better.

As you know, I have been assigned to you as your personal relationship manager. Now, what does that mean exactly? I can see from your email that you were briefed in your initial outreach, so let me go into a little more detail as to what I do and what this program entails.

As a relationship manager, I am to be your consultant, mentor, advocate, subject matter expert, counselor, and friend. I am to make this experience seamless for you as well as serve as a sounding board for everything that you would like to talk about. I am to work with you as well as our product design team to deliver an optimal solution that would allow you to live an acceptable life.

On a high level, the next steps to this process are as follows.

1. Registration: We will send you a link in a separate email, which will take you to a registration page. Please take a few minutes and follow the steps provided on this site to create your online profile, we will use this to send you important documents to sign as well as for you

to manage payment and other relevant pieces of information we may request on an as-needed basis.

2. <u>Screening:</u> After creating an online profile, you will be directed to schedule an onsite screening. From there, we will perform both a visual and psychological assessment to determine if it is safe to proceed with the operation. If the results come back positive, we will call you back for a mental imaging.

3. <u>Imaging:</u> The mental imaging, also performed onsite, will create a snapshot of your memories and provide us with all the metadata surrounding the subject we are to alter. With this information, coupled with input from your psychoanalytical report garnered from the assessment, we will be able to begin development on your solution.

4. <u>Implementation</u>: Upon completion, we will call you back for implementation.

Keep in mind that specific details of the process will be provided before each of these steps so that you may choose to opt out if needed. You will not be charged for service until ninety days after implementation should everything go forward as planned.

I do hope that you find exactly what you are looking for with us and that we may be able to provide the assistance you need. Once again, feel free to email me at all steps of the process so that I can best determine how to guide you through this treatment.

Thank you again and I hope to hear from you soon!


Josh Rikkard
Relationship Manager
*Wonderlenz* Technologies Inc.

< 43 >

I've gotta say, this guy sounds like he's got the personality of a sandbag.

But whatever, all of that is overrated.

Also, it's been a little under a month since I responded to his last email.

I have to tell ya, after hitting "send" that night, I started second-guessing the whole thing. You see, Judy will tell ya that I'm a fucking idiot when it comes to falling for shit. As a matter of fact, right in front of me, like its laughing at me, is this bottle of herbal oil I got from some bum in Little Italy a month or so back. Little Thai guy, spoke like the only people he knew were Black, like Jackie Chan doing a Chris Tucker impersonation. Big fuckin' mouth, I tell ya. He said to rub it on my penis and it'll go "bwaaah!" He even made this hand gesture that was real convincing. I wasn't sure if it resembled hardening or climaxing.

A hundred bucks lighter and now I'm convinced it's conditioner with baby oil. I tell ya, I didn't think I was in the right place of mind to make informed decisions. Hell, I still think that.

I know, I know. Something's wrong with me.

I probably sound like some sex addict by now, like the only thing that matters to me in my relationship with Judy is how many times I can pork her. But they're needs. Very big fucking needs. For me and for her. Fidelity, love, these are great, but what's a relationship without attraction? And what's attraction without sex? I could tell her how beautiful I find her every moment we're together, buy her roses, paint her naked, snap photos, serenade her, but it's like the moment we're in bed and the lights are off, only one truth speaks.

My Little Richard, the only fucker whose opinion matters, my mouth just another politician.

Lately, I've given up jerkin' off. Horniness,

< 45 >

I figured it's like needing to piss. The longer you hold it in, the more places you'll go.

Shit, I've become as chastised as Father Beck that one time when all of us kids left for summer camp.

I don't watch porn anymore. The people at YouTube must've figured I got a vasectomy or something. I don't read it either, having locked all of my literature in a cabinet filed away in a shoebox, placed neatly next to all our wedding photos.

I don't wear skinny jeans anymore. You know how Disney princes fall in love at first sight? Yeah, ain't nothing more than their dicks rubbing against their tights.

*Fuck me.* I find myself saying it a lot more. Cry of exasperation or subtle desperation?

On a brighter note, now my sock drawer is always full.

Now, did it work? I don't know, she wouldn't let me try, or she would let me try but I'd end up sounding like a pre-adolescent asking for a kiss, my face looking all pedophilic.

"Hey, honey, you wanna try having sex again?"

*Fuck me.* Maybe I should've just said that, but then what the hell would I have done if she said *yes?*

Tried? Faked it?

Would she have at least stayed if I did either?

. . .

It wasn't like she had nobody else in her life who cared.

Like her best friend Amber, who kept texting and calling and texting over and over. Judy would only glance at her phone. She'd been doing the same for all three of her closest friends in the city.

Truthfully, she didn't have many others she'd call a friend. Not anywhere on the island. Yeah, she grew up just an hour north in Long Island, having been around this neck of the woods her whole life, but, you know, she still hates everyone. Well, not hate, I put that in her mouth, more like passively tolerating.

She's sweet. Judy's the type of person who'll laugh at every one of your jokes, seamlessly covering up any trace of a cringe. She'll put her hand on your shoulder, look you straight in the eye, lift your spirits, the sides of your lips. She'll come up with a never-ending list of things to talk about, including a full mental history of where she might've seen the same style of boots you're wearing or every movie you should watch 'cause you liked *Bladerunner* or every Thai place in town you should try 'cause you like Vietnamese.

She'll smile. Oh did she have a smile! The ends of her lips would almost curve upwards, a dimple to the side, her pupils growing, her brows always at rest and without a wrinkle on her forehead. You'd feel welcome into her life, into her presence, into her social network you'd think she had.

Then you'd never see her again, no matter the numbers or Facebook pages or Instagram handles shared during the course of however long it took you to fall for her. She'd probably found you pedantic, shallow, boring, or just not interesting enough to meet a second time. So she probably just tolerated you, as she does with any lucky person she'd landed a moment with.

She did tell me once that it wasn't always like this, not before she met her ex.

Her ex, whoever the fuck he is. You'd be interested to know that to this day, I don't know his hair or skin color, religion, or even his name. I don't know why they broke up or how long they dated. Hell, she won't even confirm if he was a he. I just get this vibe from her every time I mention him that I wouldn't want to know the answer, like she'd fall apart and disappear once his name is pronounced. So I stopped, and whatever it was that happened between them to make her the way she is, that's none of my business, though I don't get how she thinks anything would be better if we moved.

I'm just saying, baggage doesn't just disappear from location to location, but you know, just an argument from some time back that we're destined to have again.

An argument I almost miss given the present.

But I digress.

So in sidestep with how she treated everyone else, she'd ghosted Amber and her other three best friends in the city long enough for em' to take the hint. They probably cared for another day or two before getting swept up in everything else there is to live for in metropolitan society as she faded to obscurity in their collective consciousness. Here, it doesn't take much to make friends disappear, especially past the age of thirty.

Maybe she preferred it that way. After all, what could anyone offer to someone in such a fucked-up state of being but pretentious pity?

"What could she offer me, a mouthful of her pretentious pity?"

We were sitting in the coffee shop downstairs, one of the few days for her where caffeine deprivation overtook public insecurity. One of the few days where she exposed any part of her facial skin to the rest of the world, scrunching up the bottom of her polyester facemask under her nose and holding it in place while bringing the mug to her lips.

"She could offer more than that," I replied. "Thought you two were close."

She set her mug down. "Close like what? Do you even know what she looks like?"

I shrugged. "Tall, blonde, female."

"Short, Asian, maybe male?" she responded.

"She's a dude?" I asked, 'cause truth be told, I've never actually met her.

She just let out a faint chuckle.

I guess I took the hint.

"So you're not close, but you've gotta have somebody."

"I've got you."

"Yeah, babe, course you've got me, but I'm

talking a chick fella, someone you could talk to about your chick feelings, you know, all this," I said, shaking my left hand toward her face.

Then when we were outside, taking a short walk around the block, I heard her mumble, as if still piecing the words together from half an hour back.

"Three days, probably. Just three fucking days."

Three days before they'd forget her, move on with whatever makes them happy, whether they came over and bear-hugged her in our living room with a bottle of Moscato or not. Three days she'd rather not fill with images of the right side of her face. Three days to fully disconnect this new reality that was her from everything that she had been before. Three days to fully kill herself and live a new life dead.

That's my guess. You see, Judy ain't the same person anymore. That kindred soul, that loving wife, that normal, functioning, social human being, vanished in the fire and emerging with a new face and personality.

Yeah, she was a shit to just about everyone else, but who cares about everyone else? She was everything she could be to me. Imperfect but self-aware, ruffled around the edges with hints of empathy buried deep inside, forward-looking, independent, a highly intelligent, proud young woman of Manhattan that doesn't need you but lets you in anyways. She was all the excitement that comes with the city.

"Three days," she repeated on and on for the rest of the walk.

What do ya think, can I even call her Judy anymore?

.  .  .

She suffered a lot in her sleep since the incident; always waking, shrieking from some nightmare.

On good mornings she'd wake up and cry for a bit. On bad ones she'd wake up and run to the mirror. I'd always walk in on her touching her face.

"I think I'm getting better, honey, ya think so?"

"Yeah," I'd lie, "yeah, you look beautiful, honey. You always do."

"Yeah, I think so too. I'll get my old face back again, I promise."

Then I'd cry a bit.

Mornings, the time of the day when you confront all your terrible realities from the beginning. And she's losing it, so on one hand if I do nothing, I'm gonna have to watch, one tear-soaked morning after another, until I'm sitting alone in this empty house wondering why I let it get that far. On the other, if I choose to go through with this and should she find out, it'll all happen the same but instantaneously.

And fuck, how dumb do I think she is? After all, the explosion may have taken her face but her head's still intact, so to go months as dry as the Sahara and then, like by some divine intervention, suddenly be pouring, how do ya explain that?

That my dick acts in mysterious ways?

That it was just stress and all I needed was, what? Some of that herbal oil?

Now, last week, we were having a worse-than-usual argument.

See, by now she had gone on medical leave, and a very generous one at that. Apparently in the world of suits, you can take as many months as needed, or maybe it's just that her pretty-boy boss is a class kinda guy.

Sure as hell tickled my insecurities. I may have let someone go for being too injured to work once. Ain't that karma a bitch?

I had reached home an hour late. Traffic

< 53 >

was blocked for about ten miles along the 278 'cause of some schmutz texting his pissed-off girlfriend while trying to down a footlong from Subway or something.

Judy was plastered. A half-empty bottle of vodka stood up right next to her and an empty one of cranberry juice was lying next to it with its purple contents coloring the rug under her ass looking like Teletubby piss.

Her back was rested against the sofa chair, which was pushed out of place, and her bare legs were spread out like a V. The smell of digesting booze, I can't forget it. It's a hell of a stench when you're on the other side of it.

I don't know where it came from, call it an accumulation over the months, but there's no poetic way to put it; I was pissed like a sailor.

Now, as angry as I was, I think I approached it delicately at first.

"Honey, da fuck is this?!"

She looked up and before I could even think, I found myself caught in the act, doing the unthinkable, especially at a time like this. I winced, loud and fucking clearly, too. Her face sober was something I've learned to handle, keep my subliminal knee-jerks at bay, but this? This was something else.

Her half-shut eye, swollen and red, the mound that covers half her face now covered by a mess of scattered bangs, and that expressionless mouth, it looked like it was sneering at me from an angle.

Jesus, did I just say all that?

Anyways, it gave her all the ammo she needed.

"I saw that, you," she was stammering. "I saw that you fuck you fucking asshole!"

"What, oh my God, you drunk!" I screamed back. "You spill shit all over the carpet, looking like you just pissed magic and you're surprised that I mighta flinched a bit?"

"A bit?!" she snapped, slurring every other word, "you looked like you... were going... to... puke."

Like I was the one who was gonna puke. Me. She's half-ready to hit the carpet with the side of her head and I'm the one who's gotta worry about puking. She was fucked up, I get it, but right then I'd had it.

"I get that you went through a lot, baby; I do. But don't act like I haven't been there every step of the way, feeling every hurt, moppin' it all up while holding my nose!" I started, feeling the adrenaline power my lips, my dick getting harder from it too. The fucking irony.

"I clean, manage all of your hospital bills, do everything you fucking ask of me, and fuck, I haven't masturbated in a month!"

"Who the fuck asked you to not masturbate in a month?" she shot back suddenly.

Fuck me. I couldn't respond. I mean, what the hell was I supposed to say? "Well, uh, honey, I know we've been having troubles but..."

"Why the fuck aren't you masturbating Jason?"

Every time she calls me that, by my full name, I'm in a world of fuck. Whatever testosterone that may have built up a moment ago had leaked through my peephole, leaving nothing but a shriveled up sack of dried testicles dangling like peas in a pod.

I don't remember the hairball of shit that might've come out of my mouth.

"I'm saving it for sex with you?"

"Honey, because…because I love you!"

But whatever it was, it resulted in a whole hour of yelling, general nastiness, and other artifacts of angry discourse I'd rather spare you from.

Well, actually, it went something like this.

"Oh wow, I'm touched," she responded whimsically. "So when's the party?"

"The fuck?"

She started stripping, starting with her jean shorts and then her shirt, words escaping between her teeth after every movement.

"You've had...to save...your fucking dick. So fuck me, Jay. Fuck me right here, with all of your savings."

Yeah, but the account wasn't near balance.

"Please, not now, honey," I begged, "I've been giving it my all, babe, really."

She was now completely naked, struggling to stand, and I had to run forward to grab her as she fell flat on her face.

"You can't," she moaned, "You can't do it, can you?"

I didn't respond.

"It's okay," she snickered, "I wouldn't be able to fuck me either. Can't even, fucking, masturbate anymore."

She started poking her finger at her pussy, pretending to finger herself. "Just, in and out, like a dipping rod. Dry fucking hole. Only complete hole I've got."

She took another swipe at the vodka before I lunged at it, ripping it away from her, spilling the rest of its contents all over the carpet. Shame, it was an expensive gift from a friend in Ukraine too.

I don't wanna continue on and on with what happened 'cause it went for an hour and, shit, for some reason, I remember every second of it. I called her terrible things; she took 'em and threw 'em back with her good arm. I called her nuts; she called me nut-less. I called her an ingrate; she questioned my motives. I called her hideous, and she…

She stormed out of the room, sobered up from all the adrenaline, enough to fly out of there like a gazelle. I didn't follow, my sanity needed recuperating.

I took the empty bottle and like a fool who had lost everything, sucked on it for every last drop, desperate, thirsty, needing everything in any direction to make it through another night of this hell.

. . .

All of last week after the fight, we shared the house like strangers in a public space. She'd be in bed an hour before me, I'd wake up with her already gone, out to God knows where, with her mask plastered over her face like the phantom of the opera in some imaginary off-Broadway remake where the main characters were all lesbian.

Dinners were eaten separately, movies were watched alone, and hell, I mighta lost my wedding ring and never bothered to look. I wondered if she would've even minded.

Pictures of what we were just last year pissed me off, like for some reason old man fate had decided we had it too good and proceeded to take it all away without warning or explanation. Like I was never married, like it was all just a good dream, like this bitch in my condo right then was just some roommate I fantasized sexually. Me, overlaying her face with a mixture of every crush I had ever had, famous or not.

I ripped them all off last Wednesday just to see if she'd notice. She never put 'em back up.

Then on Friday, I got off work to a text. I've pasted it below.

*Jason, I took a cab to my mother's place. I'm going to be there for a while.*

Oh fuck me.

*No, don't think too deeply into this, I'm not leaving you. I just need some space.*

I sighed a big one, although I would've needed a gallon of gin to quell my nerves right then and there 'cause I tell ya, when that phone lit up I could feel my heart shriveling to the size of a testicle. But she wasn't leaving me. That was good. I could live with that.

*I've had time to think it through, and I just need time away, from everyone.*

*I feel like I'm just going to hurt you more because, honestly, I just can't seem to deal with, you know, all of this.*

*So I'm going to my mom's place for three months or longer or whenever I can be with everyone again.*

*Oh, and I officially left my job at Sazera. Rick was understanding and told me to stay in touch in case I wanted to come back. I felt bad, but I just don't want to put everyone there through all this trouble right now and didn't think the leave would be enough for everything. Don't worry about money, I've got enough saved up in my personal account to last me almost a year, so I can still keep paying for my half of the mortgage.*

*I'm really sorry for everything, I don't know what else I can say right now. Hopefully, after a while, maybe therapy, I can come back and start over.*

*Maybe.*

*Lastly, I'm shutting off my phone service indefinitely. Please don't come after me, it'll make everything worse. It seriously breaks my heart to see you right now because I just feel so guilty. You never asked for any of this, but you've been so sweet. I hope you can forgive me.*

*Goodbye.*

I texted her back.

*Wait.*

I couldn't think of anything else. I sat there for a whole fucking hour rereading and stalling and rereading. Desperately, I tried to come up with something persuasive, but everything that I wanted to say only came down to that single all-encompassing word.

*Wait.*

Wait, baby, wait. Just wait. Everything will be better if we just wait, 'cause I figured if we let it, time will provide all the clarity we will ever need, just let it.

*Wait.*

Some say fate is linear. I say it's a crazy fucking dog chasing its tail.

So that night I got home and sat, alone in this empty fucking house, wondering why I let it get this far.

∎     ∎     ∎

But hell, it ain't that bad I guess.

After all, it's why I decided to reach back out to these mad scientists. No uncertainties now. No doubts, nothing. I'm in this a hundred percent 'cause what have I got to lose?

She's gone. I'm writing back to 'em in broad daylight, sitting at home, six o'clock, the time where she'd normally be loitering in the kitchen asking me where the salt and pepper shakers were, then she'd ask me what I was doing sitting there staring right at her wondering how good I have it.

She's gone. I can literally read what I'm gonna do out loud 'cause it's just me in the house.

She's gone. I have months before she'll ever come back, plenty of time to go through the motions and cover it up.

She's gone. Shit, how long did I have to respond to his last email? Have I missed the cut off?

She's gone. Fuck, what I would have done, looking back, to keep her here.

What'll come of it? Time will tell, but there isn't anywhere else to go from here, is there?

You know what? To hell with my savings

< 62 >

account! I'll make it back eventually, so shit, just get me my new set of eyes and ears and skin and I'll go from there.

All I need is what I need to believe.

< 63 >

Good Afternoon, Jay

There's no reason to worry. Please take as much time as you need. We have enough supply and will not run out if we needed to wait. What is important for us is that you make your decision to go through this at your pace, as we completely understand the gravity of it.

Now, for some housekeeping items.

We have received your registration information and see that you now have an active account. This next step of the process is your psychological screening. We conduct this for precautionary reasons, but judging from your story, I doubt it will be much of a hurdle.

To schedule a screening, please follow these instructions:

Log back into your profile.

On the left hand side, there should be a tab that says "Prework." Hover above it and you should see additional options appear.

Click on "Candidate Pre-screen".

Follow the instructions to select your best available date, time, and place.

Submit the appropriate images or documents for the screening as prompted. This section is customized to you per your initial email.

Once you've submitted, you should receive a confirmation via email.

Unfortunately, I will not be at the Manhattan office but I am certain you'll find the process quick and painless.

If you have any questions, please feel free to ask.

Josh Rikkard
Relationship Manager
*Wonderlenz* Technologies Inc.

< 65 >

## APRIL 8, 2025

I don't even know why I write to this guy like he were a person, 'cause honestly, he sounds like my Amazon Echo. But then again, I fucking love talking to that thing. It doesn't judge, doesn't give me any shit, its straight-forward and gives me what I need. No need to deal with opinions. That's the worst part of people. They've all got something to say.

So I take that back, this guy's alright.

Anyway, I followed the instructions from his last email. It all happened real quick too. Filled out the date for the pre-screen. April 5th. About three days ago at 9:00 a.m.

Snow came down hard for this time of

< 66 >

year. I almost didn't make it. Had to take the subway for the first time in years; filthy little tubes full of rats and slush and grime and mold. I swear, going down was, to me, like using the bathroom on the Amtrak. Hold your nose and flip your eyeballs up to God while you navigate your surroundings like everything was booby-trapped.

I must admit, I did wonder if anybody else in that car had the operation done. I kept looking around, looking for signs, for happy people looking at happy, shitty things, wondering if everyone was seeing what I was seeing.

One girl kept looking at her breast, so flat I could iron my shirt on it. Does she see boobs?

Some old lady kept smiling at me, does she see me smiling back?

Some douche kept eyeballing this chick who kept looking away. Did he see *her* smiling back?

An old man kept cracking up to himself, skinny little shit sitting in the corner covered from head to toe in six layers of clothing overlaid with a Mets jacket from the nineties, rocking back and forth like everyone had a giant penis for a head.

"Look at all you dickheads, all you mutha-fuckin' dickheads!" he kept shouting.

Hell, is that really what he was seeing?

I'll be honest, I was enjoying this little game.

Thirty-eight minute ride, me staring at everyone from left to right, smirking and giggling all out of the blue, probably looking crazier than that little old man.

'Cause say everyone in the car *had* gotten the *Interface* operation. Then hell, I'd have been the only one who saw the world for what it was, like a fucking prophet or God Almighty Himself.

So fuck 'em if they thought I was crazy.

. . .

I know, you're probably wondering about Judy. Actually, you're probably not wondering about anything, but I'm wondering about her, so I'm gonna pretend you are too.

And I wonder about her a lot, every damn minute of the day when I'm not preoccupied, and she sits in the back of my brain like an itch I can't reach.

Last week I tried calling her just to find out she blocked me from her contact list.

Never one for being a very logical person, I called her ten times, as if refusing to accept that I've been blocked by my own wife, who specifically told me before she left that she wasn't leaving me.

The hell she block me for then? What kind of wife does that if she ain't leaving her man?

Hell, I forgot, she did tell me she was turning off all phone services. That include texting too?

I thought about driving to her mom's place even, where she said she was staying. Nearly took a week of absence to wait outside until she would let me in so I could check up on her but, I stopped short as I didn't have a clue, still don't, as to what I would have said if the door were to open for me that would've bought me time.

*Hey, honey, so, how's your face?* Probably followed by, *keep the fuck out of this Dorothy! I'll be gone in a minute!*

Her mother loathes me in addition to her father. Long story, but another reason to leave it alone.

I don't know why; the insecurity is killing me. I wish I could tell her. Tell her how it feels to be married but without a wife, come home to a family that exists only by contract, a phantom limb that I couldn't stop scratching, a memory that I have make-shifted into my reality. I wish I could tell her about waking up every day not knowing what five years is gonna be like, nor ten, if I'll have a family then or not, if she'll even be there.

The worse part?

I couldn't even remember how she looked post-accident.

All I could think of her is what I want to see, the Judy with the face that could launch a thousand ships, that could melt iron with her glare, the universal cure for erectile dysfunction, the singular clone of all Disney princesses except for that redhead from *Brave*, God I could go on forever.

Even after all these months, nothing has changed. Most of me is still that shallow fuck who couldn't accept this new normal, no matter how much I scream and abuse him.

You know, there's this Dr. Seuss book I read as a kid called, I think it was called, *Horton Hears a Who*. And I remember these little people who lived on a seed or something like that being carried by a big dumb elephant with these big fucking good-for-nothing ears who couldn't hear 'em no matter how much they screamed. Screaming that he's going the wrong way, walking further and further away from home, from Judy, from life, and closer to a terrible, lonesome fate.

A dummy cockpit, me sitting there like a fool pretending every twist and turn, every decision I've ever made, wasn't just me turning the wheel to where the vessel was already gonna go and calling it control.

Shit, I guess we really did need this time apart. You probably think I'm nuts, but I think, if anything, I've got every fucking right to be nuts, like if there was anything that could've happened to me that would've turned me crazy. I ain't a moment's surprised that this was the one.

*          *          *

Got out at Grand, just a short walk into China Town. Thought about stopping for food but, I bet you wouldn't be surprised to hear, I've suddenly lost my taste for Chinese.

When I got there, I thought I had the wrong address. An old brick building from the thirties with a fire escape running down the front and a tattered vertical sign sticking out of the front tattooed with pieces of Chinese characters that had since faded out with brick walls recolored with graffiti and sediments and everything else the city offers with time.

At the entrance, clashing against its backdrop, a sliding door and a camera dome on top placed in front of what looked to be a speaker, the only features that hinted a clinical establishment of any sort. On the glass door, the company title was inscribed in white; *Wondervision. Your Better Reality.*

Next to it, that strange, swirly symbol again. You know, you'd think for a company all about fucking with the mind that an eye or brain or a lightbulb would've sufficed, but this?

I was thinking as much as I was standing there, looking at it like I was at the MOMA with my head all crooked trying to get into the head of the artist, before I realized someone had been shouting at me from the speaker.

"Hey! You! Here for appointment?".

I looked up and nodded.

"What name?"

"Jay Valentino!"

"Ray?"

"Jay! Jay Valentino!" I shouted.

The doors slid open and I walked in.

Shit, for such a high-cost operation, they sure could've found a better place to set up shop. Second floor of some decrepit-looking hostel without elevators and mail drops still coming down the walls that may have been outta use since the Teddy Roosevelt era. The smell of some weird Asian delicacy, the kind that all the chef's would eat quietly in the back room while the rest of us stuffed our faces with chicken chow fun or sweet and sour pork, was plastered into the fabric of the walls, probably the very smell that attracted all the city critters that made their homes in the little holes along the edges near the stairwell that I seriously doubt passed any of the city's ordinances.

Little old Chinese man at the counter.

"Upstairs, three floor! Three floor! Go! Go! Go!"

I was beginning to think the whole thing was a scam.

Then suddenly, like I went through some space-time warp, I see this room from decades into the future. It's difficult to explain. I've never seen anything like it. I may have even forgotten to exhale, and I'd been holding my breath the entire way up.

I turn out of the stairwell into an entrance that was this box made of glass. It was really fine glass, probably washed twice an hour, as I found out the hard way when half the office looked up to the sight of my cheek and tongue plastered against it over and over again like a pigeon discovering the Empire State Building. Eventually I made out the dimensions, hands stuck out in front of me like I was blind, shaking my head, trying to act natural while the embarrassment molded this wider-than-natural grin across my face that could've inspired Stephen King.

On the other side of it, pure wonder. The place looked larger than the building itself. One massive circular room, a domed ceiling emanating natural light so pristine it could've brought someone back from the dead. Every wall was made of ultra-high-definition monitors displaying contemporary film art with a focus on Zen, like this one with a man digging a hole with his bare hands in the middle of an endless expanse of sand or this other one of a masked monk meditating in the middle of a construction site where nothing was actually being built or another of a guy in a white body-suit breast-stroking in an expanse of red plastic balls or this other one of crystal-clear water running over a black stone settled on a bottom made of light-brown sand. Shit like that.

Along the back, the walls opened up to five evenly spaced tube-like hallways that looked like something out of the USS Enterprise or some lab from some sci-fi set in the year 3000 out on some remote planet moments before whatever tentacled fuck they'd be storing breaks loose to turn the entire staff into horror props littered across the floor. Furthermore, the ceilings, made of shiny carbon-like material, glowed luminously from the lights filling in from the edges of the floor and they extended to the sliding doors at the ends that opened like they were floating on pockets of air.

All around, a dozen or so people dressed in white, everyone in white scrubs with that strange-looking logo I've never seen before plastered against their chests, buzzed between each hallway like bees in a hive, not one stopping to greet me.

I made my way to the seats, each made of white leather and curved from the backrest to the floor like a paint stroke made in 3D, looking more like hand-crafted contemporary art fixtures than furniture, placed in a circular formation around a sphere of some sort at the dead center of the room. I waited for a minute or two or three, just sitting there, checking my phone for company. Usually by now I'da bugged the shit out of whoever was nearby. Strangely enough, it looked like I was the only customer that day. Started wondering out loud.

"Business must be going swell, huh?"

Nobody paid attention. They all raised their heads to me Woody-Woodpeckering their window, but nothing to this.

Suddenly, after lifting my head to the orb, and I swear I almost pissed my pants, would you believe it, a woman. A beautiful brunette with big elf eyes and pointed chin, dressed like every other Oompa Loompa, standing there staring at me.

"Mr. Valentino?"

And fuck, the orb just disappeared!

"Mr. Valentino?"

"Yeah," I stuttered back with a big-ass smile and eyes nearly popping out of my sockets. The thing wasn't just some recording, this chick was actually talking to me.

"Yeah, that's me," I responded, approaching it with my hands held forward like the walking dead, wanting to touch her to see if the sphere was intact or if it were another hologram like her.

Nope, just a transparent orb made of the same glass I got to know intimately a moment earlier, albeit angrier.

"Mr. Valentino, please don't, please step away from the glass."

"Sorry."

"Okay, Mr. Valentino, please proceed to hallway three," she pointed to my left. "Go to the end of the hall and wait for instructions."

So I did as was told. Walked right into the hallway and stood at the sliding door, waiting for further instructions.

"Please put your finger on the pad," said some guy who was probably born a robot. Shit, ya know, up to this point I hadn't met one person from this company I'd consider a normal human being, excluding the sales guy I met at the bar. There's Josh, there's that weird hologram lady, there's them minions running around for, I don't know, show?

Suddenly, a flash of light to my right. A simple monitor and a finger scanner. Not a problem.

Only that it didn't fucking scan my finger. No, next thing I felt was something like touching an electric rod for taming rhinos. I tore my finger off that pad, ready to hit anyone who would've come through that door. Then suddenly, the pain was replaced by numbness, and after that, nothing. And till this hour, I don't know what the fuck they did to my finger, but it did open the glass door.

On the other side was another room that was round and white with an orb in the center of the…Jesus Christ…why the fuck was all of this necessary?

Seriously, has society run low on human beings that can greet people and shake hands with a big-ass smile and a pat on the shoulder? What the hell was with all those cyber monkeys running around in white?

Anyway, the room was round and white and filled with little dimples in the shiny carbon-like wall, the same kind the hallway was made of, like the inside of a golf ball. Around the edges, three doors that, I assumed, led to similar rooms. I wanted to run back outside or look at Google Maps to see how they could've possibly fit this fucking spaceship in here. Most places in Manhattan could barely fit their fat uncles from Indiana during Thanksgiving.

The orb came to life, and this time, instead

of a person, I was presented a number. Room 3, the furthest one to my right. The door slid open, and I saw something that looked like a confessional booth, except futuristic, like what would be in a manned spacecraft to Mars if a priest came along. Bleached ultra-hygienic walls formed a perfectly cubed bulge that I assumed was my seat.

So I sat, uncomfortably, and when the door shut, I was face to face with a monitor just inches from my nose. A nurse appeared, the same dame from the reception desk, in the same outfit with the same curves and doll-face and everything, but she looked at me as if she didn't know who the hell I was.

"Mr. Jay Valentino?"

I mean, did she not remember who I was or was she a twin, or was she just going horribly on-script? I dunno. I can't explain it. Something about her was off, it's still bugging me now.

"Mr. Jay Valentino?"

I couldn't recall everything I was asked in the interview, but it started out pleasant.

Shit, too pleasant.

She started talking to me like we were on a date and kept asking me about stupid shit like what I liked to eat, what my favorite movie was, to recount my most memorable moments as a child, my first best friend, why I now find him an asshole, why I love *Law & Order SVU* so much. Is it really because I wanna impregnate Detective Benson or is there some sad childhood moment that makes me see myself as one of the victims? Or why don't I follow sports anymore, and what was my favorite memory with Judy.

Every question after that got progressively intimate, closer to me and where I was at. One stood out in particular when, out of the blue, the chick holds up two photos. One of Judy before the accident and one after.

"Please tell me which one is Judy? You may answer 'both'."

"Please point."

. . .

I got outta there an hour later, and boy, did I need a drink. So much running through my mind, like what the hell was with that? What the hell does my childhood have to do with anything? What was that lady? What was with that clinic?

I stepped out and looked back at the building. Sure enough, from one end to the next, probably only half of what would've fit the lobby. Five car lengths, I counted the ones on the street, nothing that could've held the lobby and the hallways and the rooms and the ceiling. Five stories, every one of 'em with boarded-up windows and a sign in Chinese draped over the front and a vacancy sign standing behind the windows at the sidewalk level that hadn't been cleaned in years, and that same Asian guy sitting behind the counter watching some soap opera in some language.

The fuck just happened? I tell ya, I thought I might have been going crazy.

Then as I was heading to the station, I realized I couldn't remember how I answered that last question, or if I even answered it at all.

Which one of the two pictures was Judy? Pick only one.

Eenie, Meenie, Miney, Mo.

That one. The fuck it matter?

Went and got a glass, and many after that, and didn't stop till an hour ago.

And now? Nothing left to do but wait for my results.

Hopefully they'll let me know today if I'm crazy. I'll fucking drink to it.

Good Morning, Jay!

I have some good news for you. After analyzing your results, we've decided to move you on to the next stage in the process.

As to the structure of the building, I can assure you that nothing there is out of the ordinary. If it seemed more spacious than it should be, it is more to do with how the interiors were designed to trick the mind. The late CEO of our company, Dr. Aldi Bosma, had always been fascinated by our perception of the world, especially how we seem so trapped in it.

See, since space is limited in most large cities, the illusion was meant to maximize what little we had, designed to project a feeling of space and comfort. During our seminars, he had cited numerous studies that have shown its positive effects on memory and honesty. Although there may well have been other reasons for the way the clinic was designed, Dr. Bosma was notoriously quiet about his grand ambitions, so

< 82 >

we could only take this reasoning by its face value.

Secondly, the questions were meant to understand how you would apply the *Interface*, and if you could be at risk of applying it for all the wrong reasons. This is, fortunately, a stringent mandate from the NBIIS (National Bureau of Innovation and Information Security), and it has allowed for our product to succeed without any undue burden with the rest of society.

Thirdly, you needn't worry. You have cleared this stage.

The next step in the process is imaging.

This is where we procure an image of your mind. Of course, we will tell you ahead of time, no human eyes at the company will see anything related to your thoughts and what the process produces. Rather, our only touchpoint will be mapping what it is you want to see over or what it is your memories produce. In all cases, we will neither have visibility into what it is you're thinking, what it is you want to replace, what it is that you remember. We will merely act as coordinators.

< 83 >

The instructions on how this is done will be provided to you during the screening.

To schedule your imaging, please follow these steps:

On the left hand side, there should be a tab that says "Prework." Hover above it and you should see additional options appear.

Click on "Candidate Imaging," something that should be available now for selection.

Follow the instructions to select your best available date, time, and place.

Once you've submitted, you should receive a confirmation via email.

Same place, same staff, by now I believe you know the drill.

Lastly, and this might feel a little squeezed in, an answer to your inquiry regarding the symbol.

The various colors represents the various sensory inputs from your interface, and the beige circle represents you, the user.

It was explicitly put in by Dr. Bosma himself, although he took along with himself to the

< 84 >

grave many ambiguities in its regard, including what the beige circle in the middle represents; the user as a blend of all of his/her realities or an independent entity.

That's all I can say to that.

Again, please let me know if you have any more questions.


Josh Rikkard
Relationship Manager
*Wonderlenz* Technologies Inc.

What can I say, that went well. Same place, same strange people in outfits, same creepy lady in the whatever-the-fuck-that-is sphere, same *Star Trek* laboratory that couldn't possibly fit into a mid-size motel in crowded-ass Chinatown.

That's some optical illusion there.

Heck, before I went in, I ran around the building to see for myself. Through the alleyways between and in the back and the front. Put in three laps, almost got my cardio in for the day. Gotta admit, still a bit of a square in a round peg situation for me but I decided not to dwell on it any longer.

< 86 >

Eventually went in. Same spiel. Chinese guy let me in and pointed up, ran into the glass, looking like one of those Fathead stickers, was the only customer in the room, poked the sphere in the center, got bitched at by the same weird robot lady in it, got sent through the hallway from a thousand years into tomorrow before entering a room with the same capsule with the same curvy seat and screen on the door.

The next part was a bit wacky.

The robot-chick from reception appeared on the screen; or maybe the AI lady, cuz there's a difference apparently.

"Good morning, Mr. Valentino."

Her instructions were brief.

"Please sit tight and you will be asked to state your requirements."

Then there was this tube just a little larger than my head. How do I explain it? White and smooth, rounded edges, like on a Boeing 747 without the shit on the inside. It came outta nowhere above me and started lowering around my head, sides sliding apart to fit me as it came closer.

Then a squeal, no, a note, a high G completely off pitch, like back in high school band when my clarinet would squeak in the middle of a concert and the sound would transcend every trumpet and bassoon and snare drum and fucking piccolo and travel through the auditorium like it were a solo. It hung in the air for a good hour, or minute, or ten seconds, I'm not sure. Some things are so fucking awful it warps the senses and all perceptions of time.

Then silence. Then AI lady spoke.

"As you answer our questions, we will scan your brain for data supplementing what you say."

"Supplementing? The hell that mean?" I asked.

"All the things you are thinking about when you answer the question. Please describe for me what it is you want to perceive in this reality."

Okay, easy question. What it is that I want to perceive in this reality. Only that it wasn't so easy, 'cause let me tell ya, the brain's like a pre-adolescent child in terms of knowing what it wants. Like it bugs you all day for candy and once you pass him a Hershey bar he wants ice cream, or he bitches all day about how tired he is just to bitch some more about watching TV when you shove that little shit in bed.

"Ah shit, I want to see, no, I want to..."

"Please take your time. We will not begin processing until you are ready."

"Okay, hear me out." Suddenly, the words came to me like poetry. Like it all fell in place at once, the way the lyrics for *Iris* came to John Rzeznik in his sleep.

"Ah shit, what was it. Okay, here it is. How about, I want to see, no, I want to *perceive* my wife the way she was before the accident. Like, I want her to be beautiful again."

A pause. Then that squeal again for another ten seconds or so before it broke into static.

"I'm sorry," replied the AI lady. "We are having difficulty retrieving the said object. How would you like to perceive the stated object?"

"Object?"

"Analyzing."

I wonder if it caught an image of me tearing the thing from its hinges and tossing it against the door. The fuck it needed analyzing for?

"How would you like to perceive Judy?"

"The hell, so how I want Judy to look?" I responded.

< 93 >

Right then I could've sworn I heard a sigh. Some fucking AI.

"Yes."

I calmed down a bit, but I still had to pause and think. For the life of me, at that moment, I couldn't remember what she looked like before. Pretty eyes, brows, nose, sharp cheeks, and rosy skin. I could write it all on paper, put it all down in words, and still not know what the hell I'd be describing.

"Um, I can't really, you know." I didn't know what to say.

"Would you have an image of her saved on your cell phone? If so, I can give you a few moments to study it before continuing."

Great idea, and when the machine moved outta the picture, I snagged my phone and flipped to my most recent snap.

There it was. It had been a while since I'd seen it.

Been a while since I'd seen those round eyes that...Shit, there I go again.

All I will say is I stared at that photo for a good minute, maybe longer, running my finger along the hair, the bangs, the cheeks, the eyes, little screen zooming in and out, in and out. Just a photo, and it still paralyzed me, in ways I cannot understand.

Lust or sorrow?

Love or longing for some bygone version of it?

"Mr. Valentino, are you ready?"

This next part was a piece of cake.

.   .   .

A while later, as I sat there with the tube off, AI lady informed me that the object I visualized came back with a match. She said it in this real cheerful voice.

"What do ya mean a match? With what?"

"With objects from your memory," she replied.

"From my memory? Jeez, how far back did you guys get?"

She stared for a moment.

"Everything," she said, smiling for the first time before disappearing.

.   .   .

A couple of observations.

First off, you'd think that if they were just gonna take a photocopy of all my thoughts, they 'oughta have some way of filtering through 'em to check for sanity right?

Oh that's right, privacy. None of them goons in white actually get to see the inner-workings of this vault, 'cause they'll probably sell that shit to all of the people at work, or the people doing business with me, or even better, working against me, which in my industry, believe it or not, is almost everybody.

Also, if they took an image of my brain and stored it somewhere, what, am I conscious somewhere else too?

You know what, I'm just gonna leave that train of thought right where it is, 'cause I don't know how much of my brain they saw, but I'll tell ya for sure it ain't big enough to think about that.

Holy shit, Judy's coming home.

She's decided to come home! What do ya know, my freaking sweet Mary mother of Jesus, she's coming back to me!

Ain't that the best news I've heard all week?

Just got a text from her too!

Jesus did I miss her.

You know, many nights I'd wake up in tears and I wouldn't know why.

Actually, I did know why, but I couldn't explain it with words. It's like trying to tell the doctor what's wrong with your knee, or what's up with your gut. Does it hurt? Is it cramped?

< 93 >

Hell, I don't know what it is. All I know is that it's putting me in absolute misery, a brew of all of the worst feelings a guy could ever feel that defies words, nothing in English at least.

Yes it hurts, yes it's cramped, no not that kinda hurt but something different. No it ain't sharp, no it ain't blunt. I don't know, it just feels.

Confusion, paralysis, the sides of my lips weighing a ton, heart pounding and shortness of breath, my darkest thoughts grabbing hold of me by the neck and refusing to let go.

Will she ever come back? Am I still married? Will I have anyone? Anyone left? No parents, no grandparents, no wife, a couple of relatives scattered throughout the country, and beer buddies I meet up with from time to time but wouldn't loan ten bucks to without a credit score. What am I gonna do if I never hear her voice again? How would I live? Is it too late to start over? A guy just five years away from forty?

I can sleep tonight. Maybe for the first time in months I'll get a good night's sleep in.

She's coming home. Maybe we'll be okay. Maybe we'll survive.

She's coming home. She'll be here in five days.

Five days.

Holy shit, five days!

The operation, this whole thing. I can't believe I spaced it, five fucking days?

What do I do? Go through with it? What, with all of this happening?

In her text she kept saying that she was sorry, but what for? Does she figure that maybe it's okay if I don't look at her the way I used to, don't touch her cheeks with my whole hand anymore, look only at her good half, stare at her breasts more than I do at her face? Maybe I will get over it, change, become a better man, fuck not based on perception but love.

Shit, is that even how sex works?

Maybe I agreed to this whole thing because of how she was reacting, like the feeling of me staring at her like she were some kind of monster was too much for her to handle. Maybe I wasn't thinking clearly, jumping at a remedy before I've seen a doctor, going by my gut feeling, 'cause you know, often my gut don't report to the top.

But I don't see her as a monster. Never did and never will and if she were one I'd make myself one too. Two monsters alone in this world, taking it on, it and all of its millions of judgmental little people, together.

Okay, shit, let's see what options I have. If five days ain't possible, I'll just write an apology email for wasting their time.

< 96 >

Good Morning, Jay

Congratulations with regards to your wife coming home.

As to the five-day deadline, I am certain we can make it work. As a matter of fact, I've spoken with our delivery department, and they've confirmed that we may have the bandwidth to bring you in for your operation no sooner than tomorrow or the day after. Believe it or not, the operation is quicker than you think.

To schedule your implementation, please follow these steps:

On the app, please locate "Implementation," something that should be available now for selection. There, you will be taken through a wizard to book an available date for your operation.

After you've scheduled your appointment, there should be a tab that appears at the bottom of the confirmation screen that says "Prework."

Hover above it and you should see additional options appear.

You will be required to watch a thirty-minute long-video outlining what to expect when you arrive.

After the video, there will be an operations guide for you to read. This document will cover the exact procedure for your operation as well as all of the legal ramifications involved. Please read carefully before proceeding.

After reading the operations guide, follow the instructions to fill out a disclaimer. This will be your legal consent, confirming that all the information about the operation have been provided and that you have taken the time to review it.

Once you've submitted, you should receive a confirmation via email.

Furthermore, after the operation, you will likely notice a few marks on your head in the all the relevant areas where we will insert a chip. They aren't large, but in most cases, they are quite noticeable. If you'd like, we can refer you to a cosmetic surgeon. She is located in the upper east side of town and, although relatively new, is highly sought out. We have sent many of

< 98 >

our customers to her and all have reported extremely high satisfaction.

Anyways, regardless of what you choose, I wish all the best to you. Let me know how it goes.

Josh Rikkard
Relationship Manager
*Wonderlenz* Technologies Inc.

Honestly, I really don't get why all of my communication with this guy has to be through email.

I mean, what's with this company? A business that makes stuff from some millennia into the future and I can't even place a call? What happened? You think they got so lost in Tomorrowland they forgot about today? Hell, not even sure if this guy's a person or a robot, like that AI lady from the lab. Maybe he was only designed to process emails?

Ha, I joke, badly, but that's the jitters talking. Honest. And let me tell ya about these jitters.

< 100 >

How do I begin? Well, to start, I don't do well with the knowledge that in a few hours I'm gonna have my head drilled open, even if surgically with a tiny drill. I don't know why it never occurred to me what the hell these guys actually planned on doing, like all I could think about was the final product. I mean, it occurred to me but I kinda brushed it aside, like how much I'm still paying for this operation, all the liquor I'm gonna have to miss out on and all the cheap liquor I'm gonna have to settle for until I make even again.

Then watching that thirty-minute video last night, boy, whatever they're gonna sedate me with this afternoon I sure hope they could stick some in a goodie bag for the road, 'cause I don't know how I could sleep knowing the hows and the whats of this procedure.

Tiny holes drilled and filled throughout various parts of my skull. Little phantom electrodes buried in fifteen places in my brain, thin enough so that, apparently, they'd practically fuse with the outer tissue, and an ultra-thin *reading* chip (for consolidating and sending information) inserted near the back of my head, powered by, and I still couldn't believe it, my brain! Apparently, at any given

< 101 >

time, the human brain produces around 0.085 watts, enough to charge a smart-phone in seventy hours! And definitely enough to keep a micro-micro-microchip, or as they called it, a *picochip*, running on its own. Unless it doesn't, which would amount to a hilarious but unnecessarily drawn-out way of proving someone a moron.

I, for one, would love to try this on all of our elected officials.

But I digress.

The guy in the video summed it up in some crazy way. Something about how we are now evolving the brain with a built-in Wi-Fi? Wi-Fi for the brain, can you believe it? What do these guys think our brains are, computers?

For real though, if what this guy says is true, I'd get booked so many times for public indecency with all the gigs of porn I'd be able to consume with my eyes closed just sitting on the green line. Me and half of the guys in my car. Best quality ever, you could imagine yourself there probably, maybe even with uploaded sensory. We'd drive strip clubs out of business, every bathroom stall in the world would be like fucking Vegas.

Again, I digress.

The guy did say that it'd be quick and painless, like going to sleep and waking up. No explanation. No details about what the surgery will be like, who's doing the drilling, who's doing the implants. No, just him, this thirty something year old poster child for Aryan nations, this Flash Gordon turned Republican senator, winking at me as if to say, "trust me, kid you'll be fine."

He also mentioned something at the end, something about testing or what not. Admittedly I don't remember it too well, but I'll cross that bridge when it comes.

Do I have to shave for this, by the way? Looks like it'd help, 'cause God forbid my hair gets stuck on the inside of my skull. How would I pull it out?

And was that guy real or another cyber-reality trick?

I skimmed through the operations guide before signing the disclaimer. That's right, skimmed, not read, 'cause what's the worst that could happen anyhow? Me dying in the process? Then who'll be left to sue these guys? Besides, if I were to get fucked over I'll just sue and read all this shit then. Nothing is going to stop me from doing this, not with everything I've gone through.

I submitted the form, felt good for all of an hour before bedtime. Watched an episode of *Seinfeld* to keep my mind off of today. Didn't work, so I downed half a liter of Cuervo with a pint of orange juice.

Passed out on the couch, slept like an infant. It wasn't until I woke up three hours later in the dead of night, completely fucked out of my mind when everything hit.

Fifteen holes, little pieces of fabric woven into my brain tissue, reconstructive surgery making me a mutant of some sort, something straight out of the *Twilight Zone*. Strapped into a chair while someone opens my head, examining every fold in my sponge like it were nothing more than a collection of wires and silicon.

Someone opening my head, that never sounds any better no matter how you say it. Drills digging into my skull, little holes exposing my motherboard (I just googled this term) to the world. Touch it one way and I'll turn a Mets fan, touch it another and I'll turn queer. So much for self-control. They'll practically be in the cockpit. Hell, one of 'em could even convince me to vote with a touch of the index finger. The worst part is, I wasn't even sick. I chose this path despite having every opportunity to back out.

I chose this path because I couldn't face the alternative.

I tried going back to sleep before every other faction of my conscience rebelled and rightfully so. Then, a series of lucid dreams, the kind that your mind works up while you're caught between the world of wakefulness and sleeping.

Some chick who walked into my office with rosy cheeks and crystal blue eyes and bangs, the kind that drape to the edges of her forehead like a silk curtain with only a few strands hovering over her brows, and asked me for a job. Before, I would have referred her to human resources. But right then I just stood and drooled like a dog. Then I was at a bar, a female friend, that bartender who smiles a million dollars every time she looks my way, some brunette with fat lips and an adorable chin I met when grabbing a drink with some guys at Southie's, asking if we had anything planned for the evening. I found myself staggering for another drink, and I limped into the kitchen only to find a redhead standing by the fridge offering me a cold beer, and I wanted

< 105 >

to throw something at her if she weren't such a beauty.

I screamed at her, calling her and all of them bitches. I swore they weren't tearing me away from my wife, but then I saw Judy approaching from behind and she was wearing nothing and holding a bottle of vodka, the fine one she had been sucking on that other night that seems so long ago, with half her face gone, the skin melting into the bottom of her chin and covering the right side of her neck.

I wanted to hug her but everybody else, all standing beside her, looked too enticing. I reached and everyone disappeared.

She grew older and the rags on the right side of her face started to dry. I saw her entire being turn forty, fifty, sixty, seventy, and she slowly became nothing more than the giant wad of skin that was the right side of her face. No matter how hard I tried, I couldn't touch her, I wouldn't touch her, and my arm shriveled up before my eyes all the same as it kept trying.

I woke to sweat and tears streaming down the side of my head. It was two a.m., but I noticed the glass I knocked over stumbling to the kitchen. Another lucid dream, but I see Judy getting her things to leave the room.

< 106 >

"Where you going, honey," I asked but she didn't respond. She just stood there by the door until I asked again. "Honey, look, I can explain!"

She turned around.

She was Judy from before the accident, the Judy with the face that could turn me on like a switch, and she asked me what the hell was wrong with my head.

I touched it and there was blood on my fingers. I ran to the restroom to find my head, shaven, covered with holes and the insides visible with blood leaking slowly off the edges, as if all of it had already emptied and I was now powered by nothing more than the implants woven into the outer tissue of my brain.

But I woke again, the night of the accident, and then came an explosion and then came Judy running at me with her hands covering the burnt mess of tissue that was her face, screaming at me to help and I could only back away despite how I tried to open my arms to catch her, my body moving to some exterior force and my will suppressed.

I woke again, and again, and again. I reached and reached but never to any avail. I screamed and begged and swung and screamed at my arms for not reaching far enough and at my hands for not grasping hard enough and my legs for not running faster. With every time I woke I saw her further and further away.

They say guilt feels painful. I beg to differ. I would fucking plead for it to hurt if only to feel, and if I could feel I could be in a little more control of myself. No, guilt is exhaustion from frustration from expecting more only to come up pitifully short with every other part of your body running away in fear and your mind stopping to say, "hold the fuck up."

Hold the fuck up. Don't you love her for who she is?

Hold the fuck up. You really going through with this?

Hold the fuck up. Who you saving? Your relationship or yourself?

If only I could hurt, feel, suffer as much as she is suffering, maybe I'd hold the fuck up.

But yeah, that was my fucking night. Next time I'm taking Ambien.

Getting my head drilled open, guess that ain't the only place from where these jitters are from.

And now I'm only an hour away from leaving my house and making my way to the place. This is an exciting day. Maybe after everything I'll wake up again. Maybe all of this was just another lucid dream, and I'll be next to her the day after getting home from the hospital, hoping she wouldn't take off her mask.

< 109 >

Hello, Jay

We wish you luck with your operation. I assure you, however, luck will not be needed, as you shall find the process quick and painless.

Every customer I have worked with in the past had expressed to me a degree of anxiety similar to something of this sort. They would, however, always come around a day later and they would inform me of how little pain they felt, how it was in and out.

As for if you ought to get a haircut, there is no need to worry. Although I did mention a patch, the technology we use is extremely precise and will only remove the minimum strands of hair that need to be removed.

In fact, speaking of hair removal, I was able to get you a time with Wanda, the cosmetic surgeon on the upper east side of town. As you should be done by 3:00 p.m., she can see you at 5:00 tonight. She practices with this new technique for scars that only take a couple of hours, including hair transplantation if needed, and she was willing to keep her shop open late. Again, from all of the reviews I have seen, she is a very kind and competent woman. I am sure you will find her methods extraordinary.

As for why everything must be done through email, it is for quality assurance purposes. All communications must be documented, and given the regulations placed on us by the federal government, email was the most cost-effective way for our organization as it is less costly to store and requires less transformation. I do apologize for it if it inconveniences you.

Also note, everything I have just written in this email is detailed in the operations guide.

Lastly, I do hope you get better sleep later tonight.

I will talk to you again soon.


Josh Rikkard
Relationship Manager
*Wonderlenz* Technologies Inc.

## MAY 5, 2025

Brand new day.

Just got up, and how about that sky? That sun? That warmth?

Or is the sky blue? Is the sun out? Is it warm? I don't know. For once in my life I'm questioning what I perceive because I'm aware that everything I see is just a projection from my mind, something, I guess, that might not always be telling the truth. 'Cause that's exactly what the operation did, right? Merge my brain to a bigger brain that tells my eyes and nose and fingers and ears what is real and what is not, whether it is or isn't?

< 112 >

I kid. It might have crossed my mind for a minute while falling asleep, which, let me tell ya, was the best sleep I've had in years. I don't know if they programmed my brain (or as they call it, the Interface) to sleep better, but I didn't have a single dream. Got home, sat on the couch, put my feet up on the footrest, and fast forwarded eight hours into today.

The *Interface*, would you believe that name. I can actually call my brain that now and not sound like some arrogant tech bro. My brain isn't just a brain like you normal folks, it's the *Interface*. Just sayin'. It's a big, smart machine that's so powerful it can distort my five senses to create something nobody else could see. Say goodbye to shrooms, introducing controlled schizophrenia!

Again, I kid.

To be honest, this morning just felt like any other morning. No migraine, no discomfort on my scalp, and what do ya know, a full head of hair.

Not a mark that would've given away yesterday.

*　*　*

So, let's talk about yesterday.

I noticed the glass this time around. Funny how that works, isn't it? Couldn't explain it. When you're aware of it, you see it, and you wonder out loud like a nutcase how the hell you could've missed it before. Maybe it wasn't washed as good this time around? I don't know, but I almost felt smarter in the moment, like somehow, I'm a stronger person 'cause I can see *that* glass. Maybe even a pigeon learns after a few rounds with Trump Tower.

Everything after that ran like clockwork.

Waiting room took no time at all, with the AI lady popping up like a jack-in-the-box the moment I sat my ass down, followed with being led to the same exact room past all the usual busy people in white. Funny though, up till then, I could never really remember what their faces looked like, and by the time I would enter the space hallway, they'd be gone.

But that wasn't exactly what was on my mind.

See, I was walking real slow down that hall. Call it nerves, 'cause my legs might've buckled a few times as my mind came to terms with what was really about to happen, that in a few minutes my head was gonna be drilled open, that something was gonna touch my brain, and no matter what angle I took, these nerves would never rest. But, anyways, got in the pod, watched the doors shut with AI lady appearing to me one last time with that sweet smile she always puts up, seemingly digitally engineered to calm any panic-stricken schmucks like myself.

She instructed me to breathe in.

Breathe out.

Breathe in.

Breathe out.

And then I woke.

．　　．　　．

A time warp, think of it as a time warp. Only way I could explain it. In and out, closed my eyes and opened them. No dreams, no concept of the time that passed, nothing.

Breath out.

Breath in.

Breath out.

Then I just sat there, like an idiot, literally asking when everything was gonna start. Right then, the screen in front of me came to life.

At first, all I saw was myself, like a mirror, impatient, waiting for the thing to start. Then a green checkmark appeared overhead, followed by a string of text telling me to go to the lobby and await further instructions. It was then that I rubbed my head and felt over a dozen mosquito bites, fifteen to be exact, sixteen if you include the welt on the back.

They weren't fucking around. The operation had passed.

All the symptoms I thought would be there were not. No headache, no itchiness, no dizziness, nothing that would've made me wonder if somebody had just drilled open my skull and buried shit into my brain. Nothing. Hell, even my head was still in the exact position I had left it.

Jesus, what the hell happened? Was there a surgeon? Some contraption that came over my head? How could that have taken twenty minutes? Seriously, the video I saw the night before didn't explain shit. Just the results but never the process.

By now, I thought I'd be going on about being all dazed and confused, rambling on about how everything was spinning because this was supposed to be fucking open-brain surgery, right? But I wasn't dazed. Like I said, I didn't even know it happened. As far as I can remember, I went in, sat down, took a few deep breaths, and left, and I would've sworn to every soul in the waiting room that it took just three minutes.

And before I could leave, everything went from weird to insane, because the next part was the testing phase.

.　.　.

So, I walked out into the waiting room and instantly noticed that something looked outta place.

The sphere in the center of the waiting room. It was gone.

In its place? A reception desk. Behind it? The AI lady, typing into her computer, live and in person.

Live and in fucking person!

I had to take a moment, move back into the hall a bit as I looked at what I had thought was just another illusion, like as soon as I got close it would turn back into a ball.

Five steps forward. Three steps back. Six steps forward, close enough to put my hand on the desk. And I did, quickly at first, a slight tap with the finger, and then my hand. And I felt the smooth surface, cold and rounded on the edges and rough toward the center. I leaned against it, grabbing the edges and attempting to shake it as if it would make any difference, resting my ass on it.

"What are you doing?"

And this whole time, she was looking right at me.

I smiled. She smiled back.

I got off and took a step away, not only out of embarrassment, but out of shock. Shock at how clearly I could hear her voice, smell the lavender from her perfume, feel her presence. I mean, I didn't think she was a real human being. Just a few hours earlier, she was just some projection in this crystal ball in the middle of the room. Unless it wasn't a few hours? Unless I've been out for God knows how long, and these fuckers had the time to put this all here. But to do what? Fuck with me?

"No, Mr. Valentino. I assure you this isn't the case," she says. "Nothing has changed. You are still standing in front of the sphere and I am still merely a projection in it."

"Wait, what?" I asked. "What the hell is going on? I mean, why am I feeling up a table instead of a sphere? Why are *you* real?"

"This is what we call an *altered reality*," She explained. "It's your *Interface* at work."

< 118 >

"My Interface?" I pointed to my head. "So, these *things* you all just stuck in my brain?"

She nodded. "I'll speak to you in a moment, Mr. Valentino. I've got another customer to help."

I turned my head and noticed at least two other customers in the room. They sat in the waiting room around the reception desk, a young woman and an older male, each without acknowledging the other, each in their own trance staring straight, like wondering what the deal was with the sphere.

And I couldn't put my finger on it, the place felt bigger. Nothing that I could see physically. Everything was set up the same. Same walls made of monitors that wrapped around every side of every room with the same man digging his hole that never gets any deeper and the same monk in the same abandoned construction site and the same guy in the same pool of plastic balls. Same hallway sticking into the room with glass walls that I made love to twice, same dome, same natural life-giving light, same proportions, same dimensions.

But different.

"Justin?" she called, and then Justin, the

older guy, got up and walked with her into the space hallway for whatever step in the process he was in. Walked with her, like she got out of her seat and led him, and the guy just followed without glancing up.

"Please have a seat," she said to me with a pat on the shoulder as she moved past.

I put my hand to it.

*Did I really just feel that?*

It took me a bit of effort to take that seat, walking around blind and feeling everything with amazement. The seats, the reception desk, the lady waiting her turn, the part of my arm she hit, the floor, myself. For a moment, I wondered if I were still under, if all of this was a dream.

Before I could investigate any more, AI lady came back in.

"Mr. Valentino?"

I stood up straight. I wanted to touch her again. No, not in any perverted way, although it mighta been a flash in the back of my head, but out of curiosity.

"AI lady.." I started.

"Kris," she said with almost no change in demeanor, "please, Mr. Valentino, call me Kris."

I took note.

"AI lady, can I touch you?"

She didn't respond, and hell, she didn't even react. Must not have been programmed into her, 'cause she just went on talking.

"Sir, what you are looking at right now is a part of the post-operation user testing. Please listen."

She proceeded to tell me to go back the way I came from, to stop and look around on the tenth step down the stairwell, in the lobby, outside the building at the entrance. If in an hour I do not get an alert on the app, it all went well.

She let me know that all further instructions from there would be on the app, how once I got to the plastic surgeon I should show the receptionist the QR code they sent me via text.

"Good wishes with everything Mr. Valentino," she said with a smile and turned away.

So I tried following her instructions, but I nearly forgot 'em all when I got to checkpoint one.

That junk stairwell that led to the main area made of concrete and rat feces? Now laminated oak steps that glimmered against the light curving downwards in a large spiral surrounded by digital monitors lining the walls with random bits of news and numbers and more still lifes of random people in random places doing random things. I walked ten steps down, just like she told me, and looked up and saw a domed ceiling that went up somewhere close to ten feet made of walls that were made of some shiny white material that glowed with a haunting white light. Left and right, up and down, shit, I might've forgotten her instructions, though it wouldn't have taken any as I could've just stood there for a whole hour, dumbfounded, looking like I've warped into some new dimension that I couldn't piece together.

And it didn't end there.

Right as the stairwell opened up, I came face to face with this epic lobby, three times the size of what I remember walking into just an hour earlier. It looked like the entrance to some corporate office building from tomorrow or a contemporary art museum. Same white walls, mega digital monitors of images of landscapes and waterfalls and sand dunes displayed to the sound of a flute that played from hidden speakers, light escaping from

< 122 >

the sides, black sculptures and potted plants scattered throughout. The ceiling a lighted dome, the same one from the stairwell and the lab upstairs, a single black rug that ran to the entrance atop the white floor that was so white it was impossible to remember what it was made of, just that it was so smooth I could see my reflection in it.

I realized I was definitely still in Chinatown, 'cause the entire wall on the side of the entrance was glass, as was the door, and I could see that I was still in the present, with the same models of cars speeding left to right and right to left in front of the same beat-up restaurants and motels and laundromats that lined the backdrop.

And the little Chinese guy? Still a little Chinese guy, except that he was sitting behind a white reception desk that looked to have grown out of the building, with the bottom edges curving and blending right into the floor and it stretched nearly the entire length of the side wall. Instead of sitting back and watching TV in his wad of Goodwill clothing, he was buried into his computer, wearing a white lab coat like everyone else upstairs. Behind him, a flat television screen that ran the entire length of the desk with *Wondervision* displayed in black letters against a blank white backdrop.

I swear, if there's one word that describes the place, it's *white*. Blinding white, surreal white, like a whole world trapped in a camera flash, like you can walk in and out of the building a different skin tone. After standing at the bottom of the stairwell in wonder, head spinning in all directions like radar, I proceeded, cautiously, toward the entrance.

*What the fuck.* Those three words defined every step I took, every glance, every thought that formed in my head as I made my way down the black strip.

And it didn't end there either.

In a moment I found myself looking back at the clinic from the sidewalk, and I don't know if I can explain it all in words, but Christ fucking Almighty, I will try.

I saw glass, all glass, black glass, structured to resemble half an egg, a fucking massive one, that shot twenty stories high into the sky, towering over the block with the bottom buried into the ground. In short, a big black fucking egg made of glass.

I saw the surrounding buildings. I saw that they were still there, except that they

< 124 >

looked cleaner, shit, not just cleaner, they were completely different buildings! In place of the dilapidated shitholes of the 1930s that everyone knows and loves and pictures when someone says "Chinatown" were these corporate structures, futuristic ones with glass walls and slide-open doors and business logos re-imagined to resemble accounting firms and banks and tech conglomerates. And I kid you not, it was the whole damn row!

I paced up and down the street. I counted ten parking spaces, a gap in between each of the five parked cars that filled the entire length of the building just an hour earlier.

I moved in between the spaces that were the cars, I walked in them, I danced, I skipped. Then at the ends of the lab, the empty spaces disappeared. It's like the world shifted thirty -five feet from west to east just to fit this fucking thing.

I saw a young woman who'd turned the corner down the block and started walking towards me. She passed the parking spaces without notice, walking at the same pace, moving in tandem to this new normal as if nothing had changed. Then more people passed, and for an indeterminable amount of time, I just stood there looking on all retarded-like as nobody seemed to notice how, seemingly, in just the last hour the whole place had been bought out and remodeled by some prick corporatist property owner trying to move Wall Street further east of the island.

And I saw, in large white print, pasted to the side of the building, unmistakable, displayed in all its glory:

### Wondervision Inc: Welcome to Your Better Reality.

My better reality?

Like Judy?

What the hell was all of this?

What the hell did they do to me?

So I went back inside, ran past the lobby and back up the stairwell, stopping once to gaze upwards at the dome and the monitors and back into the clinic with the people in white and the circular seating and the hallways that looked too big. The AI lady was gone. Nobody looked up at me. I turned back around and it was the stairwell from a Ridley Scott movie, then forward and it was the clinic from *Deep Space 9*. Back and forth, back and forth,

I couldn't fucking move. What the fuck kind of test was this?

And the shack that it was in from before, was that real? Seriously, was it? 'Cause I don't know how we could go back to that and say, "yeah, this makes more sense."

▪     ▪     ▪

I spent my journey on the green line heading to my next appointment ruminating about what had just happened; the operation, the reception desk, the AI lady, the stairwell, the lobby, the whiteness, the black egg of glass, the corporate offices surrounding the building, the doubling in length, the indifference of everyone else, the difference between an hour before and after. All these events played on repeat over and over and over, eating up every particle that is or was my rational mind.

Then, somewhere along the line, I must've hit a plateau. Seriously, there's only so much cognitive chaos a mind can handle before it has to shut down.

Reboot.

Reprocess.

And then I saw it all again, but from a different angle.

"All just in my head," I thought to myself. "Or rather, all inside the *Interface, my Interface*!"

That's it, right? None of that was real. Just an illusion, my supplemental brain, the little microchips they shoved through my cranium, it's all part of it. Isn't it?

Just little bits of information sent to my fingertips, my eyes, my nose, my ears. Or, what? Is it the other way around? That nothing is being sent? Just my brain intaking everything coming in from all of these little sensors that covers my body and giving me a different picture?

Wait, I thought that all that was gonna be altered was Judy's face! What the hell, are they building new realities for me now? What were they testing anyhow?

\* \* \*

I missed my stop and had to reroute from the other side, burnt another two bucks to exit and go back in from the other way.

Wanda was nice. Talented, competent, and, let me tell ya, drop-dead gorgeous.

Young, slender, wore her frizzled black hair out and proud with a checkered headband that kept it out of her face, smooth black skin,

< 128 >

and lips of glossy red. Her eyes were piercing, the kinds that can speak poetry, seduce me with a twitch of her brow, calm me with a blink, her eyelashes like veils and her pupils like little black holes.

Everything else was covered with a blue scrub and a white lab coat. What a shame.

I won't go into much detail talking about arriving, how the clinic looked, 'cause who hasn't been to one? Plus, most of the time leading up to me meeting her was basically spent in some other corner of my head.

But Wanda, goodness gracious, I tell ya, this woman could replace my entire day's worth of memories, like I woke up and then I was sitting up on her lab table, her soft hand rubbing my head, her eyes staring at me like she knew I was trying to figure her out.

So I sat on the bed like a horny middle schooler, nodding like an idiot to everything that came out of her mouth, grinning like I just learned how to.

"Yes Doc, yes Doc, not a problem Doc, not much Doc. My wife? Oh yeah, her."

In a moment, I was directed to a rolling bed in another room.

I felt a pinch in my arm.

I woke up.

I felt my head. The bumps were gone, just a head full of hair from end to end. A little itch, but that was it. I thought to myself, never having wiped that stupid grin, my troubles were over.

Whaddya know? I pulled it off.

So I left the center at around eleven p.m. after a long stint with all the post-operation evaluation and shit. On my way out, Doc Wanda came over with an envelope.

"For your wife, just in case," she said. Apparently she's been talking with Rick. I shoved it in my pocket, barely giving it a thought. After all, we've been down this road before.

Walking back home, I'd forgotten all about that crazy clinic.

In a short while, I'd even forgotten about that beautiful chick doctor.

All I could think of was what Judy was gonna look like when she got home.

.   .   .

So what am I now?

A cyborg?

< 130 >

Ha! Just thought of that. I'm officially part human and part machine, am I right? A cyborg with an antenna sticking outta his head. Guess tin foil hats wouldn't do me much good now, the government would just have to go online.

Wow, everything that's happened, how do I begin to process it all? I'm trying to work but I'm just not jiving with the tasks of the day, not the way I used to. I've got a hundred unread emails and half of them are marked important, and there's this order that needs to go out in an hour to some pissed-off customer, pissed off because I was late last time because I was too busy to open my cell phone or check my calendar. That or I might've been drunk, but to be honest, I don't even know the line between drunk and sober anymore; like was that water I had ten minutes earlier or another glass of vodka?

But I've realized something. There's no way in hell I'll truly be able to take all of this and understand it or what it means for me or humanity or anything deeper than how far I need to reach to find normalcy in life again. So I'll just let it happen, sit and strap in and look forward and forward only. All I'm gonna think about is this balance, this beautiful normal that we sacrifice so much for, and eventually, maybe I'll have time to make sense of it all.

So things will get better now. They have to. If all goes to plan, Judy will look as she did before the accident, and I will be able to treat her that way, the way she wants to be treated, the way she deserves to be treated.

I'm gonna fuck her brains out every night until she thinks she's a fucking queen. She's my queen, she's my empress, and she will only hear from me what she wants to hear, feel what she needs to feel, like the way I'll only perceive what I'll need to perceive, so that we can keep living the way our life together should be lived.

To sustain, to be, to love, to survive.

In one word, normalcy.

< 132 >

Hi Jay

First, I would like to congratulate you on a successful operation!

I had just gotten in after a slight illness, so I do apologize for not having responded yesterday. I did manage, however, to read your latest email. I must say, there is quite a lot to respond to.

To begin, about the operation itself, I am glad you found it as quick and painless as I had told you it would be.

You seem either very surprised or very curious, judging from the nature of your words. Rest assured, the procedure is standard, so much so that, believe it or not, it doesn't require human interaction.

Now, keep in mind, like I mentioned in my previous emails, most of the information I am about to give you is in the operations guide, but I will still try to explain it to the best of my ability.

< 133 >

So here goes.

When you entered the pod, gas was already running. It was clear and odorless, developed two years back to knock out inmates in solitary confinement who had developed sleeping disorders or had gone insane before being modified for medical purposes. The gas would've taken approximately two minutes to reach peak effect, suppressing all nervous system sensations as well as consciousness.

You say that you don't remember even going under. All I can say to that is that the anesthesia did its job well. Quite simply put, you were knocked out instantly.

Now, let me elaborate on what occurred during your subconscious state. Adjustment arms, or long robotic arms with padded ends long enough to push you one way or another, would've emerged from all directions to hold you in the correct spot. A cylinder contraption would've been lowered over your head, complete with a cap full of tiny drills at the end of tiny moving arms and a scanner that would've mapped out your brain. The operation from there would've been quick once the target sections had been identified, where each drill would've retired once getting past

< 134 >

your cranium and an apparatus the width of a sewing needle would've taken over, stitching the microfibers and microchip into the correct parts of your brain. Then, once complete, they would've retreated, the seat would've laid you down, and a tiny tube would've plugged the holes (save for the one over the microchip) with a quick-hardening composite mold that shoots out from its sides. Then, upon bringing you back up, the same procedure would've been performed for the one near your occipital lobe at the back of your head. This would've been done to prevent the very minimal chance anything would leak into your brain by keeping the tunnels horizontal so to offset the effects of gravity. Lastly, an advanced compound similar to Restylane, a "skin filler" used for cosmetic purposes, would've been applied to fill in the holes on your scalp.

As for not feeling anything, thank your *Interface*.

If you want any more information, I can send you material if you're interested.

Now, let's talk about that mysterious user acceptance testing.

< 135 >

Your operation was complete. The first person you saw when walking into the lobby was the receptionist, live and in person. You saw a circular reception desk in place of where the sphere used to be.

Kris, the receptionist, or who you called "AI lady," was merely a product of your *Interface*. So was the desk, so was the woman sitting down.

The man walking in for his screening, however, was real.

Everything after that, the stairwell, the atrium downstairs, what Dr. Nguyen (who you call the "Chinese Guy") was wearing, the building from the exterior, all of it was just a product of your *Interface*.

Did you imagine anything? Well, hard to say. Everything went through the same channels as before the operation. Everything was processed in your brain and displayed to your consciousness, just that certain things were superseded with perceptions produced by a slightly altered algorithm. To everyone else, the glass building, the sign, the space between the cars, the carbon-fiber walls and ceilings inside and the television monitors and the receptionist and the old lady, would've all been imagination, but for you, it was a controlled reality.

So what were we trying to accomplish with all of this?

We are required by NBIIS guidelines to submit data detailing our user acceptance testing (UAT), and the auditors look for thoroughness and that the testing was completed onsite. From the start, this presented us with a unique challenge. As what the *Interface* generated for the patient to perceive was a sum of all of his or her memories and current perception of reality, we were not privy to seeing it as it would be akin to reading their thoughts, something strictly forbidden per NBIIS.

Without the ability to see what was being tested, we had no way of programming pass or fail. Therefore, we had to build an entirely new environment from scratch, or what we call the *standard test*, independent from their memories and replicated for all customers. It was a program temporarily lodged inside the Interface and executed after implementation. From there, it created the world you reported perceiving.

As you went about the points of destination laid

< 137 >

out by Kris, the program was busy collecting data, recording who and what you were seeing, creating your conception of reality, and verifying everything; from Kris herself to the lady in the chair to the man walking to his appointment to the stairwell to the lobby to the block from outside.

It verified that you felt her touch on your shoulder, the sensation of it, the softness, the realism. It verified that you could see the service desk and the lady sitting in the chair. You even beat the test to the punch by touching her before we could bring her to you as she was scheduled to trip out of her seat while getting up, prompting you to assist her.

It verified that you saw the glow coming from behind the carbon fiber walls in the stairwell, the monitors and their displays of modern art and stats, the luminescent domed ceiling above, the gloss on the wooden stairs.

It verified that you could walk the circular path to the bottom, that you would have believed you followed its winding nature.

It verified that you felt the breadth of the lobby, the light protruding through the glass wall and the world outside.

< 138 >

It verified that you noticed the cameras, the art, the designs, Dr. Nguyen and his desk, the design of the floor to the ceiling, the company logo. It verified if you saw the glass egg that shot to the sky from the outside, the change in space, the corporate buildings along the block, the logo and the parking spaces.

It verified that you saw it all, that you were convinced, that the *Interface* was indeed working before releasing you into the world, that you were experiencing only what you were intended to experience, and that you were experiencing it to the fullest extent of what you were meant to. Mostly, it was the best we could do without having Judy physically present.

It would've then compiled all the technical procedures and results and stored them before combining them with everyone else's and submitting them to our auditors in August.

And of course, I repeat, nowhere in this process would any of us have laid eyes on what you were seeing and thinking. The testing server would've handled everything.

As to why the exact nature of the test itself was kept from you before the operation, this was something that is still up for debate and is subject to change in the future. Our late founder, Dr. Bosma, championed this unconventional idea of letting your instincts and curiosity guide you rather than creating anticipation, believing the shock would lead you in a more thorough inspection of the world around you. Anything missed, as Kris had indicated, would've prompted a call for you to come back for a more guided procedure.

The idea was this: had we informed you as to the exact nature of what you would've been seeing, we feared it would have compromised some of this precious curiosity, making the process more involved and cumbersome and limiting than what could've been achieved with the pure force of human wonder.

Of course, not everyone in the testing department agrees with this approach as, I will be the first to admit, it has its potential for flaws. But to date, it hasn't failed us in passing audits, and that was enough to convince Dr. Bosma.

And it may have been a bit much, but as with every audit, the more data the better.

Lastly, this test environment has been deactivated as it expires after submission.

I know this was a lot of information, but it is standard protocol for me to ensure you leave the process understanding it in full.

I am glad things turned out okay with Dr. Wanda Jennings. Aside from her looks, I do hope you find her as an exceptional surgeon in her trade. In fact, you may hear of her more going forward, as she has begun making quite a reputation for herself in the field.

Please let me know about how it goes with Judy and if everything went according to how you wanted it to go. I will continue to do everything from my end to ensure you get what you need, so please feel free to continue with the updates.

I hope to hear from you soon. Good day and good luck!


Josh Rikkard
Relationship Manager
*Wonderlenz* Technologies Inc.

*Dear Doc.*

I guess he's just gonna let me keep calling him that. Ha! Go figure. I wouldn't mind being called one myself, but these guys deserve it more. Honestly, that thing I said about what they'll be doing for me? Making me whole again, giving me the ability to see? And some other shit like that?

Well, they've done it. Cured me like what Jesus did to that blind guy. Heard that story in church last weekend. Yeah that's right, I'm going back to the house again. Well, sort of, trying to. It was one trip and it's really something Judy wanted to do.

< 142 >

Honestly for me, I sorta go to look supportive and threatening, like I'd knock the lights outta any fuck who'd so much as give her an eye. Not that I don't believe in the good book or the guy in the sky, I'm just not a big reader or student of anything, so going to church was always a bit like going to school. I'd fall asleep, snore, make a scene, embarrass everyone I'm with, maybe piss off Jesus; poor guy getting nailed to the cross just for me to sit there thinking about poking my wife the moment we got back home, stealing glances at her face, wanting nothing more than to rip that mask she wore off so I could let the world see what I saw.

Except nobody could've seen what I saw. Not her, not the clergy, not the congregation, nobody. Instead, they walked around her, brushed right past without making eye contact to either of us, going straight to their own groups of friends and neighbors and colleagues and fuck buddies 'cause who the hell wants to deal with those pesky feelings like compassion? I swear, even in the house of God, everyone's first instinct when faced with it is to grab for any excuse to not have to give a flying fuck like it was hard currency, more precious than time and money, made to be held close and invested for some bullshit social capital rather than spent on useless things like people in need.

And Judy is a person in need, in need of the same shit everyone else seems to always be in desperate shortage of. Empathy, love, security, and the real friendships that twist the three together. In a nutshell, a flying fuck, something that's hard-earned when you and everyone around you perceives you as some kinda monster based off of some perception made without a second thought, inquiry, or doubt.

But fuck 'em, she's got me. She's always had me, and now, finally, since the day of the accident, I have her too. Back home, with me, working together to make the last six months of hell disappear.

.  .  .

Honestly, I didn't know what to expect at first.

As a matter of fact, for the next few days after the operation, I went about like nothing happened; going to work, day in and day out, sifting through the day to day dealings, a beer

< 144 >

with the guys at Southies, everything under that priceless umbrella called normalcy.

Flowing under the current though, I admit, there was a little anxiety. It may sound crazy, but I really didn't know how I would react if everything went well.

I didn't know if I'd throw my arms around her and kiss her like she came back from the dead, or if I'd stand with my mouth open all stupid and shit like I was when looking up at the crystal glass egg-shaped building that was the broken down Chinatown motel questioning reality, or if I'd be smart.

Smart, like, reacting as if nothing had changed. Running my left hand down the side of her face and asking if it still hurt while staring right into her eyes without blinking, pretending her face was still the same deformed mess and that I'd somehow become a changed man.

Changed, to accept, to have somehow evolved to see what the standards of society wanted me to see: her inner beauty, her presence, her soul, the sum of all things that should've made her more attractive to me than anything else. To hold her like a piece of me were gone, like I was trying to take it all back,

< 145 >

without seeing her face, without touching her ass, as if she could've been anything at the moment and I'd feel all the same.

To have somehow evolved to see her in all those ways rather than what I had reprogrammed myself to see, because I couldn't think of anything else at the moment that would've given it away more.

On reflection, I think I might've been just coping, giving myself a running start into the lie of a world I'd created for us, hoping I could convince myself that it was the truth, and then live my life with her the way it was meant to be lived. In happiness.

Or it all could've been a flop, and I'd have to stare at her boobs or something to calm myself.

■   ■   ■

She came home a day later than she said, six days after my operation rather than four. Not a call from her parents, not a return call from her, not even a reply to my text messages.

Six days. The first four flew by quick, but days five and six were like weeks.

Yes, I could've called her parents, but let me tell ya, I never call her fucking parents. It'll have to be a real emergency for me to go there. Fucking pricks, they'd probably not answer on purpose 'cause as far as I could tell, if history could provide any clues, they probably blamed me for what happened to her. I knew as much from trying to get in touch with her when she was over there. They didn't even think to give me a heads up to leave her alone.

But after day four, I was ready to bite that bullet. I was desperate. I couldn't go another minute without her, not another fucking minute. It was pure agony; the waiting without answers, the gallon of whiskey I'd lapped up, the mess I've left everyone at work, my mind spinning back to that hellish snowy night it all started. So on day six, I was ready to check my pride at the door and drive over there and knock. And if they didn't open, I was ready to camp out on their lawn until either they called the police or Judy came out to talk. And if they called the police, I was ready to make a big enough scene so that Judy could hear me through the window and realize how far I was willing to go to make it right with her.

I had put on my shoes and was looking around for my keys. I Google Mapped the fastest route there and rehearsed every angry line I was gonna deliver. I was dialing my rage so that it would be effective but controlled. I was on my way to grab my wife and bring her back, even if charges were pressed, so long as I could see her.

Then when I opened the door, a woman was walking toward me from the end of the hall. I stopped, frozen in place, and I swear, I seriously worried for half a second that I'd never be able close my gaping mouth. It was Judy, my Judy, the real Judy, smiling from ear to ear, both eyes wide like a doe and brimming with ebullience, her cheeks rosy and red, her bangs swooping in ever so gently over her paint-brush like brows.

It worked. I don't know what else to say. It caught me so off guard at first that I found myself ready to fall to my knees.

My Judy, back from the dead.

"Hey, honey," she whispered. It sent shock waves through my chest. It's been so long since I've heard it, that voice that could provide me a lifetime of nourishment. She dropped her things. I walked over with every intention to throw my arms around her and squeeze the life out of that delicate little body, relish every second of the moment the way I do with the

< 148 >

bottle after weeks of attempted sobriety, leave her shit in the hallway and bring her back in and put her down on the bed and go at it all day and night until she realizes that everything had returned to normal.

But I just stood there, millimeters away from her, touching her cheeks, her hair. We just stood there gazing into each other, smiling like fools, looking for all the things to say but not wanting to say anything to ruin existence right then and there, when everything seemed to come back to balance, and everything was right again. Maybe this was enough to let her know that everything had for sure returned to normal.

And then when the time came, I said my first words.

"Babe, does it still hurt?"

．　．　．

Well, I couldn't just go back to normal, at least not immediately.

I had to keep myself in control, fight the urges, and stand up to my hormones. Remember, as far as Judy is concerned, I still see her face as it is; burnt off, half-destroyed, I think I've said enough. When I wanted to touch her face, I'd poke. When I wanted to kiss her, I aimed for the left side of her cheek. When I stroked her head, I'd have to remember all the places where there was and wasn't hair. I almost wished that I could turn it off and on to my convenience, that fucking *Interface*. "On" when I'm trying to fuck her and "off" when I'm not. "On" to show her how much it didn't matter anymore and "off" to cover up what a lying asshole I am.

Eventually, however, I realized that all I needed was time, patience, and a little bit of practice.

Eventually.

On that first day, after the moment she came home, we didn't hug, we didn't kiss, we barely spoke. Not that I didn't want to, but the vibes I was getting from her hadn't changed, not since she left. Sure, she was smiling, sure she was happy to see me. But underneath it all, there was still an undercurrent of distrust. Like I cheated on her or something, like me having once a sexual preference for her prettier self to her current was akin to infidelity, and that although she stood there brimming ear to ear, she did so in the shadow of every reason she left.

So instead of embracing as I had wanted to do for so damn long, where a hug or a kiss even would've been just a portion of it, I found myself carrying her suitcase that was bigger than her back into the room while she followed from behind without saying a word.

I don't remember what happened after that, not immediately anyhow, but I do remember there was this point where we were sitting on the couch having finally settled down a while later. It was already evening, and neither of us had eaten. Food wasn't exactly on the top of my mind, not with the suffocating cloud of a billion other little things I would rather entertain.

So there she was, all stretched out on that white leather couch, next to the window, her favorite thing in the house, wearing her black yoga pants and over-sized sweatshirt that she always wore, and she had in her hand a glass of merlot from a bottle she must've bought on the way. She wasn't looking at me. Instead, she was staring out the window, over the city, eyes pointed at the evening sky as the last rays of sun retreated towards her left. She sat there with the lights off, and I wanted to keep it that

< 151 >

way, because she looked so at peace when the light was somewhere else.

I was sitting in the armchair directly in front of her. It was just one of those moments where I didn't mind the quiet, and knowing me, those moments are virtually non-existent. I was sitting with a glass of whiskey, neat, Johnny Walker Black, my third one in the hour, and I didn't feel a thing, too distracted to feel the drunk. At that moment, sitting with this aura, this glow against the city lights as the night fell that made it almost surreal, that even without the *Interface* kickin', she would've looked just as she'd looked then.

Shit. Let me tell ya something about a man in heat. He either becomes a sex offender or Shakespeare in love.

"How'd you get back?" I finally asked, breaking the silence.

"Took my old Volvo, from high school."

"Wow, I'm surprised your folks hadn't sold that piece of junk," I replied. She only shrugged. I let a few more minutes pass before trying again.

"So, you never answered my question."

She turned around. She looked back at the window. She put down her wine glass. Why do I remember that specifically? I can't tell ya. For whatever reason, after the operation, when I'm paying attention, things that happened are as clear as day.

"Sorry," she said real soft, barely whispering. "What was that?"

It hit me that these were just her second set of words since she first called out my name in the hallway that day, and just hearing words from her mouth in her voice at that moment sent my neck hairs into a stiff.

"I asked if it still hurt."

"Oh," she said, plain and simple, before raising the glass of red to her face again.

"No, it doesn't hurt. Didn't really hurt before I left either."

"That's good," I replied, bobbling my head up and down in that annoying way we guys do, like we ain't impressed or unimpressed. "That's real good. Good, good, good."

"Yeah," she said, holding her glass to her lips, chewing on it the way she would. Then she stopped. Slowly, she turned towards the backrest of the couch.

I tell ya, wiping my eyes, I can still see it now like it were still in front of me. I can see her spirit set, the light from her eyes going

< 153 >

out, the shadow of the couch covering the left side of her face.

She followed the rest of the room as all went dark, having found a special friend in it during her time away, a concealer better than anything on the market.

Had I turned the light on, she woulda sucked it all away.

Had I touched her, I woulda felt nothing.

She didn't cry, she didn't groan, she didn't fall asleep. She just disappeared, and not all the power of the *Interface* could've brought her back.

Well, at least it didn't hurt.

*   *   *

The second day came. I woke up realizing I'd slept alone and went into the living room to find her fast asleep on the couch. She was still dressed in that same outfit from the night before and the wine glass lay empty on the floor.

I prepared breakfast; wild rice with eggs over easy on top with a hint of soy and tuna, our favorite, and the best remedy to any bedtime fight. Delicious stuff. Sometimes I find myself adding a hint of mayonnaise into the mix as a treat without her looking, the same way I'd see her add a shot of vodka into her coffee.

Actually, that was me. Also me.

I brought the food to her. I set it up on a sofa table, you know, the kind where the bottom part slides under the couch so the platform slides over the top so you could eat without having to do something so strenuous like reaching for your beer. I tell ya, genius invention, better than the smart phone, brings me a lot more joy than anxiety.

Anyways, I sat the plate down and went about my business. Got my computer out and set it on my lap, ready for a long-overdue full day's work. But I never really made it past opening the thing, and I ain't talking about turning it on neither, but literally unfolding the screen and looking up.

She was sleeping better than she had ever slept before, like she was floatin' on a cloud. From the neck down, you would've thought her dead by how still her figure was, not even rising and falling the way sleeping bodies do. But then a few inches up and all came back to life. I couldn't explain why either. What was it about a sleeping face so still that could make it seem so alive? Maybe it was the lack of agony, like a sudden calm had taken over her eyes, her lips, her brows. Then again, it was probably just the *Interface* talking.

I wanted to curl up next to her, touch her, kiss her. I wanted so much from her being there, so much more than pretending I wasn't seeing what I was seeing so that I could keep up this lie. So much more than turning away, so much more than restraint, so much more.

Forget sex, I just wanted to tell her she was beautiful.

Forget beautiful, I just wanted to tell her she was loved.

Forget love, I just wanted to tell her anything.

Anything and everything about my last few months without her, every day, every hour (excluding the *Interface* shit). About how many times I wanted to visit her, how I wanted to take back every word I said that made her leave, and how I remember each one like they would forever be a part of me and all the shame I carried on my back side.

She woke up finally. It was practically noon. Rather than minding the food, she walked over and stood in front of me.

She wrapped her arms around my shoulders, gently at first, then a squeeze.

Then I felt it, delicious and quenching. Normalcy.

< 156 >

＊　＊　＊

So another day passed. She spent it doing shit nothing, reading books on her Kindle and streaming shows in her room on her iPad like she used to when she wasn't napping.

Some things improved a bit.

She ate the food I cooked her for one. Well, some of it. Threw out two-thirds of it 'cause either she wasn't hungry or wasn't feeling my culinary work. Plus, leftover food is disgusting.

Sad. She'd always loved my cooking. Never left a scrap on the plate before she left.

She'd also begun talking a little more, talking about everything that could be said without saying a thing.

"Well," she'd say with a smile after I'd asked her how she slept.

"Looks good," she said of the plate of fried okra with glazed chicken breast over a bed of quinoa before ingesting just a third of it, leaving the rest to the disposer.

"Looks cold today," she said after looking outside.

"Looks warm today," she said after looking outside again.

"You look busy," she said when I went to work.

"Off work?" she said when I closed my laptop.

I tried to talk back, attempting conversation.

"You bet your ass it is, eat it before it's cold!"

"Sure is babe. Says it's in the low fifties."

"Sure is babe. Says it's in the low fifties."

"Sure am babe. Some miscommunication with that freight broker outta Chicago."

"Sure am babe. Done for the day."

It was like before, those dark ages, that gap of time between the operating room and her leaving; existing, acknowledging, and nothing more.

Right after lunch or so, she laid down on the couch, overlooking the city with a glass of red, wearing that same oversized sweater and those same leggings from the night before. I felt her eyes on my back. I turned and caught them and held on for nearly half a second too long before swinging my head around in fake discomfort.

Throughout the next hour, all I wanted to do was turn back around and stare. All I wanted to do was walk up to her on the couch, rip off that ugly fucking sweatshirt and those leggings and eat her alive. I wanted to taste those lips again, inhale that perfume, run my fingers down her cheeks until they turned red, breathe in everything she was breathing out, fuse, become one.

I also wanted to fuck her, but shit, I was gonna take whatever I could get.

I had to sit with my dick tucked between my legs to calm it down, my balls probably looking like the color of the sky and talking to my heart 'cause I could hear it beat like drums. Seriously, I had no fucking clue how long I'd keep it up.

It was beginning to look self-defeating, like one of those Chinese finger traps. The harder I'd try, the worse shit got. The more my hormones would speak, the more she'd hate herself, and the closer she'd get to the door once again.

"Fuck this," I thought as I turned around. She looked up. I walked over, got on my knees, leaned over, and delicately placed my fat lips on hers. Softly at first, then a little harder as the lavender perfume filled my nose. I suddenly grabbed the back of her head like I was eating her face whole.

She didn't struggle. She just let it all happen, like she'd been waiting all day for me, wondering why I was sitting there, back turned, checking her out like a creep from the corner of my eye, whacking myself off between my legs.

But shit, it was just day three.

Three days had already passed.

*   *   *

Let me try to explain this in another way.

Let me start off talking about the next two weeks by starting with how it ended.

Let me talk about that night at twelve a.m.

Midnight, where we were lying in bed, panting, smiling, my tongue hanging out the side of my mouth like I just had a seizure. Clothes were strewn on and off the bed, condom wrappers torn in two pressing against the skin on my back.

Midnight, where I turned over to Judy, expecting what you'd probably expect from her at this point. Shock, probably with a big -ass stupid smile, like the "how the fuck did he do that?" kind of smile.

Like the "where did that come from?" kind of smile.

"What changed?"

"Did that really just happen?"

< 160 >

The beginning of this saga before she left, where she ended up desperately tugging on my dick to bring it back to life while I stared at her boobs like they were her face, her body sprawled out, wasted on the floor as if daring me to fuck her like a real man would to his woman with a half of a fifth of vodka running through her veins, her storming out and never looking back for two months because of it, and now here, after all that time, here I am having finally gone at her like a fucking piston and all she could do was fall the fuck asleep.

And she was very fucking asleep, still and motionless. You could hold your finger under her nose and only barely feel the carbon dioxide, its passing feeling like nothing but a tickle.

She looked so peaceful, her eyes no longer squeezing shut to the nightmares that had haunted her before. She looked like she'd found some comfort in the subconscious, like she'd found a way to dream herself, the way I fixed myself, to see herself.

Where I turned back around, still smiling all big, 'cause who the fuck cares how she reacts, right? I finally cracked it, the whole operation, all that stood between us.

But it took two weeks. Two weeks to get there, to earn it.

Fourteen days from that third day where I finally thought I was getting somewhere.

Where I had almost ditched the whole plan just to get laid, my hands running behind her back, my mouth all over her neck, my hands slowly creeping to her bra. Then, a force against my chest.

"No," she said bluntly.

"No?" I replied abruptly, unable to squeeze out the full question.

"Just no," she said, completing it.

"No," I replied, getting up and looking around all lost while she crouched back in the corner of the couch, looking back up at me like I were some kind of predator.

"Of course," I repeated, hands raised as if telling her to chill the fuck out. "Sorry, babe, just that."

I paused. She wasn't looking at me anymore. Instead, the right side of her face was tucked back against her and the couch, left eye pointed at the window. She had tucked it away from me so fast, her head snapping into position the moment she leaned into the

< 152 >

headrest. A defense mechanism of some kind, involuntary movement of self-preservation she'd developed in her time away, no doubt there'd be more.

Was I angry? I couldn't be angry. Not at Judy, not for everything she must've been going through. But was I frustrated? A little.

She had left me. Left me without even a hug goodbye or a face to face talk. A text message, and then for the next sixty days, abject loneliness.

Yeah, I needed those two months! What for the operation and all the prework that came with it! But still, would I have gone through it if she were still there? Had she trusted me to work it out with her rather than abandoning me for her parents? Did she, for one moment, think about what she was leaving me to? How, like a dutiful husband, I stayed, loyal like a fucking dog, wiping her ass and making her food and becoming her fucking butler for all that time until she decided I was good for nothing and left me questioning everything I may have or should've done?

And now she was back, and without even a sorry or thank you, she could only push me further, as if I wasn't already on my trajectory out that door. Fuck the operation, fuck the *Interface*, fuck the marriage, fuck Judy!

Yeah, so maybe I was a little angry. Or maybe that's just me thinking in hindsight, but the feelings are all the same.

But despite the rising heat in my face, I found enough control to bite my lips and sit back down at the kitchen counter, open my laptop, and attempt to work. Only that I never got back to work, not immediately anyways. Instead, I sat there talking to myself, saying the same thing over and over again like therapy.

"You think she's hideous, you think she's hideous, you think she's hideous."

I might've even said it out loud, maybe once. But by then, she was back in our room, doing God knows what, being miserable for the both of us.

The rest of the day was un-eventful. As soon as I got done with work, I went to Southie's and put down two shots of Grey Goose and washed it down with four glasses of bourbon.

The next morning, I woke up in the hall. I was flat on my stomach, nose deep in my own breath, my cheek wet from the drool. I woke up to old lady Margie who lived next

< 154 >

door, nudging me, asking if all was fine, if she needed to call an ambulance.

"Have you never been hungover before?" I asked, really not meaning to sound like a dick.

A pause.

"Dick," she snorted before disappearing into her own room.

My key was in the door. Looked like I got close.

When I got in, I was greeted with the smell of ham, bacon, and fried eggs. Jesus, I'm licking my lips thinking about it now. It's depressing, really, but this wasn't the first time I came home at seven a.m. in such a state, and somehow, she'd remembered exactly what to do.

No bullshit, no crap, just some greasy food swimming in maple syrup and butter.

"I've already eaten," she said with a smile as she headed back to her room. There were two plates, sizzling hot and piled from edge to edge, sitting on the table. There was a liter of hot coffee still in the pot, a fork and knife assembled next to a wet mouth-wipe, shakers of salt and pepper and sugar, assembled in a ring around where I was to sit.

< 165 >

I glanced at the kitchen. Clean as if nothing was made, just as I've always wanted it after prepping a meal. Clean and tidy, as was the room, as was the table. All I needed to do was sit and gorge in blissful peace.

Coming up for a breath of air, mouth full of everything wonderful about that morning, bacons and pancakes and fried eggs mixed in heavenly glory, I wasn't sure if I was still angry or if I'd even forgiven her or whatever. It was enough, just for that moment, to make me forget about everything that had driven me to drink the night prior, and in hindsight, probably enough to hold my tongue in place and keep it from making any noise that would've sent everything to flaming hell.

After a stretch, a belch, and a rub of the stomach, I crashed hard on the couch.

I slept until four p.m. before waking up to my stomach talking.

I woke up to see Judy on the other end, curled up and reading. For a split second, I thought about trying again, with all of my hormones egging me on, still not over the defeat from a day earlier.

Instead, I just got up and made my way to the kitchen counter where my computer still sat. I heated up some leftover *Happy Dragon* (my Chinese food hiatus over) to share and spent the rest of the evening responding to the five hundred pissed-off people I'd brushed off.

The next day, things went back to her sitting next to the window while I worked, talking without dialogue, living with each other rather than together. Then another day went by, then another, and then another, and I weathered each and every one of them like a trapeze artist on a tightrope.

It's funny how a simple moment of calm can rewire an entire trajectory, like how a meal and a day-long nap could temper me enough, just enough, to hold my tongue and think. Think and make a decision. A decision to put all that shit that happened with the operation, all the weirdness of that fucking lab and that test and AI lady and everything else, in its own little storage container for later use. Same with my resentment. It sounds easy, but it took years of anger management and therapy to get it right.

I didn't know if it would make anything better, but at the very least it kept everything from getting worse. Worse, like her walking out again, and me sitting in the empty

< 167 >

apartment in some twisted déjà vu, buried in misery, knowing that this time she wasn't coming back.

No. Instead I let go of time and let it take us to wherever we were meant to go, putting my faith into it, worshipping it, all the while doing my best to just be the best husband I could be. Be her rock, be her smile, be her shelter, be her home, let time do the rest. I let go of my strategy. I was gonna treat her exactly as I saw her, because hell, who was I to let myself get in the way of the normalcy I paid so much for?

Now I admit, I did have my moments.

One night, I might've visited an online community for advice. They were fucking useless, but then again, that might have something to do with how I was wording my ask. "Wife's face burnt to shit, now she hates me. Help?"

Another night I'd opened my trap texting with my buddy Bard, the barkeep at Southie's. He told me it reminded him of his wife during labor. Dumb as bricks, and he wondered why I couldn't find it in me to thank him.

Another time I even tried texting her best friend Amber for advice (we share all of our contacts with each other for emergency purposes). She sounded a mix of excited and pissed off she was back.

*OMG she's back? From where?*

Yeah, I forgot Judy put her on her blackout list when it all happened half a year back.

*WTF, I kept texting her, like, four months ago and she never responded! Why was she ignoring me? Is everything alright?*

Fuck.

So I decided to move on. Didn't reply, won't reply, at least until Judy is feeling comfortable in her own skin again to reach out and reconnect. God knows when that'll be.

For most of the two weeks, however, I let time take the lead. Funny what happens when you do that, because it just freezes in place. Well, not freeze in place like people can't move or whatever, but in the sense that everything becomes so damn repetitive. Like yesterday starts looking so much like today, which you know will look like tomorrow. Judy getting up at ten to come out into the living room to read or watch sitcom reruns on Netflix while I worked until noon, I would make a quick lunch and afterward take her out for a stroll around the block until 1:30. We'd get back and repeat the morning until evening at six, when I'd make dinner and sit with her to watch some random show or movie classic with a glass of wine and scotch until midnight, when I'd turn around to find her fast asleep on the other side of the couch or, in time, lying all snug and comfortable on my lap.

Let it go and time can take two weeks and make it a day.

Then it was the middle of last week, Wednesday I think. We were out on a walk, heading to Central Park. I wanted to take her all the way to 59th, call it a day trip around the Onassis, the lawn, the Met, wherever we would end up. I don't know, I might've been desperate to break the routine, 'cause I've honestly had enough of the block surrounding our place. Barely made it into the park before she wanted to head back. That facemask was too hot for her in the middle of summer.

"You could try taking it off, babe," I suggested.

She shook her head.

"Babe," I continued, "would ya just take it off? Just for a moment? If it's too hot, just take it off for ten seconds. Nobody's gonna turn and stare, and if they do, I'll make 'em blind."

She didn't respond.

"Besides," I continued, "ain't you sick of life between the four sidewalks around our building? Please, babe, just this once."

She started to walk away again, then something took ahold of me. Before I could think, I was holding her, both hands pressed tightly against each delicate little shoulder, and I was holding her very still, still and silent as my arms had acted quicker than my mind.

"Please," I said, "Look at you, look at us. We're never gonna walk further than two blocks from our place?"

"I'm not stopping you," she responded.

"No," I said, "No, no, no, no, babe, you're trying to start a fight. I'm not biting it. This ain't for me."

Of course it was.

But I felt her shoulders relax; I had her attention.

"Babe, come on, I'm not going home. I'm here for you, with you. And right now, I wanna to take you to the Met. I wanna take you down to that French pastry place on 59th and 7th, the one with those Macrons you'd spend half a week's hard-earned money on like they were made of gold or something. I wanna buy you three boxes of 'em and stuff them in your rosy little mouth until the crumbs are falling between the cracks of your lips.

"Well, that or a coffee. Fifty bucks for a box ya know? It's fucking criminal.

But seriously, babe, I wanna take you somewhere, somewhere you could take that mask off and let the whole world see your smile, your eyes, the shine they bring, the way they glow against any direction of light. And if they react, I'll personally show 'em what it's like to walk with half a face missing, swear to God."

Nothing. She was never the kind to fall for that kind of shit, even had I actually said those words.

No, I was just holding her, looking at her the way I've been looking at her every day and every night since she came home.

And somehow, she noticed.

Somehow, she was able to read the words I couldn't say, like they were superimposed like a teleprompter on my eyes over the glare.

I reached for her mask. She didn't stop me.

I gently peeled back the layers and layers. They didn't stick. Rather, they came off like untying a shoe, one strand freeing another freeing another.

Behind one strand, cheeks so smooth with a perfect blend of pinkish hue and peach, without a wrinkle, satin covering the delicate structure underneath.

Behind another, brows that crescendoed right above the eye commanding presence and effortlessly shying into oblivion towards the temple, hinting intrigue.

Behind another, a nose, an eyebrow disappearing into its right contour.

Behind another, dark lashes shot out of the corner of the eye and curved into the sky.

Then, her hair, her black hair that breezed behind her ear and back over her shoulder, catching the rays of the sun at all the right angles.

Then, the rest of her lips, her sharp lower jaw.

Jesus, this is starting to sound like Amish erotica.

Anyways.

At that moment, I wanted to throw those bandages away, into a can, over a pile of wood. I wanted to set them ablaze, let fire bring back the face it destroyed.

I held her there, close, and instructed her softly over and over, like a meditation instructor. I instructed her to look at me, to look only at me, focus on me, the blue sky, the abandoned buildings, the empty street. Focus on us, just her and me. I brushed her bangs away and held them against the back of her head. I swear, if you could eat someone alive with your eyes, I was fucking ravenous.

By then, her shoulders had collapsed. She'd given me total control. So I brought her in to my chest. I didn't know what else to do. She was so limp. It felt like she would've fallen any other way had I let go.

Thank goodness for every shrink who put up with my shit for hours on end and their ways of settling me down. I've seen 'em all one too many times.

As I held her close, I noticed people were staring. Oh were they fucking staring!

There were three of 'em, this creepy old guy, this chick jogging, this wise guy with a red tie sitting on the bench, looking at us like they've never seen PDA before.

"You fucks got somewhere to be?" I shouted.

They kept walking. The old guy's lips

scrunched up in a smirk, I could've run up and knocked it right off, that bastard.

"What's going on?" asked Judy, taking a step back, looking around for those nosy fucks.

Others passed, quickly, the way you would a drunk, half-naked bum in the subway station. A swivel to look, a swivel back straight as if pretending you were facing that way the entire time, and two swivels back when you thought nobody was looking.

"Give me my mask, Jay," she said, quietly. I obliged.

We never made it to Central Park. It was too much for her.

If only took a second to undo all my work of bringing her back to the world.

A world outside of those pieces of linen.

.   .   .

Her mother tried to reach us last Friday.

Seven a.m. Judy was still asleep to my right, and I happened to peek at my phone to notice she'd called me three times. I didn't even hear it ring. My settings took care of her for me, not that I blocked her or anything. It just goes straight to voicemail for certain people.

< 175 >

Then came the text messages.

*Where the hell is Judy?*

Yeah, that's how she talks to me. I wasn't kidding.

*I've been trying to call you guys!*

*I've called YOU ten times!*

Three times.

*Where the hell is she?! Is she home?!*

"Judy?" I said, gently nudging her.

She moaned, that soft kind, that perfect pitch melody, exposing the delicate nature that is her soul before her waking mind takes over.

"Get off! Stop pinching me!"

"Babe, it's your mom."

No response. She was back asleep. She's got this knack for that, shifting in and outta consciousness in seconds, a wonderous gift of evolution in the modern era.

*She's asleep, will text you when she wakes.*

Who the fuck calls this early?

An hour later, we were eating brunch. I'd made some steel oats with blueberries and raisins, egg white omelets with turkey bacon and spinach, a whole sourdough bread on the side, and two cappuccinos made fresh downstairs. I had my laptop set up next to me and was reviewing some bills of lading for a shipment

< 176 >

in the afternoon, using a full hour to eat as I shifted between my screen and my plate.

Then my screen flashed.

*Can I speak to Judy?*

"Judy," I said, in between annotating and spooning a mouthful of hot cereal into my hole.

"Your mom wants to talk to you."

She looked at her phone before responding with a sigh, "Yeah, she's called a couple of times."

"A *couple* of times?" I replied real smug.

"Be nice."

"Just saying."

*Jay, seriously, is she up?*

What the hell was she so antsy for?

"Judith, she's driving me nuts. Would you just call her or something?"

She didn't respond.

"Judy, babe, would you call your mother? She's just gonna keep bugging us—"

"I'm not fucking calling her," she snapped.

I looked up. This I loved. This attitude, this anger, this resentment, directed at her old lady instead of me. It was relishing. I about licked my lips.

"Why not, honey?"

She was being about as communicative as

usual, burying her forehead into her palm and caressing the left side of it.

"Don't wanna talk about it?" I asked.

She didn't respond.

I sat back and decided to take a quick stab at it, easy figuring given the nature of her parents. Middle class but owns three luxury cars with one parked in the driveway, rugs from China with calligraphy they claim to mean "divine peace" when it probably reads "do not dry clean," meditation room constructed only to show friends, *hate has no place here* signs in a neighborhood 100% white. Aristocratic upper long-island snobs, all exterior and nothing beneath.

"Did someone try to come over?" I began theorizing. "Oh, let me guess," I shut the lid on my computer and plopped down in front of her. I was brimming from ear to ear. "They wouldn't let anyone over, right? Somebody wanted to stop by for dinner. Your mom probably made excuses, citing the house being a mess, the shit she has to do tomorrow, you know, all that work retirees do when they're sitting on a boatload of inheritance with no dependents. She probably told everyone how you were still living in Manhattan, probably how you never visit. She probably said all that not knowing the door was opened to your room, and you fucking heard everything."

She didn't confirm or deny. She just let out a sigh, rocking her head back and forth while staring at her phone which happened to be turned off. It was as good as gold.

"Alright," I replied after a minute of silence, "let me handle this."

I grabbed my phone from my side of the table.

I replied.

*Judy doesn't wanna talk to you, but don't worry about her. We're going for walks, visiting cafes, eating home-made meals and fucking.*

We weren't just yet.

*I really missed her gorgeous face while she was gone.*

*She won't respond to you. She's really pissed at you two at the moment; I'd wait until she's completely recovered and her face restored back to normal.*

*Your normal.*

*Until then, kindly fuck off.*

I showed her the string of texts.

She smiled, a real one, the kind that catches you off guard, where you don't even notice.

Nothing happened from there. Her mother didn't respond immediately. She was gonna need an entire day of Vicodin and squabbling over it with some friends from hot yoga before she could form the words. I went back to work; Judy went back to doing nothing. The rest of the day went as fast as any other.

Then came evening. A stroll around the block and the purchase of a bottle of cognac. She was leaning particularly close to me while we watched some shit on Netflix. A kiss of the lips, and the rest of the night happened in the way this long-ass section began.

An evening of delicious normalcy, my phone going off so many times with texts flying over from her mother, it about doubled as a vibrator.

.   .   .

Judy wanted to go to church.

It caught me off guard. The woman had spent the better of the last two to three weeks sheltered in place, like hunkering down from an epidemic. Now she wanted to go all of three blocks south of Central Park.

She'd been before, maybe twice to mass

before the accident. Never one to be crazy religious, as she was raised secular with a culturally Jewish mother and a progressive Catholic father, she'd only go on an invite by Amber for a pickup game of indoor volleyball at the church gym or for special events where there'd be a shit ton of food in the kitchen. My kind of gal; always knew her priorities.

I'd just come back from a quick Saturday morning trip to one of my warehouses in Jersey.

She was perched on the couch, which was by now her woman version of a mancave. Box wine on the floor under the armrest, favorite books in front, her tablet resting on the backrest plugged into the outlet behind, socks and slippers and all of her favorite blankets tossed all over every other inch of the thing. 'Bout needed a shovel to dig out a space for my ass every night when we'd watch something or read or chill in silence.

She was perched there, looking out the window, wrapped in a blanket from her neck down, and her face glowed against the fragments of light that slipped through the gray covering the sky and through the speckled glass that nobody washes nor has washed in a year.

I put my stuff down and crashed at her feet.

"How's the weather?" she asked.

"Ain't hot, ain't cold," I responded.

Then laughter. I got up and walked over to the window and saw a group of kids. Well, "kids," or a group of guys and gals in their twenties or thirties or whatever age range accounts for full heads of hair and skinny jeans and inane laughter over what some friend did earlier in the day and what an idiot this other friend is and where they're meeting him that night and something else about some chick or some douche at some overpriced gym they frequent.

"They sound like they're having fun," she muttered.

"I'm sure they are," I muttered back.

She laid her head back into the backrest and let it roll towards her left shoulder. Her eyes were open wide but in the way where they weren't looking.

"I used to have fun," she said.

"Yeah," I responded, "yeah you sure did. We sure did."

She kept this charade up until dark.

It was fascinating to watch her from a distance. On one hand, I could see nothing; her playing with a piece of fabric she pulled from one of the pillows, gently wrapping it around her index finger, every muscle from her torso to her face suspended in time, where I could knock her over and she wouldn't notice.

On the other, I saw everything. I *felt* everything. The back and forth, the struggle, her demons and angels, the light from the window and the comfort of the cushion, the now and what could be, what people would say, what they would not say, the fortitude of her chest against every conceivable micro-expression aimed in her direction. I felt it all.

"Babe, you gonna tell me what's on your mind?"

"Nothing."

I didn't have a choice.

The yearning. I might have missed the signs, but something told me it'd been building over some time. For half a year, she hadn't ventured further from her house in Long Island, the condo, the block surrounding, and the inside of a cab and her car. Half a year where she battled her darkest self alone. Then she came back to me. Learned to trust me again. And then, that night, right then, she might've relearned to trust herself, against what may or may not await.

"Babe, seriously, what's wrong?"

"Oh my God, nothing. Just give me a moment."

Might've. After all, I could only guess.

After dinner, she agreed to climb to the top of the building with me. The rooftop had recently been opened to residents after some construction, and the view from it was breathtaking. In a span of a few minutes, the skyline darkened. Then, one by one, the lights flickered on, refusing to go to sleep. Over a million people filled the gaps between each glittering structure. We could feel their presence.

I leaned against the railing, Judy with her arms around my waist and her head resting against my back. Right there, I hadn't felt what I was feeling since the day of our wedding. *Interface* or not, half a face or a full one, at that moment, nothing would've changed a goddamn thing.

"Maybe," she finally spoke.

"What?" I asked.

"I've got a place in mind. Tomorrow. Nothing fancy, but, it'll be a first step I think."

"A first step," I wondered out loud, unable to contain the smile.

"Where is that?"

< 184 >

She didn't respond. Instead, she just gazed at the lights, a slice of life she kept at such a distance, now finally within reach.

*   *   *

We sat in the back row. She figured it'd be better this way, spare the poor priest from seeing her face naked. Two blocks south of Central Park, it was the furthest she'd ever gone in public without her mask since the accident, the furthest without the exteriors of a car to hide in. We'd gotten up at the butt crack of dawn for coffee and bagels at some random café downstairs and walked the entire way there. Baby steps, as nobody in the city wakes up until noon on Sundays, but they were like her first.

Nobody said a thing to us after the service was done. Walked right through us like we were invisible. I might've called out once to a gentleman who bumped into me as he left and he didn't even look back. So I guess it wasn't all bad. Better to not exist to these people if doing so would only mean judgment.

I guess it's hard to blame em. After all, I forget from time to time, or at all times actually, that I don't exactly see the same Judy as

< 185 >

everyone else, and I pitied them. In a way, it seemed to have made me the only person she could be around. The only person who didn't look away, who'd look at her in the eyes like she existed. The only person she could hold herself to against this world.

I know it's selfish, but our marriage hasn't been better.

Things went uphill from there. Yesterday, we made it all the way across Central Park on foot. This weekend, I'm taking her to a Broadway play and dinner. Next, we might reconnect with her long-lost friends we've ignored for the better part of the year. Hopefully, they'll understand. Afterwards, work, a child, a family, and everything wonderful about a normal life.

Normalcy, I can almost touch it. I'm finally feeling that delicious feeling that things are gonna work out.

Hi Jay

I'm sorry it took me so long to respond.

Mind you though, we certainly do appreciate these updates. I could tell, there was a lot to say, and I am glad it helps.

I don't have much to add other than to tell you that I am glad, through all that has happened, we were able to support you and help you return to the life you desire.

There were, however, two items of housekeeping I would like to address.

First off, as you have been informed, payment is due after the operation is conducted successfully. A bill was sent to your account, which is accessible through the app. We have made it quite easy as all you would need to do is read through the contents and click "accept." From there, select your payment method.

You can use the account you linked to this

< 187 >

application by choosing the first option, which will be "bank transfer," and the funds will automatically be withdrawn overnight. Do make sure you have the full amount as written on the bill before proceeding. If you would like to pay by credit card, select "Pay by Card." Also, for your convenience, we offer the ability to finance the lump sum if you so choose. If you do wish to go that route, select "Pay Later," and follow the system instructions to set up your payment plan.

Other than that, everything else you need to know should be on the bill. Let me know if you have any questions.

Secondly, feel free to continue your correspondence with me as much as you need. As your relationship manager, I would like to stress that our journey does not end here, and that I can be a set of ears for all you go through from here on out. I anticipate it will be at least a year before everything returns to normal in full, and I am keenly interested in how things turn out and if there may be any issues regarding the product.

That's it for housekeeping. Now to answer your questions.

You were asking at some point about your memory, and how it appears so much more enhanced since the operation.

For what I am about to say next, please, allow me to preface.

So much of how you understand the world, how you see Judy, and how you separate her from a doppelganger, comes from memories. To ensure 100% match with the target subject at all times, therefore, we found the best way to do so was to create a digital instance of the patient, or in this case, yourself.

I understand that this might sound a bit insane, but please bear with me, as I promise it will make sense by the end of this email. As a result of the operation, your *Interface* has become a duplicate version of you, living out his reality fed by all of your perceptions. In other words, he has become a mirror of your consciousness.

So let's talk about mirrors.

Your reflection mimics every movement you make down to an exact precision. Light bounces off of you and into the glass, feeding an alternate visual living on the other side, the

< 189 >

same way that all of your receptors fill your mind with a conception of reality, sending it to your *Interface* for processing before returning an enhanced rendering of what you perceive. Further, as you know, your *Interface* self retains a copy of all your memories to make sense of everything you perceive.

In other words, for both of you to coexist, mirroring each other's experiences, all facets of your mind must be the same, including memory.

Consider the following scenario.

Say I went through the same operation as you. My memory is now uploaded to the Interface, and it now mirrors everything that I see. What I needed to alter is, at this point, irrelevant. The two individuals that you need to focus on are just me and my uploaded self.

Say I see someone at the corner of the street, a man with gray hair and a brown moustache. An old friend from a long time ago. I do not immediately recognize him but my uploaded self *does*.

What do you suppose would happen?

A few seconds of memory imbalance could

skew what each one of us does. My uploaded self would now be approaching my conception of this man those few seconds before me, and I will be honest, I have no clue as to what the *Interface* will do from there.

Create a new conception based off of my memories so that we are no longer in sync?

What would it do with my conception of new information?

Have it replace its own, or would me and my uploaded self both begin perceiving two realities at once?

I'm just not certain. We were only told by our superiors that this simply cannot happen.

Therefore, we introduced a process called *Parallel Memory Synchronization* (PMS). To explain, when you send your perception to your uploaded self, it will feed you with a conception, including a combination of the objects of *perception* and your *memory*.

I will not be receiving from my *Interface* an image of the man with gray hair and a brown moustache. I am receiving an image of Alton Brown, an old colleague of mine from three years back.

Further, coming back to your experience, *thoughts* are also included in the PMS. This may not have been explained to you earlier, but your visualizations, ponderings, and all other conscious brain activities are also uploaded to your *Interface* in the same manner as your sensory perception. Although they bypass the same algorithm that re-interprets the data coming from your senses, they are just as indelible to ascertaining complete synchronization between the two minds (brain tissue and silicon). Therefore, be it you or your digital self, all perceptions of Judy in whatever function will conjure the same memories at the same speed.

In other words, you now have a fully enhanced memory of everything you see, smell, hear, touch, taste, or think as the *Interface* feeds you a *complete understanding* of the reality you are feeding it.

At least that's how I interpreted it.

Well, I do hope you enjoy your newfound memory. Let me know if you have any concerns over what I have written in this email.

Josh Rikkard
Relationship Manager
*Wonderlenz* Technologies Inc.

Judy's mother paid us a visit.

It happened just this weekend, and I couldn't get it out of my head.

I'd just come back from picking up some fresh tomatoes to make Spaghetti Bolognese, with a slightly altered recipe courtesy of grandma Valentino, when I got the text. Now, I've been trying to avoid reading any text messages from her mother, but this wasn't her number. I swear, this lady couldn't figure out how to connect to her own Wi-Fi at home, but somehow figured out how to spoof her number.

*This is Valerie.*

*I'm on my way over.*

*Please tell me your address.*

*Or street crossing, tell me your street crossing.*

*Or just give me a restaurant or business or something.*

*Jay, you there?*

*Jay?!*

I responded.

*How are you going to tell me you're almost here?*

*When you don't know where I live!*

Then she called me.

"Mother in law!" I exclaimed.

Then followed a shitload of passive aggression before I could make out what she was saying.

"I know where you live, Jay, I just don't know your address!"

"So you know where I live, you just don't know where I live?"

"Well, I know the general location! It's Manhattan after all. You either live north or south, east or west!"

"So you know I live in Manhattan. You found me."

"Look, whatever, just please give me your address."

< 134 >

By then I'd made it into my room and had set everything down. Judy was out on another run. Her running shoes, which were always set near the top right corner of the shoe rack, were missing.

"Hold on, hold on, mother."

"Don't call me your mother."

"Mother by law. You hoarded Judy for three months but you never saw my face. Did I come barn rolling into your crib looking for her? No. Did I call? Did I text? Did I harass you at the butt crack of dawn?"

Pause.

"No, you're right, you didn't come over and I thank you for that," she replied. I could hear her breathing; she was trying hard to restrain the bitch. "But, Jay, you really think you were feeling the same pain that I'm feeling right now?"

The front door creaked open. Judy had just gotten back.

"Jay!" she snapped.

"Huh? Oh yeah, totally, not totally. Sorry, what was the question?" I stalled.

"Do you really think that you were feeling the same pain? The same pain that I'm going through right now?"

< 135 >

"How the fuck should I know?"

"Of course you wouldn't know. You love her, sure you can say that over and over until you go hoarse. One second, let me park at this gas station."

She parked.

"You good?" I asked.

"Yeah, okay, listen," she replied. "You can tell me you love her, Jay. I believe you. You can tell me she's your world and that you'd do anything for her and I won't blink an eye."

She continued. "Look, I know we aren't exactly friends. I won't even go into it, but I believe you when you tell me you love Judy. Honestly, I wish it were not that way, but that's just the God's honest truth. But Jay, don't you ever compare your affection for her to mine."

"The hell you mean?"

"I am saying that if I take Judy from you, you could always find another wife. You tear her from me, and I can never, ever, find another daughter. She's a pretty Long Island girl you had the good luck of meeting. She is my daughter, my goddamn daughter. I get to see her."

"OH! Such passion," I responded, my pupils nearly making out the inside of my forehead. "You got to see her for all of two months! Would've been better to give that same speech to all of your friends from yoga!"

"Yes, I messed up, so I'm coming to make things right. You aren't a parent, you don't understand."

"Well maybe love is love, Valerie. Love from a parent, love from a husband, and it looks like she picked my version to yours. Maybe it's not about you. Maybe it's about Judy, what she wants. Have you ever considered that?"

"Please don't talk to me like that, Jay! I'm just a mother who wants to see her own daughter, a mother who just wants to make things right!" She was sobbing so hard it sounded like she couldn't breathe. "I swear, this one time, and you won't see or hear from me again. Please, just give me your goddamn address."

That was quite a deal. Plus, no matter who it is, there's something about an old lady crying.

Curse my Italian upbringing.

"Judy!" I called out after hanging up the phone. "Your mother's coming!"

●  ●  ●

Thirty minutes passed. That dumb bitch was lost.

Judy wasn't having it. She'd taken a shower and was in her closet throwing on anything that would cover her, just enough to call herself dressed; a red Under Armor t-shirt paired with a black skirt, black flip flops and pink head-phones. She grabbed her apartment keys, and her purse, and walked back to the front door without a glance in my direction.

I ran up to block it.

"Babe, where the what the fuck are you doing?"

"Move," she demanded.

"Babe, your mother's coming. I know it's been half an hour; she's probably lost in one of the boroughs, but she could also be right around the block."

"Hope you two have a nice chat."

"Babe, she's here for you."

"I'm sure she is."

"Hold up," I said, gently putting my hands on her shoulders. "Hold up, hold up, babe, hold the fuck up. Can we please sit down, chill, have a drink."

< 198 >

"Booze, that's your solution to everything, isn't it?"

"It's 50/50. C'mon, hon, would you just listen?"

"You're hurting me. Let go!"

Through much negotiating, I was able to bring her to the kitchen counter.

"Judy, look. You know me. I'd entertain a serial murderer before your parents. But," I paused.

"But what?" she responded, left arm grabbing her purse string, ready to turn around at any moment's notice and bolt.

"But I dunno, she sounded sincere."

And just like that, in the blink of an eye, she swung around, her full attention back to getting the hell out. I had to run after her down the hall, only for my phone to vibrate.

"Judy, babe, she's here!" I called out. "You either come back or run into her on your way out! Either way, she's not gonna leave without talking."

A moment later, I was seated at the kitchen island, sipping on a Manhattan and pretending to play with my phone. The two of them sat on the couch, Judy refusing her mother the decency of clearing out a space.

The conversation was depressing.

"Judy, take that off."

Judy had wrapped her face up again, and shit, did she do a hell of a job. She didn't have time to finesse it to only cover her right side, so she just wrapped the entire roll three times around her entire head, leaving herself only as much as a crack for her left eye.

Her mother had spent the better part of the first ten minutes begging her to take it off.

"Judy, please, I'm your mother.

"Judy, please, you never wore that back home."

"Judy, please, this feels—"

She stopped to breathe; deep inhales and exhales taken as if timed.

I wanted to say something, give the old lady a hand, 'cause honestly it was downright cruel.

There was something about the scene. Valerie, my mother in law from hell, a woman used to weaponizing her tears, sitting there looking all too human. Her face shriveled, like all the tears there were to cry had been wrung out, the wrinkles on her forehead deeper, the dark around her eyes darker, the Botox barely holding itself as she aged by the minute.

None of it mattered; the yoga classes that failed to hold up her gym rat physique, the Dollar Store hair products she forgot to apply, the makeup smudged all over her cheeks. Her portrait of herself finally aging to objective time, leaving the thin, crippled, suffering woman she is and had always been in place.

I couldn't hate her then. I just can't hate something so human.

She tried to change the subject a few times, reason over what happened at home.

I guess I only got part of it right. I was right about her public denial about her daughter being home. Having known her mother, that was an easy one.

But I guess actions aren't as simple as the people committing them. That's where I got everything else wrong.

I was wrong about Valerie.

She hadn't kept Judy hidden out of embarrassment. No, rather she kept her hidden out of fear. Fear because she knew the kind of people her friends were, what they would do, what it would cause. Fear that they'd come running over in groups, saying things so horrendous and mentally scorching that it would drive her away. Fear about what others would

< 201 >

say to each other, what Judy would turn into amongst community members, amongst friends, amongst those of her mother's synagogue or her father's church.

She hadn't kept Judy hidden out of embarrassment. She kept her hidden from pity. Pity, the burden it puts on her, the burden it puts on others. A shadow in an otherwise perfect little community. A stain on her image, her otherwise perfect image.

Judy had always been incongruent after all; treat someone as friend in public but talk shit in private; be this confident person amongst coworkers and peers but break down naked next to a pool of vodka pouring from a tipped-over bottle at home. In many ways, I guess it hit me right then. She wasn't that different from her mother.

Or from me. Shit.

From what I could make out, her mother had likely given up everything; book club meetings, ladies' nights, yoga, whatever; all in an effort to focus on her daughter while maintaining her privacy. And let me tell ya, in her community, decline an invitation once and they'll get over it. Twice, and you're the talk of the town, the subject of discourse over fifty dollar plates of salad.

< 202 >

I was wrong about Judy. I guess she didn't appreciate.

I could almost see a little of it here. Living like a bum, skipping on rent, pushing away everyone who cared, leaving the place a mess, drowning in the same pity she refused from the public.

It may have only taken a single moment in a day that looked like every other. Maybe a smirk, a sock on the living room couch, a half-nibbled plate of breakfast (not surprising given her mother's culinary skills), something that must've set off the hidden fuse. Then all of her mother's social sacrifices, everything I just wrote, must've spilled with Judy lapping it up in all the ways you would expect.

Then again, I could be wrong. After all, I was only able to make out bits and pieces as her mother's frustration worsened and Judy's silence grew in volume.

"Tell me what I should've done then," was the last thing her mother said, finally sobbing as Judy looked on. "Tell me, what I should've done."

She just kept saying that over and over and over, mumbling it to herself, all the way down the elevator.

It's strange, but for the rest of our time together that day she wasn't treating me half bad.

For one, she held onto me the entire way down the elevator. She buried her head into my chest, sobbing and mumbling, without seeming to mind that it was mine.

Then, when we made it to her car and she'd calmed down a bit, she suddenly offered to buy me a drink. Looked me dead in the eye and asked while gently touching my arm.

Too busy grieving to hate? I dunno, but I didn't fight it.

I took her to Southie's. Bard wasn't working that day, so I sat us at a small, raised table for two near the window and ordered some fried pickles, cheesy tots, a bourbon, and a beer.

I ordered her a salad and chardonnay.

She downed the glass of chardonnay and then my bourbon before even acknowledging her plate.

"So, what did she text you?" she asked gently, sitting back in that awkward way when alcohol knocks you like a fist.

"She told me she was coming home in five days," I replied, inhaling half my beer. "That's it. And then, she did."

"Of course," she replied with a whisper while motioning to both her empty glasses and looking at the bar keep. "Could you show me?"

So I did. She took a glance.

"Did you read these?" she asked.

"What do ya mean did I read em?" I snapped back.

"Did you read these?" she replied calmly.

"Well, of course I read 'em Valerie. They're written in English and all," I replied.

I grabbed the phone from her and took a glance.

The text was slightly different from what I remembered.

*Hey Jay*

*Long time*

*Honestly, don't know what to do, nor do I have anyone else to talk to. All my friends, my family, you, I've pushed away.*

*Maybe you're too mad to read this, and I'll understand if you are.*

*But I'm miserable, and I'm beginning to realize how coming here has been the worst fucking mistake.*

*Well, actually, never mind. I'm not going to waste your time with all of it. Just letting you*

< 205 >

*know I'm getting out of here in five days. Have a good day.*

*Oh, and you might not believe it, but I love you.*

*Bye.*

"What are you getting at, Val? She wrote she's coming back in five days," I said.

Only that wasn't true.

"I guess it surprises me a little she'd phrase it like that," she replied. "She's usually straight-forward. I've never had to second-guess her emails."

"That wasn't straight enough for you?"

"Did she say she's going home?"

"Well she did, didn't she?"

"Yes, I'm not questioning what she was trying to say, just how she said it."

"Why the fuck it matter how she said it?"

She didn't answer my question. By then the bar keep had restocked us with a cold glass of chardonnay and a bourbon, and she went straight to demolishing her third glass.

"It doesn't," she said with a wave of a hand. "I'm just having such a hard time."

She choked on that last word, pausing to hold her steady. I hesitated, but, eventually reached over to touch her hand.

< 206 >

"Yeah, I want her back too," I said, knowing it was only half true. "You know, if it makes you feel any better, I think your intentions weren't all bad."

She looked at me with a hard gaze, like she was trying hard to remind herself she hated me. Slowly, it softened, and she looked away.

"Were you eavesdropping?" she asked.

"Yeah, I was."

She shook her head. "Well you've got it all wrong. My intentions. You don't know my intentions. I don't even know my intentions. I just act out of fear, but half the time I don't even know fear of what. Fear of everyone pitying Judy in front of her or pitying me behind her back. You just don't know with some of these people. Maybe if I did know my intentions, I could at least be honest."

"I'm telling you; she could sniff out bullshit," she said with a chuckle shaking her head, "Jesus did she have a knack for it. She's always had a way of knowing."

She put her hand over mine. "You know, I'd rather you just go on assuming the worst. Maybe me being a terrible mother will bring you two closer together. Common enemy."

It worked before.

"So then," I began, "I'm assuming you aren't here to make amends?"

"Sure I was. It just ended with all of this."

"Well, that's what I was talking about, all of this," I replied, waiving my hand between us. "I'm assuming you aren't buying me beer to bury the hatchet. I mean, I admit, I've said some terrible things."

She didn't respond. Her attention was elsewhere, her gaze disappearing into a void the way they do when alcohol kicks in. She poured another mouthful of chardonnay between her cheeks.

"You know who you remind me of?" she asked, slurring her words a bit. "You remind me of her high school sweetheart Michael. He was such a cute young man. Bright, ivy league bound, a promising path ahead, great family. You remind me of him."

Michael. So that's his name.

"'Cause you're everything he isn't."

Okay, by now I was ready to cut the conversation and leave. I had a hundred in my wallet and would've put it all down and let the barkeep keep all the change. Sixty bucks to not listen to this crap.

But Michael, her mysterious ex. Whatever she was gonna say, I sure as hell wasn't getting another chance, not from Judy.

"But I guess she's with who she's with."

That bitch.

"Why do you suppose that is?" I asked, shooting the whiskey to calm my nerves.

"He died."

Fuck, not even booze could calm that chill that ran down my back.

"Hold up," I started, "Judy told me they broke up."

"Sure," she replied before pausing to stare at her empty glass. "I guess that's one way to put it."

I'm not sure how else to describe it. I felt my heart sink. I mean, it isn't a big piece of our marriage. But it felt a good chunk, like the very concept of our marriage was off, like if our entire relationship could be defined by the sum of all its parts. Even missing a piece so small can turn it into something unrecognizable, a completely new conception of our life together that I hadn't the state of mind to wrap my head around. She didn't *break up* with him, he fucking *died*. She never fell out of love, neither did he. He probably still occupied a place in her heart all this time. I mean, how does this *not* feel like cheating? What else don't I know?

My insecurities began flaring up like my psoriasis, an itchy little patch that I couldn't rid that only grows the more I try. Fucking Judy. Why? Why did she lie? Or is her mother just full of it?

"You know, there was a park we'd visit every summer," she continued, showing fuck-all concern for my state of shock. "About two hours away on a good day, upper New York right below the Catskills. There is a lake house we owned, still own actually, and leading from it, a hiking trail that would zig zag across the trees to this gorgeous little waterfall flowing into a canyon. Hidden little secret, we liked to pretend it was a place that only our community knew about. Judy would sneak off there by herself from time to time or with friends."

"So we drove there as a family one summer, bringing Michael along. He loved it; he looked like he'd never seen mother nature before. So one day when he was out with Judy alone, and I guess they were stone hopping over the top of the waterfall. Kids would do that, it was just

< 210 >

a stream after all, good place to snap pictures too. That day, however, he must've…"

She paused, taking in air before continuing.

"It's not a long fall, but the base…the base was treacherous."

She tried to make a triangle out of her fingers. "Lots of jagged rocks, real sharp."

She paused as another chardonnay arrived. She took a swig of it.

"Judy came back screaming. Oh my God, it was terrible," she said, shaking her head, staring off blankly.

"You're right, a very bright young man," I wanted to say.

"He should've been the one. They were perfect together. I don't know, I think till this day I feel responsible, like I let it happen, like Judy was robbed of a future with an investment banker or a doctor or a lawyer or a politician or…"

She trailed off into a mumble. The four drinks on her empty stomach hit sudden and hard and she was beginning to slouch forward. A minute more and that salad was gonna get another brand of dressing.

I paid the tab, and rather than dragging her back to my place, I booked her a room at some boutique hotel a few blocks down. Let me just say for the record that I was sure a boutique hotel would've been much more comfortable than my couch, and you know, we've gotta look out for our seniors.

As I settled her in her bed, she grabbed my arm, looked into my eyes, and told me, slurring like a serpent and spitting, something I wouldn't forget.

"You know, I never answered your question, about why I was talking to you or something."

She pulled me closer.

" I... I wanted a moment with you, to tell you, no matter what I think of you or what her father thinks of you or whatever," she took her finger and swung it on my nose. "Judy loves you. She probably hadn't ever forgotten about Michael, no, but for whatever reason, she's glad she's with you. She told me as much, or something like it. But I guess, in a way, you're her new Michael. So I guess you're my new Michael too, whether I like it or not. You're a lucky man, Jay, but I guess..."

< 212 >

She sighed, like she really didn't want to say those next words.

"I guess she's lucky too. Because I don't know if the real Michael would've put up with..."

And then she was out like a light, leaving me there to deal with what was gonna to be the nicest sentence I've ever heard come out of her mouth, throwing me more off guard than all of her nastiest.

My God, what has my relationship with this woman come to? And did we just make peace? And what the hell did she mean by the "real" Michael?

Then things got weird. I walked to the front door and noticed a mirror on both sides of the entryway. I saw something that threw me stumbling back, nearly knocking over a chair.

Another person, a guy, no, a teenager, a boy, someone almost a decade or two younger than me. A fresh-faced kid with black, curly hair and bushy eyebrows and a chiseled jaw wearing a button-down white shirt.

Michael?

I went back. He was gone. Just me. Just

me again. Just me and an infinite number of me's reflecting upon reflection after reflection after reflection.

. . .

I haven't seen her mother since that day. Sure hope she got home alright. I went back to check the next morning with a small tray of coffee and some doughnuts, figuring it'd be nice to keep this truce going. Front desk told me she checked out early, so I sat in the lobby and polished it all off myself. Two donuts and two coffees. Wasn't how it used to be; I've even had to buy a new belt since the operation.

Anyways, I wanted to call her but didn't know what I would say other than the obvious.

*You leave early?*

*Got you some donuts and coffee and ate em.*

*Hope you're getting home safe.*

What's crazier is that I've ceased to hate. What do you do in times like this? I mean, even considering the concept of hating your in-laws, for most couples, should've knocked a marriage down. So what does it mean that ours is still standing? That this hate found its way into the foundations? If this is some kinda truce, will it change my dynamics with

< 214 >

Judy? After all, her mother did mention it. "Common enemy." She spoke of it like she'd done me a favor with all this rabid antagonism over the years.

So I just texted her what I felt, the first thing that came to my mind after all this ruminating.

*Thank you.*

And that was it.

SUBJECT: RE: JUDY'S MOTHER
SENT: JULY 2, 2025, 4:45 P.M.
TO: JAYBIGGS1987@HOTMAIL.NET

Hi Jay

I am thankful for the feedback on how your *Interface* is functioning and am glad it has, for the most part, worked as it needed. I do hope this continues and you will continue to report these findings to my superiors so that they can be put to ease.

I also would like to thank you for your payment in full. I am glad we were able to cross that off of our list early.

In relation to your question about the mysterious man in the mirror, I admit, I am drawing a blank. If your *Interface* is working correctly, you shouldn't perceive any objects out of the ordinary other than what was altered. In my opinion, it's most likely stress, or some other factor unrelated to the technology. In any case, do let me know if you see anything like it again.

Josh Rikkard
Relationship Manager
*Wonderlenz* Technologies Inc.

< 216 >

## AUGUST 1, 2025

I guess I should've known that this was coming. How the growing brand recognition of this company could make it harder to keep Judy's suspicions at bay. It's starting to dawn on me now that I might have to proceed with a little more caution for an indiscernible amount of time.

It's starting to dawn on me, and it's all thanks to Amber.

Remember her? Judy's best friend in the city? The one she ghosted? The one I accidentally reached out to forgetting she did?

Probably shouldn't have done that. It put us back on her radar.

< 217 >

So about a week ago, literally right after Judy's mother's visit, I got this text from her.

*Can I meet you guys tomorrow?*

*How about lunch?*

*Meet somewhere in midtown?*

*Also, Judy hasn't been answering my texts and I just wanted to make sure everything is alright with her.*

I didn't want to say yes without asking first; Judy would've had my ass for dinner.

*Sure, just tell us time and place.*

***

We arrived ten minutes ahead of schedule the next day at this Italian place in Hell's Kitchen, 8th avenue, right underneath Columbus Circle. I'd picked the location 'cause it'd been a lifetime since I'd had food from the motherland, and this place had a certain ambiance for small gatherings.

We picked a place near the windows. Habit of mine, it was always important that my guests don't catch me by surprise. Like this one time in college when a date didn't show up 'cause she'd seen me from a distance scratching my nose, only she didn't think I was scratching my nose 'cause of the angle and shit, and, well, yeah, I was single for another three years.

Also, come to think of it, it might've been the only table left.

Judy didn't exactly chew me out the way I'd thought she would the night before. I guess she'd given up to a degree and didn't hold a lot of hard feelings towards this woman.

I mean, don't get me wrong, she did give me a little hell. Like when she asked me with a pillow over her face, "are you going to make me meet everybody in New York City by the end of the month?"

To which I replied, "No, babe, not your cousin Lani."

To which she replied, mumbling, "we'd better fucking not".

Then negotiations.

"Why can't you just go alone?"

"She's *your* friend, babe!"

"Why'd she text *you*? And how'd she get your number?"

"I don't know, babe. I might've butt-texted her once. Anyhow, she texted *me* 'cause you didn't pick up your phone! Jesus, what have I become, your agent?"

It didn't go on that long, and by noon the next day, she'd come out fully dressed in a red velvet blouse, skin-tight jeans, knee high boots, gold hoop earrings, her priciest purse, and no facemask.

"Aren't you gonna put on your mask?" I asked between sips of my espresso, thinking she had it in her purse.

"I left it at home," she replied.

"Why?"

"I've told you why. She only sees herself."

"And you're best friends with her?"

She only shrugged, "*was* best friends with her."

Then, with a sigh, "I don't know, it's weird, but it's kind of nice hanging out with people like her."

"Like her?"

"Yeah, people who can provide me a social life while leaving me alone at the same time."

"What the hell do you mean by that?"

I guess I was about to learn because right then, a squeal from behind cut our conversation short.

"Judy!"

We spun around, and everything started to make sense; everything from the six-inch heels, the fat sunglasses, the outfit that was either layers of black saran wrap or a ten

< 220 >

thousand dollar dress that locked every part of her stiff from her quads to her boobs that were too large to be real, the layers of product on her face, the velvety hair of unnatural black, the shimmering gold that made up her earrings, the white leather handbag that looked purchased a minute ago. From looks alone, you'd think she was either a cover girl for Vogue or its fucking owner rather than another department store accountant.

And there I was in a t-shirt of some sports team of some college I've never heard of, acquired at ten bucks from TJ Maxx a week prior, paired with jeans I'd had since college.

"Amber, oh my God!" Judy called back.

For the first minute or so, I barely existed. They traded hugs and laughs like Judy hadn't totally ghosted her for over half a year and spent the better part of yesterday evening and this morning bitching about having to come out and meet.

Well, guess they were best friends again. Christ.

My eyes wandered a bit and I caught sight of people staring with hideous glares. I whistled between my teeth to grab their attention and return the favor. One by one they turned

< 221 >

around like good little puppies, some still mur-
muring amongst themselves like it's a fucking
wonder why anyone would hug someone with
such a face. That's right, it's always times like
this when we're out in public around other
assholes that bring me back to reality, where
I'm forced to strain and bite my tongue extra
hard to keep myself from causing a scene that
would land me another trip to the shrink.

"And you must be Jay!"

I looked up and before I could stand to
shake her hand or whatever she'd pulled me
out of the chair with this bear hug around my
neck like I was some long lost brother, her
tits pushing up against my chest (they weren't
fake), that smell of cherries and apples; it
almost felt like infidelity.

It did feel like infidelity.

In fact, as soon as she let go, I snapped
back down on my ass and covered my lap with
the tablecloth. I swear, puberty grabbed me
harder than most at thirteen and it never let
go of its grip. I had to order a glass or two of
something, hoping it'd intoxicate it to death.

A family serving of penne rosa, a bottle
of red wine and three glasses; the server kept
staring at Judy as I called for an extra set of

< 222 >

silverware and a plate. I about grabbed his fucking necktie and hanged him from the ceiling fan for doing so if I were even a tad less civilized. Yeah, my urges tend to drift into violent territory when locked up in a box, but can you blame me? I began to wonder how much more of this bullshit I could take before I went on a murder spree, me shoving those microchips lodged in my brain through their skulls without anesthesia only to realize I did it wrong.

Anyways, despite my fuming, Amber didn't seem to notice. As Judy said, she doesn't seem to notice anything that hadn't anything to do with her.

To say that she's an extrovert is an under-statement. Extroverts talk to you. She just talks, like her head would blow if she didn't let out content, like it's a one-woman show where every moment of awkward pause would mean cancellation, like a news channel that manages to fill every hour with shit whether it was rel-evant or aimless, mattered or not, original or a repeat of something from another segment presented with a new set of words.

"Oh my God, I've got a story" leads to "that reminds me of another story" leads to "speaking

< 223 >

of which, have I told you about this story?" leads back to "oh my god, I've got a story."

There were the stories of running into people she thought were Judy and making an ass of herself, people she thought were celebrities and making an ass of herself, people who were actual celebrities, and making an ass of herself. There were the stories of perverts, who were all the clients who wanted to get between her legs; her creepy boss, who peeks into her cube and leaves; her neighbor's dog, who kept sniffing up her crotch. There were stories of hot waiters, cute middle eastern guys with the half-shaved look working at the halal stands, and a shortstop for the Yankees she got with three nights ago at a rave.

She'd also talked about her boyfriend; his name is Jaycee.

As a matter of fact, by the time I'd finished three helpings and half a loaf of bread, she got around to taking her first bite. Judy had only been sipping on her wine, nodding her head with a smile, and laughing seemingly at random. I made some observations. It was always during the third pause, she'd turned the delicate balance of tuning out while pretending to listen into a formula.

A social life while being left alone; it finally clicked.

"That's incredible. You've sure had a crazy week," I managed to squeeze in as she was chewing.

"Mmm yeah, so I feel like I've been talking this whole time." Yeah. "What's been going on for the last however many weeks since we've met?"

Weeks?

"So, Judy was caught in a gas explosion back in January," I started.

"Oh no," said Amber, one hand against her mouth.

"Yeah, she—"

"Jay, let me speak," Judy said, resting a hand on mine.

So she did. She spoke about the accident, things I didn't even bother to ask about, like where she was when it all happened and how she was hit and what was the last thing she remembered. She spoke about walking in to buy a bottle of water after filling her tank, the sound of the blast, how everything went black, and how little she could remember after that moment. She recalled how lucky she was that her thermal jacket kept most of the heat away from the rest of her body, how she was still alive because of it. She started talking about her face, and that's where she paused.

"What happened to your face?" Amber asked, throwing back another mouthful of merlot.

Judy could only run her finger around it.

"Oh stop it, honey, you look fine," she continued with a wave of her hand, "you're gorgeous as always."

Judy only smiled, like this was expected or something. I on the other hand couldn't contain my shock.

"Yeah, she's beautiful, right?" I cried a stupid grin plastered on my face.

"No totally, you're lucky to have her! I could barely tell!"

I swear I could've kissed her for saying that. I wanted to shake Judy right then and there, ask her what the hell she was worried about, why she'd ignored her for so long, a friend like that! I was astonished. She was looking at Judy dead straight, without a flicker in her eyes. It was something that not even I, her loving husband who's supposed to see through that kind of shit, could do without altering my mind, and right then I felt, mixing into my state of relief, a slight pang of guilt.

"But, honey, I'm so sorry for what happened, I really am. Ohhh—" She put her hands to her chest, her face scrunched in a way that looked like she was sitting on a cactus rather than in empathetic pain, and her lips were curled up like she forgot she was still smiling.

"I wish you had told me!" she cried.

"I know, I know. I just really wasn't in a place to meet anyone," Judy replied silently.

"I get it, I get it, I totally, totally get it," she said, placing her hand on hers. "Listen, I'm always here for you, okay? You're beautiful, hey look at me, you're gorgeous. And, I'm so sorry this happened! Ohhh!"

She brought a napkin to her eyes to soak the tears, half cursing under her breath as the mascara wiped off. But then, in a few seconds, she was done. Smiling, as if patiently waiting for Judy to give her permission to move on to another subject.

I was cracking up inside. This lady had texted me to see if everything was alright with Judy, and she just treated it like a formality before looking for a way to grab the spotlight again. I figured I didn't need to ask Judy why she ignored her all this time.

But still, on the other hand, it was a

miracle for Judy to know someone, at this stage, who didn't give a damn about what she looked like. Hell, I hate to say it, but Amber may have been the only one.

Then a pause followed. For a moment, Amber seemed to have faded into the environment, like she had nothing more to say.

Then out of nowhere, she popped a question. "So, have any of you heard of *Wondervision*?"

I smirked. I was definitely not hearing her right.

"Hear of what?" I asked.

"Wondervision Inc. Guess you haven't. It's this biotechnology company my dad helped finance years ago before it was bought out by that other tech giant, *AISys*. They basically perform these surgical implants in your brain that tweaks your reality, something called the *Interface*. Like, it's insane. It makes it so that you literally see and feel things that are not there, or don't see or feel things that *are* there, or *aren't* there for cases where, you know, you're like schizo or something."

Shit, I did hear her right. She was talking about *Wondervision*, the *Interface*, *our Interface*, right in front of Judy!

"Wow," I answered, summoning all the

< 228 >

meager acting skills I had, "that's, that's really insane."

I turned to Judy. She was interested.

"So what about it?" she asked.

"I got it done!" Amber replied.

"Really!" I interjected, almost a little too loud. "What for?"

She took a sip of wine, inhaled, and continued.

"So, as Judy knows, I suffer from depression. I've fought it for most of my life, since high school actually, and it's chronic. Like, I could go years without it ever being a problem and it'd come back out of nowhere. Recently, it's come back in a really bad way."

"Like what?" Judy asked.

"Like, I don't know, bad. Like I was taking pills just to stay sane, or happy, or normal, or whatever you call it, in front of people."

"So, I think staying at home was especially bad for me 'cause it was almost like an emotional trigger. You've been to my place, right, Judy? You've seen my window; it literally faces a brick wall."

"Anyway, last month I was almost fired for coming in late again. It was getting harder and harder to get out of bed, and I found myself, out of nowhere, spiraling downward, and hard. I worked it out with my therapist that, although the dark room wasn't the 'cause of it, it was definitely a trigger. So I told my dad what was going on and he set something up with some people he knew."

She drained the rest of her glass.

"And now, check out my room!"

She held out her phone. A room, her room, a window that covered the entire wall that overlooked the city from some unknown building, a glowing blue that was the sky shooting in rays of light, emanating the lines that outlined the walls, her furniture, her floor, her ceiling, and bringing to crisp contrast all of her modern black furnishings like her carpet, her pillows, her television screen, her pet cat. It looked like a penthouse from any real estate magazine cover catered to the city's richest people.

"Did you move?" asked Judy.

"No, same place. This is what I see because of the operation! I'm telling you. It's like augmented reality at a whole different level. I don't just see the light coming in from the window, I can *feel* its warmth, *hear* the cars in the distance, *be* in the environment. To me, when I walk home, I walk home to *this*."

"But then how are *we* seeing what you're seeing?" I asked, my brain working overtime to craft my questions so to not give away any unnecessary knowledge.

"Oh, my dad gave me this app where I could connect to my own *Interface* and take photos of shit I perceive. It's really neat because you can play through your entire history of memory and snap photos of points in time. Not necessary though. I guess since my memory of anything is basically 100%. I've found it hard to shut up about stuff that's happened ever since getting the operation done, 'cause now that I can remember everything so clearly, I have, like, literally so much more to talk about. It's like describing a film in real time!"

"Do they give this to everybody?" I asked, pointing to the app on the screen.

"No, it's actually banned from sale. It's only allowed for demo purposes and for select salesmen who've basically signed away their lives to the company or privileged individuals. Guess my dad's one of them."

I almost wanted to ask if her dad was missing an arm. Luckily, I'm not that stupid.

"Has it helped?" asked Judy.

"It has. It's helped a lot. Like, it's not a cure, but it helps me manage it better. I'm waking up earlier at least."

"How does it work?"

So she went over the entire process. She talked about the prework, her RM, the entire implementation process, the strange clinic.

"Oh my God, you're not going to believe me, but it's like a fucking facility from the year 3000 inside a building just a little bigger and older than the block this restaurant is in! I literally ran circles around that building trying to figure out if I was tripping on something, 'cause it was impossible. Oh! Let me tell you about this weird holographic lady!"

She talked about AI lady, the procedure itself.

"I about shat my pants once I found out what they were going to do, but honest to God, it was like walking in and out. That was it!"

She talked about what was done to her brain, the Interface, how it became an extension of her current brain. She talked about the crazy test she had to go through afterwards. Guess she took it differently than I did.

"I, like, touched every one of those screens

< 232 >

down the stairwell. I think I even licked something but I can't remember. I mean, why not! They're testing my sensory!"

Guess she wasn't a huge fan of writing to her RM.

"My guy, his name is Derek, he would annoy me every other week asking for updates after updates, even after the operation! Like, I'd pay more money to just be left alone!"

When she was done, she looked Judy dead in the eyes and said, "You know, maybe you should get one too, Judy. I can get you a heck of a good deal. I mean, if *you* aren't satisfied with how you look, at least you could see yourself differently, right? Plus, they've started taking insurance for anything medical related, like my procedure for instance. I'm sure we could get you this operation free!"

"No, I'm fine." Judy replied quickly. "It doesn't change anything does it?"

"What do you mean?" asked Amber.

"I mean," Judy continued, "I'd just be lying to myself, embracing something that isn't real. Plus, it's pretty pathetic, really. Denialism at its worse."

"Mmm...I disagree," replied Amber.

< 233 >

"You're not denying reality, just fixing it so you can put up with it better. And why would it be pathetic to feel better about yourself?"

She suddenly placed her hand on mine.

"Pathetic would be, like, if this guy got it to see you with bigger boobs or something."

Then she turned to me, smiling and gave my arm a rub.

"But of course I'm joking. He looks like a sweetie pie. Some other guy."

\*       \*       \*

Judy didn't want to walk home, so I called a cab. For the entire ride, we kept to ourselves, her sifting through her phone and me going through unattended voicemail using my earpiece.

We got out a block or two from our place. There's this mom and pop grocery store called *Del Monte's* that I'd always frequent for fresh vegetables and I needed a couple of cans of tomatoes to make pomodoro sauce; I had to save the big bag of basil sitting in the fridge going bad.

Of course, it wasn't until we were waiting in line to check out, surrounded by other people, that Judy decided to spill.

"So, about that thing Amber was talking about. Have you heard of it before?"

"No, babe," I responded, wondering to myself why she'd think that. "Why would you think that?"

She looked at me pleadingly. She wanted something out of that question, a type of certainty, the kind you can only give when you're telling the truth.

Then they relaxed. Best to change the subject, I decided. A second longer on it and I would've been in danger.

"Babe, what, do you think I did something?"

I'm an idiot.

"No," she replied, uncertain. "No, you wouldn't."

"Wouldn't what?"

"Do what Amber joked you could do."

"Holy shit, Judy!" I set my basket down and stormed out, waiving at poor Mr. Del Monte, who stood there wondering if he'd done something to piss me off.

I started walking home as fast as I could, ahead of her. I'm not sure if I was running away from her or the truth, but whatever was fueling me, anger or fear, it was strong.

Down Manhattan Ave, right on 115th, another left onto Frederick Douglass into Harlem, passing my place 'cause Judy would be there in short order. What was I doing? What was I thinking? Was I overreacting? Would this 'cause suspicion?

I was fast approaching a liquor store. I wanted a drink. No, I needed many. I needed clarity, enough of it to parse out this cloud of questions, this general blurb of anguish that moved me further and further away from home. I needed just ten little bottles of assorted beverages to suck dry one by one, each iteration another point of clarity.

A shot of Smirnoff. *What was I running from?*

A shot of Jack. *Where was I going?*

A V.S.O.P brandy. *Am I coming to the end?*

A Jose Cuervo. *Does she know?*

A Johnny Walker Black. *Will she find out?*

An Absolut. *Has she found out?*

Remy Martin. *How smart is she?*

A Bulleit and a Woodford. *Hold up, where the fuck am I?*

Instead, I took a hard left across the street and found a bench, sat down, and raised my

< 236 >

face up to God. He was probably busy attending to Judy, and I wouldn't blame Him.

What kind of just god would make time for someone like me?

Honestly, I'm not sure what that psychiatric screening was for, 'cause it obviously missed something. Maybe rather than asking me pointless questions comparing before and after photos of Judy, it should've just parsed through my memories and told me straight up I was too much of a shitbag to go through with this.

I did make it home. I did make things right with Judy, well, make things right in the service of maintaining the wrong. I just held her and told her I was sorry, that I was just offended given how hard I've tried to show her I cared, how hopeless I felt, how I would never ever do something as pathetic as operating on my mind to see her with larger breasts, to look like someone else, edit her to satisfy my own needs.

'Cause what kind of monster would do such a thing?

Hi Jay

I have a few things to unpack.

To begin, the screening you took was merely to measure your interpretation of objective reality. The idea is to ask a series of relevant and irrelevant questions pertaining to this to keep the respondent honest. The questions were designed to ensure you were close to a certain score, which is measured not only by what you *perceive* as reality but also by your *fidelity* towards it. Remember, the goal of the operation is so that you can better live in the world, not create a different one altogether. We just had to know, based on your first email, that your motives are such, as we have little control or visual over what the *Interface* will generate based on its analysis of your brain.

Secondly, the reason we performed the screening without uploading your brain is due to complications related to analyzing your memories for all the flags without us directly viewing them, at least not yet. We did, at one

< 238 >

time, consider putting in place something like our UAT program, but controlling what you see in the environment is very different from picking out pieces of your entire memory. This year, another solution of some sort did receive a green light, but it's slated to release years from now and I wasn't informed of its specifics. Besides, as of now, the regulations from NBIIS accepts this old-school form of screening, so the incentive to innovate isn't there.

That's all the questions I picked up.

I do look forward to reading your next correspondence.


Josh Rikkard
Relationship Manager
*Wonderlenz* Technologies Inc.

< 233 >

I've had it up to here.

Yeah, I get it. You can't see where "here" is.

"Here" is the surface of some unknown liquid. It secretes whenever I find another potato chip on the floor or another tipped-over glass of red on the carpet or another smorgasbord of assorted female undergarments and accessories and pillows and brushes lumped on the couch. It secretes whenever we yell at each other, or when we don't yell at each other and I let the rage echo through every side of my skull. It secretes whenever I ask her a question and she doesn't look up, whenever she steals a book I'm reading, whenever she uses up all the

< 240 >

battery on her computer and snags my charger while I'm working. It secretes whenever the food I make sits cold after a few bites, or whenever the bills come in for the month and everything's gotta come out of my paycheck. It secretes by the day as my wife turns into a roommate, a chore, a nuisance, and less of someone I love.

Fuck it, imagine me pounding my chest, right here. That's how deep it's gotten in just the short time since we've last talked. I'm fucking treading in it, and I don't know how much endurance I've got.

. . .

Judy never seemed to have gotten over the lunch we had with Amber; her friend had implanted a dangerous idea.

The advertisements, the ones that are suddenly popping up out of nowhere, the ones that always end with "your better reality," nourishes it, provides it with fresh paranoia.

Or is it my paranoia? Honestly, I don't know anymore.

Maybe I've been thinking too deeply into things, like the time when she groaned about the wrinkles on her right cheek, counting them, pointing them out to me as if I could see. Maybe I'm overanalyzing when she commented on her hair being over-combed to her right side, or when she snagged my hand and put it against her face and ran it up and down while glaring into my eyes after a session in bed, as if desperately looking for any sign of disgust. Maybe I misheard her when she asked me how much the cost of the operation would be, as if I would know.

Maybe I'm thinking myself off the dotted line. We can rationalize, can't we? Maybe there's a good reason for everything above, that she forgot she didn't have hair on her right side or had simply combed over everything from the left, that cheek rubs are stimulating, that she was just curious about the operation for herself.

Probably just my paranoia. Probably just small things becoming bigger things 'cause I know, intrinsically, they ought to be.

After all, it's all true, ain't it? That there isn't a wrinkle on her face, that I can easily let her run my fingers along her cheek over and over and over, that if my eyes could speak they'd beg her not to stop, that her hair flows from her left shoulder to her right, dipping in just above her right brow, never over-combed, never breaking flow. It's true how it cost me everything in my savings, including the cosmetic surgery. It's true how I'd been staring at a lie this whole time; these fifteen microchips woven into my brain, a program sending me images and sensations superseding my own, a Judy who'd never stopped for gas and water that shit-scene winter night.

Was it too obvious? How would I have given it away?

Shit, with everything I've done for her, *what* would've given it away?

These thoughts I try to keep down, try to ignore, weighed down by reality and guilt. How I stayed by her side, how I tried to keep her close, how I graciously let her back into my life without demanding so much as a kiss on the cheek, letting her run all over me while I bent backwards to make her feel happy and at home and secure. What, to her a guy couldn't just love his deformed wife without an operation? Is this what she expects out of me after all these years?

Yeah, it's deranged. I'm pissed that she'd even assume I would go through this operation for such shallow ends, whether I've done it or not. And then again, what gets me more, is that she's right about me, *if* there was any suspicion there to begin with.

And so I need to know, desperately, that it's all in my head, and that all she's been thinking about these days since that lunch with that bitch was sandwiched between one of the hundred books she's been reading or in one of a million shows or movies or documentaries on Netflix or Amazon Prime or what have you.

I couldn't ask her; I was too afraid it'd only make things worse, like accidentally trudging in dirt when her mind was actually clean. But keeping it down had only created this vicious cycle, one where suspicion can only grow, where my resentment follows, resentment towards her, towards myself, towards everything.

Everything and the tiny dots of merlot running from the couch through the carpeting.

.  .  .

It was Sunday evening when I sat down with her to talk about getting back to work. After the accident, she'd left her job on, from

< 244 >

what she tells me, good terms, so I thought she oughta cash them in for her old desk space.

Like I said, business was booming, and I wasn't worried about money. I just didn't know if any brain surgery of any kind could change what she was becoming before my eyes. Also, I figured the quicker we got back to our routine before the accident, the less she'd think about me, the less she'd wonder or suspect—if she was suspecting anything to begin with.

I approached it really delicately too, sliding into the topic slowly and gradually.

"Boy we oughta make a Sunday ritual of that Peruvian place, huh? New kid on the block putting up a fight against the heavy hitters, best chicken I've had on this side of Manhattan. Say, speaking of chicken, have you called Rick?"

Rick was her old boss at the department chain, *Sazera*. Met him from time to time, happy hours and company celebrations when plus one's were invited. Nice fella, and from how Judy spoke of him, it sounded like he treated her well. Too well at times. Like he might have broken a couple of rules to get her a raise. Like he might've given her an extra day of leave than allotted. Like he might've forgotten she was a married woman. In fact, when she called him a few days after her surgery, he was willing to give her an entire six months of paid leave so long as she promised to return. I remember telling her what a class guy he was and got kinda pissed when she nodded.

Anyways, not too nervous now about her going back because of, not to sound like a dick, circumstances.

"Why would I call Rick?" she replied, eyes caught in her book.

Why the hell would she call Rick? Like I had to explain?

"Look at me, babe," I demanded. She complied.

"Have you called Rick, your old boss at the department store? The place you worked?"

She set her book aside. As she brought her knees up, it slid to the floor, followed by a magazine, an e-reader, a tablet PC, pens, papers, and magazines. A good minute went by as she stared at the floor, like she was coming up with the next thing to say. Yeah, she fucking knew what I was talking about.

"I don't know," she whined, "you know he's never seen my face after the accident?"

"Yeah, I know. So meet him in person, schedule a face to face. You know where his office is."

"What if he's hired someone to replace me?"

"Can't know if you don't ask."

"What if he freaks out after?"

I realize that written down like this, it could be misinterpreted as her actually giving a shit about calling him or even meeting him for her old job back. But let me be clear; I know Judy. In the time spent with her this horrible year, I've learned to read her like a book, more than all the years we've been together. The way she sat against the armrest, head rested against her fist, one foot crossed in front of the other, playing with her hair, twirling her index finger around a thin collection of strands, her eyes focused on them, relaxed like nothing was being said at all. She was written in bold. It wasn't so much that she didn't want to talk about it, but that she cared so little for it that she could talk about it all day.

"Babe, you've gotta start working again sometime! This can't be the rest of your life!"

"Who said I wanted it to be the rest of my life?" she responded, almost playfully.

"Honey, look around. You've practically

grown roots in the carpeting!" I pointed to the trails of stains from spilt glasses of red wine around the couch. "I mean, I get it's hard but you're growing into this!"

"This what?" she asked.

"This!" I waived my arms around, pointing to the mess that was once the living room.

"I can leave."

"No, fuck, wait."

I took a step back; this was going badly. "I don't want you to leave, don't want you to fucking leave." I moved closer, my hands out, approaching her in the way she does when she sees a friendly squirrel; gently, lovingly, without one step too loud to scare her off.

"What the hell are you doing?" she asked. I stopped in place.

"I don't want you to leave," I repeated, "I just want everything back to where they were."

She dropped her hair, looked away and let out an exhale before turning back around to face me, a face of indifference giving way as her pupils wandered everywhere outside my gaze.

"I want the same," she finally said, twirling a finger around her face. "Obviously, right?"

"But, Jay, things don't go back to where they were, like if that's how it even works. They

< 248 >

just fall in place. Today, tomorrow, and every day after. Like, a year ago, I had a human face, or at least one I could stand. Didn't have to wonder who was looking, who cared, who was disgusted, who pitied me. Today, I'm this. Like, even if I got a new face, if you came up with half a million tomorrow for a transplant, I'm still not going to be the same, both physically and mentally."

"So, what," I replied, "you're just gonna melt in this place?"

"No!" she yelled. "Of course not! I'm moving forward at my pace, Jay, *my pace*. It's the *only* pace that will work."

I couldn't respond to that, like she structured that response to where there was literally nothing I could argue that would *not* make me look like an asshole. I needed a drink.

"Okay, honey," I finally said after fixing myself a glass of vodka. "*Your* pace."

"Thank you," she replied. "But I'll text him tonight if that makes you feel better."

It did make me feel a lot better.

"Thanks," I said, turning back only to find her sitting upright without having moved, twirling and untwirling her hair with her index finger, over and over and over.

The following day was a beautiful one, the last one before the inevitable string of shit, according to the forecast. We were set up in on the back porch of some small coffee shop in Harlem, me with my laptop and notebook stacked on the wooden bench table and Judy sitting in front of me reading her book.

"So, you text Rick last night?" I asked as I sat down with a fresh coffee.

She nodded.

"He say anything?" I pressed.

She shook her head. And that was it.

On our walk home we passed a billboard. *AISys: Re-imagine your reality.*

Nothing but the same goddamn billboard that had been there since the company's founding, the same one we might've passed a few times a day. I turned to Judy, discreetly trying to shuffle her along, snap her out of her trance, staring at the words like she'd just learned how to read.

I'd spent the first hour after getting home cleaning the living room and ordering dinner. By the second, we'd finished half the pizza. Judy, having only taken a few bites out of her slice, went straight to her spot on the couch with another glass of Merlot.

That was the first day. Now multiply it by seven, each one an assortment of the same details in various orders in various locations told in various ways. No need for specifics as it'll just be redundant.

Insanity. It's never interesting, never a single moment, but a steady repetition, a body of many points in time of feelings of anxiety and acrimony and desperation with no discernable beginning or an end, each event as trivial as the next. It's a realization that you simply couldn't take another day of the same shit, the same shit with no end to it in sight, not without something drastic.

One day, an advertisement was blaring over the television. Looks like their PR guys bought out an entire channel and spent a full day on repeat, one episode after the next, all about the *Interface*, its guarantees, its possibilities. The day after that, an article in the New York Times. Then a nightly news broadcast, coming literally out of nowhere as we were shutting down and heading off to bed. Then a posting in the metro station, a magazine, a podcast, your corporate CEO on a talk show. I swear, if I weren't smarter I'da thought these guys were spending all of their advertising

< 251 >

dollars just to tell Judy to look at me and look at me twice.

And boy, did she, or wait, it could've all been in my head, but how else do you explain someone who never followed the news or gave a damn about *AISys,* a company so established it might as well have invented the word *technology*, to suddenly take an interest in all of its advertisements, specifically the ones about the microchips in my head? How she'd pause at every infomercial before flipping like crazy through every other channel in the guide, or how every time I'd catch her reading something she'd always be on the exact page of their advertisement no matter if it was a magazine, newspaper, in print or digital, or how every time we'd pass that fucking billboard on our way to the coffee shop she'd glare at it like it was trying to tell her something.

"What's that?" I'd ask casually as she flips the page or switches the channel or looks back down.

"Nothing," she'd say.

"Got something to do with me?" I'd ask.

"Nothing," she'd say.

"Babe, Amber was joking!"

"Babe, you can't think I'd go that low!"

"Babe, we've been over this!"

Nothing, nothing, nothing.

"Babe, after everything we've been through, after everything *I've* been through, *for you, for us*. Sticking it out huddled up in that dingy little piece of shit room every fucking day while you wallow in self-pity, never asking for an apology for leaving me nor expecting one or even a *thank you*, never expecting *anything* but for you to trust me, and after all that you have the nerve to accuse me of *this*? Who the hell are you? Why the hell have I stuck it out this long?"

Nothing. She wasn't reading my silence, my front teeth over my lower lip chewing so hard I could've bitten it off. She wasn't reading it in the same way I was trying to read hers.

"What do you mean nothing?" I'd ask.

"It's nothing," she'd reply.

Nothing. What she had done to this word, saying it to mean nothing and everything at the same time.

"Nothing, just another ad."

"Nothing, for now."

"Nothing, just a weird billboard, never noticed it before."

"Nothing, don't worry about it, just give

me time to work it out in private, let me resolve this alone, figure you out like I don't know you already, who Jay Valentino is, what you're capable of doing when facing something as challenging as respecting me and everything about me over your image of what you want me to be. Let me think about the time you first looked at me when the bandages came off, the red on your face from all the straining on your neck to look straight, the stare I had to put up with every day from you, my parents, others, myself. Let me think about the possibilities that someone as self-absorbed as yourself would suddenly find these wrinkles, this scalp, this clout over my right eye attractive. Let me wonder what lengths you would've gone to convince yourself you're some loving husband while banging some other woman in your head, scrubbing clean the house, and cooking me casseroles and lasagna's so you can play the role."

"Nothing, I just like watching late night talk shows and this CEO happened to be on."

That bitch. Self-absorbed, if that's what she thinks I am. She probably felt it too. No, she must've. Even if brief, like that day in the supermarket before I pulled that soap opera

< 254 >

exit. There's no way of suspecting without at least a hint, buried somewhere in her psyche, looking at me, watching me, judging me, telling her everything about why I'd do something so shallow.

So shallow, like everything I've done for her wasn't out of love.

Pick up a sock, maybe another. Order out Chinese and stick her uneaten pork fried rice into the refrigerator. Get on my knees and scrub the carpet pickled with little red spots that won't disappear. Oxi-Clean feeling more like soap and water than an actual compound. Me throwing myself back after an hour of struggle only to see the stains remaining as visible as Judy sitting on the couch watching me clean.

"I told you I'll take care of it," she'd say, face buried into her phone.

"Fuck me, you will," I'd mumble, throwing the rag to the side.

During the afternoons, shipments would go wrong and I'd be forced to the warehouse, wondering what would happen if one container skimped the regulatory process, if one client dropped for another because of a misquote, or if one order was lost at sea. I wondered all this as mortgage payments and bills came due and competition amped up and the entire operation I built from scratch skated on thinner and thinner ice, even as we were expanding into other territories. For every moment that I was there, half my mind was back at home, wondering if I'm going to come home to a surprise with Judy sobbing and covering her face, me trying my best to deny or explain why I went through it and how much it cost and why I hadn't told her sooner.

I think I'm sounding a bit repetitive. I guess that's just how my head is rolling right now.

Normalcy, how close it was and out of reach it remains, like some cruel god dangling it above my head and laughing as I fall on my ass swiping at it.

But no matter how desperate it sounds, I had to try.

"Judy, Rick say anything?" I'd ask one evening.

She'd shake her head.

"Judy, Rick say anything?" I'd ask, a morning later.

Still nothing.

"Anything?" Nothing. "Maybe a voice-mail?" Nothing. Over and over again.

"Her pace, her pace." I'd repeat it to myself curled up in bed, my innovative alternative to crying myself to sleep.

I wanted to follow up with so much more, each time, sitting or standing there, looking all constipated, rubbing the back of my head, a ten year old throwing a tantrum through body language.

"Judy, Rick say anything? No? Well would you mind texting him again? Or call him? Try calling him, his work phone. He probably got a new cell."

"Maybe try emailing him, or better yet, message him through one of your dozen social media apps. You've gotta have him on at least one. Linked-In? Try Linked-In. It'll look more professional through Linked-In. Or maybe Tinder. You know he'd jizz his pants if you came up, just wear your facemask when you meet him in person. Shit. Of course I'm kidding, Judy. Seriously, don't give me that look. A little much? Maybe."

"Okay, okay, babe, whatever, forget that. You've gotta try something, anything, 'cause I can't do this anymore. I can't pay the bills alone, I can't keep raising you, looking at you this way. I fucking can't. I can't because I feel

< 257 >

like I'm losing my mind one day at a time, losing you, losing *us*."

Or.

"Well, your choice I guess. Forget I asked. It's nothing."

.   .   .

I can't say for certain how on this god-forsaken path I fell off the train and why it all happened in one week. That's the thing with sanity. Whether you have it together or whether you don't, it can feel the same so long as you drink yourself silly and repeat how wonderful you have it. Then all it takes is a Saturday morning brunch gone wrong, and you find yourself standing before all the bills you forgot to pay.

And that total was steep.

Somewhere during the week, I'd found her old boss on Linked-In through her profile.

Eric Joy. Area manager, *Sazera LTD*, promoted from general manager since the last time he'd spoken with Judy. A guy who, from looking at his profile picture, you really wouldn't want your wife around alone. Crew-cut hair all black and full, blue eyes, chiseled jaw, leaning against something real white in a three-piece blue fitted pin stripe suit, staring at you like he wants to fuck. Shit, it was probably the same photo plastered to his bedroom ceiling to help him cum quicker, and judging from all of his Instagram photos (yes, I went there too), he could write an autobiography and it'd read like *Fifty Shades of Grey*.

I sent him a message.

"Hey Eric, how's it going, man? Reaching out because Judy told me she texted you about five days or so ago about returning to work and was wondering if you ever got them? She's doing well now and, from what she tells me, eager to get back to work. Let me know if you're still looking for an accounting manager."

Then on Saturday, a day later, he responded.

"Hi Jay! How've ya been? Good to hear that Judy is doing alright. I haven't gotten any text messages from her yet, but I'll be on the lookout. It's been really difficult finding an accounting head that could fill her shoes, so no, we haven't filled the position. Why don't you guys swing on by sometime tomorrow or the day after and we can talk!"

She never fucking texted him, so that night, I held nothing back.

I walked into the living room, having

finished up washing the dishes. I sat down next to her, took the remote, and clicked "mute."

"What are you doing?" she asked.

I gave her my phone, my conversation with Rick on full display.

"What am I looking at?" she asked after staring at it for a while.

"Did you ever text him?" I asked.

She looked up and stared. For a few seconds, she remained suspended in time, not once blinking. From her gaze, I couldn't tell if she was looking for something to say or waiting for me to yell.

"Did you?" I asked again.

"No," she replied, laying back against the headrest, reaching for the remote as if this piece of shit answer were all I was looking for. I grabbed it first.

"Judas priest, it's like talking to a teenager," I said with an exhale, "you told me you did."

"Well, Jay, I guess I lied."

"Yes, that's pretty fucking clear, so *why*?"

"I told you, hon, I needed time."

"Oh, that's right, *your* pace," I said, standing up and pacing. "Might I ask then, *why* even tell me you were going to text him?"

< 260 >

"I mean, I really was going to. It wasn't going to be anything really formal. I just wanted to get back in contact, let him know I'm okay, and maybe eventually, when I was ready, ease myself back into working for him."

"But then what?" I asked.

"I forgot," she replied matter-of-factly. "I was stressed. I didn't know if I could meet him or what he would say if he saw my face or…"

"So you forgot or you were too stressed to follow through?" I interrupted.

"Honey," she never calls me that and it pissed me off. "I can't explain it, I just couldn't follow through. Maybe it feels like I forgot because I've stopped thinking about it and couldn't remember."

"I've reminded you every fucking day this week; what do you mean you can't remember?" My voice, I couldn't keep it down.

"Please, stop shouting," she said, her fingers against her forehead.

"And how far along are you, in terms of being ready to work?" I asked. "Say, should I give you another week, month, year, ten years, a lifetime? You think a lifetime would be enough?"

I think I was shouting.

"Jay, what the hell is this all about?"

"Well," I picked up an unopened bottle of wine from the floor, "for one, I'm sick of cleaning these goddamn stains off the carpet. You see them? All smudged and shit because of that piece of shit OxiClean?"

"Well, write a complaint or something."

"Jesus, Judy, it isn't about the fucking Oxi Clean! Look at all your shit on the couch! Your shoes, your slippers, your books, your magazines. You've made this couch obsolete for me! And it's not enough that I have to deal with everything going on at work, I've gotta come home and cook and clean and make you happy! Happy, as if it's even possible with you when all you want to do is wallow in self-pity because of what happened to your face!"

I was definitely shouting.

"Well guess what, Judy, it happened, it happened, it happened, no matter what, you can't change that! A year from now, it happened. Three or four years from now, it happened. A fucking lifetime could pass and it happened! Time won't just wash it away! So unless you wanna die this way, *you've* gotta be the one to make that move *now* so we can reconstruct our lives from the ash-heap that's our marriage in its current form!"

< 262 >

And all this time while I was on my soap-box, she started shaking her head, snickering, and blowing up in laughter.

"What's so funny," I asked.

"You. You've set up all the pieces so you could give that stump speech." She got within inches of me. "I could hear you rehearsing in your sleep."

"Yeah, it's a pretty damn good speech," I snorted back.

"You never once said a thing to me," she began, "not about the stains on the carpet, not about the mess, not about having to cook for me or anything. You just let it happen. You know why? I know why. You didn't say a thing because I might've actually listened."

She was hissing.

"I might've cleaned up after myself, cooked, wiped down the house, helped you out with groceries, all that shit I used to do, and *you* would've hated that because *then* you wouldn't have been able to hold it against me."

"And what's that exactly?" I snapped back. "Hold it against you so that I could get you back on your feet?"

"Yes, Jay! You think I wanna spend my life melting away in this room? You think I *enjoy* feeling like a monster every time I walk out in public? You think I wouldn't give anything to get back to the life I had, before the accident, before it made me a *fucking* pariah? I *told* you I needed to do it at *my* pace, when *I'm* ready, but right now, I physically *can't* get back to normal, not at the rate you'd like. This wasn't about me getting back on track. This was always about *you*. YOU. You, wanting everything back to normal on *your* terms."

She shot up and began picking up all her shit on the couch.

"Well, seeing that this bugs you so much, maybe I could start. Here, I'm throwing this out, keeping *this* on the bed; *this* goes in the kitchen."

I wasn't going to lose this fight, not after all that.

"You know what, I bet you still think I went through it, don't you?" I said.

She dropped everything in her hands. "What are you talking about?"

"What Amber was talking about," I replied. "*Wondervision* or whatever you call it. That operation, the microchips in the brain, that external server that processes all

< 264 >

perceptions, where I would be able to see you differently, like how you used to look before the accident. You still think I'm the kind of guy who would go through it. Ever since she made that goddamn joke at the end, you've been giving me all this attitude, like I've gotta justify somehow to you that I wouldn't have gone through with it!"

"Well did you?" she asked.

"NO! Of course not!" I snapped.

"Then why freak out?" she asked.

I couldn't respond quickly enough.

"If you didn't go through it, you didn't go through it. I admit, it crossed my mind once, back at the grocery store after meeting Amber, but that was it. Sounds like it's been crossing yours too."

"What are you saying?" I demanded.

"What do you think I'm saying?"

"I think you know what I think you're saying!"

"Try me."

"I think you're saying that you think I'm that kind of person who would do something as fucked up as what I know you're thinking I did because of what Amber said. That never mind everything I've done up till this point to make our marriage work. Never mind it! I couldn't possibly be an actual good husband without having edited your face in real time."

"You're just talking to yourself, Jay," she said, shaking her head, "I should record you."

"Well fucking do it! I dare you!" I shouted, little pebbles of tears forming. "Put it out on Facebook or Instagram, I don't give a shit! You can look like the victim, it's all that matters to you anyways!"

We fought for probably half an hour more, her cleaning, laughing, shaking her head in disbelief. It ended with her slamming the door to our bedroom shut and locking it from the inside. I ran back to the kitchen and nearly grabbed a drink before thinking against it 'cause God knows what I might've done drunk at that moment. So I just poured myself a glass of water and dumped it around in my mouth, half of it getting all over my face and on the floor. A glass of cold water, it didn't help much in putting out the fire.

I slept on the couch that night. Slept; more like curled in a ball holding a pillow like a toddler throwing a tantrum. I got up three or four times to meditate, pace, or do pushups,

< 266 >

before finally pounding half the bottle of cabernet that I'd picked up from the floor earlier.

And I was empty. There were no words left for me to use. Had that argument gone on, it would've all come out as me grunting and stomping like a neanderthal. There were no thoughts in my head, no internal monologue, just a cloud of hot gas.

I threw the last glassful in my mouth and finally passed out around the time the birds started chirping again, leaving the glass turned on the floor, fresh residue of red leaking onto the carpet.

\* \* \*

I was calmer the next morning, having woken up around noon and getting out of bed at three-ish. Judy wasn't around, and despite expecting to feel bad for the night before, I honestly felt relieved she wasn't there. The hangover wasn't bad. Half a bottle of red and all I could feel was a light dizziness from poor sleep and a bit of a runny stomach. Guess my body's built up a bit of a tolerance to the poison of some sort. I dunno, probably need to see somebody about it.

< 267 >

For fifteen minutes, I just sat with my head propped up against the backrest, staring into the ceiling, trying to figure out what to bring myself to do. Sort things out with her? What would I say? Hell, what were we even fighting about anyways?

At first, so much of it was a blur, like even though I didn't have my first drink until a few hours past midnight, it felt like I'd been drunk that whole evening. Then the *Interface* kicked in and everything I said, did, all the stink of last night, came rushing back as soon as my mind cleared.

Wow. Thought I could filter my memories. What if they were things I'd rather ignore?

Hell, maybe I didn't want to and I didn't even know it, like some little guy nestled deep in my consciousness, finally taking control and telling me to face it this time around, and he played the entire shitshow starring all of my emotional insecurities, and he played it in slow motion while holding my eyelids open and wrapping me down with duct tape.

Record what I was saying. The irony. Guess Judy wouldn't have known how unnecessary it was for her to follow through.

Disgusted, I went about putting myself

< 268 >

together, showering, flossing, and brushing, all while avoiding anything that could carry my reflection. Threw a leftover slice of pizza in the microwave and nibbled on it while ruminating over everything.

Judy just needs time.

Judy just needs time.

Judy just needs time.

Her pace, her pace, her pace.

Funny how things are after a fight like that. Where now that your cards are all out on the table, you could care just a little less about how everything turns out. Maybe it wasn't even anger all along, that long week of building frustration. Maybe it was just anticipation.

Now it's over. Both of us completely exposed, with nothing else to do but wait and hope.

Wait and hope. Her pace. She just needs time.

Then I noticed my Linked-In page was still open, and remembered Rick, our proposed meeting. Judy could be back to work as soon as next week if it goes well! Fuck it if she didn't want to go. I was going alone.

Unshaven, golf shirt over some basketball shorts and old tennis shoes, pizza sauce still on my beard, I was in a cab praying the store didn't close early on Sundays.

.  .  .

Things got weird from here.

I arrived an hour before closing time at the flag ship store in Midtown, where Judy used to work.

I admit, even after being here a few dozen times, I still ended up wasting a few minutes standing in the atrium, trying to adjust my eyes to the expanse of black and white and black and white; sleek black fixtures, glossy white floor, black exposed ceiling with track lights, white mannequins wearing black party skirts and stilettos, black articles of clothing for sale, white articles of clothing for sale, wavy white walls made entirely of an endless screen with moving black silhouette figures approaching and receding and pacing left and right and shaking their asses. I swear, I might've walked past a million dollars' worth of merchandise in the first few steps. It was one of those clothing stores where a floor rep could earn as much commission as a luxury car salesman, the kind with no customer service desk or lines, just good-looking people, some in white outfits and others in black, holding tablet PCs, pacing between the aisles.

Anyway, this next part I still cannot explain right, even after having rehearsed at least a dozen times, but here goes.

I was moments from giving up and calling it a day, having wasted thirty minutes wandering the floors of the place, when I spotted him standing near the entrance, talking with some old guy dressed like shit. Besides his suit, beige two-piece over the usual dark navy blue with pinstripes, he looked the same as every time I've ever met him, with that same haircut, same cheesy ass smile, staring at that old guy in that same way, like he wanted to fuck him.

I walked up to him, not minding the other gentleman, who saw me approaching out of the corner of his eye and motioned with a nod of his head. Rick turned around.

"Yes, sir," he said, the other gentleman stepping aside.

"Uh, hey, Rick," I said.

"Hey. Do I know you?"

"Um," I was bit surprised, "of course, I'm Jay, Judy's husband."

Didn't seem to register.

"Judy," he said, pondering out loud.

"Oh come on, stop it," I said, "Judy Valentino, the woman who used to work for you."

"Well," he chuckled, "I wish I were that kind of person but, nobody works for me."

"Nobody works for you, the Area Manager."

He was laughing, "you've got the wrong guy buddy, I'm a sales rep." He waved to the floor.

"Well, is there another Eric Joy who looks just like you working as the general manager?" I asked, half joking, half irate.

He shook his head. "We don't really have a store manager; everything is run up in corporate."

I started getting angry, I could feel it in my temples. This fucking wise guy, what the hell was he trying to pull?

"Oh come on Rick, I've had a hard week. My wife, Judy Valentino, you don't remember her at least? Worked here for two years as your head of accounting before quitting in February because of the accident?"

"Well, I don't see how that'd work, as we don't have an accounting department either."

"Jesus Rick, give me a break, how would you run a business without an accounting department?"

"Everything's digital."

< 272 >

"Wow, okay, one second." I said, furiously grabbing my phone, "Look here."

They both looked over to see. I didn't mind, I was so caught up with the moment I couldn't have cared less if that creepy old guy was eavesdropping.

But there was no message.

"What…what the fuck?" I said very loudly.

I couldn't find it, my last one being from some hot shot freight broker looking for business from three weeks back.

"Hold on," I muttered as I proceeded to close my browser to refresh, logging off and back on again and scanning through my emails for a notification, my finger twitching faster and faster as I went. Still, no message.

"Look, sir," Rick was beginning to sound impatient, "I'm actually off the clock and was heading out for a drink with this gentleman here. I'm sorry about what may have happened to your wife. Please go to the website and apply if she's looking for work."

My mind powered down; any words would come out as gibberish.

"Alright," I muttered. "Sorry, must've made a mistake."

Nothing else to say.

So I walked out, dazed in oblivion, wondering what to wonder about, why Rick was acting the way he was, lying out of his teeth about everything. I still don't know. Maybe he was trying to hide something from that other guy?

But what the fuck then was up with my phone? Did he delete that message? Could he even do that from his phone?

I wondered until I could wonder no more, finally breaking down and seating myself in a bar in some restaurant with a cold, sweating lager placed right in front of my head buried in my arms.

While pouring it down my throat, I took another look at my phone and almost choked it all back out.

A new message from Eric Joy.

*Hey, sorry if you didn't find me at the store today, I forgot to tell you I was at the other location. Let me text Judy this week and see how it goes. Thanks!*

A new message, right above the one he sent me the day before.

\* \* \*

In retrospect, he never did contact Judy.

I didn't message him either; I didn't know who or what to trust or what the hell happened with my phone or him or that old guy standing next to him. Be it my *Interface* or my brain, something's wrong. In all cases, I admit, I've done away with it like I've done with all the weirdness from this whole experience; put it in a box and sealed it tight for later.

Don't have enough shits to give right now. They're all for something else. Just thought I'd talk about it as an FYI.

That Sunday after visiting the store, I got in, drunk, crashing before acknowledging Judy, or whether or not she was even there.

The next morning, I awoke to the sound of her sobbing next to me. I didn't ask why, didn't need to know. I just put my arm around her, rubbing her shoulder, telling her over and over and over.

"Your pace, your pace, your pace."

And suddenly that was fine with me. Her pace. I'm not sure how it came about, this point where I've come to accept it. I guess emotions can be like bowel movements. Shit builds up and comes out through one of your two holes, and you go from ugly to nice in a matter of minutes. I'm sure there's a better way to describe that.

Or it could be my anxieties, quelled by chewing on her flimsy reassurance that she didn't suspect anything, suckling it for all its comfort. Maybe I've made it a reality, *my* reality, choosing to believe that it was all in my head and that my little secret, the *Interface Therapy*, the *Interface*, all of it was still safe with me. I guess with peace of mind, however illusory it might be, I don't have any reason more to care.

Or maybe there are no reasons.

Maybe I'm just done. Just like that. Done and without a reason for being so or a care in the world for why. Done like this single word can be all the reasons and explanations in and of itself, like the mind just reaches a point and decides to move on. Done, like I wouldn't give a shit if Eric Joy texts or forgets, if Judy is back in the office next week or year, if I've gotta clean and take care of this woman or if she starts picking herself back up. I'm done with chasing normalcy, some word I use for how things used to be.

How things used to be. I guess Judy's right. It's every goddamn day of existence.

So I'll kiss her before bed, fry her up an egg-white omelet in the a.m., a sandwich at

< 276 >

noon, pasta in the evening, switch up every other day with something new I found online, work while she reads, pick up shit, and ready the couch for her every day like room service until it all becomes routine.

Out of selfishness, she said. As if anything done out of love isn't lined with a shade of it.

You know, there are many roads to a steady life, so long as you're flexible with what it is, and know what it isn't.

I know it can't be her leaving me again, me going at it all alone. I know it isn't another fight, where we tear each other to bits and wake up convincing ourselves it wasn't us; me, in the moment, letting all of my insecurities out in the open run around with all its filth like sewer rats. Normalcy will just have to be anything but a life without her.

Let it all go, the impatience, the need for certainty, and save it all, those priceless little shits, for what I can control. My temperament, what I see and feel and smell around Judy, my greatest lie, my best truth.

## SEPTEMBER 30, 2025

So something is wrong with my *Interface*.

It happened yesterday when I rode a bike-share to Chinatown. Don't ask me why, I just needed a reason to get out of the apartment, probably spurred by the battles with the thermostat with Judy wanting it twenty degrees lower than what the average person would keep it at and me freezing my ass off and calling her insane. Or it might've had something to do with what my doctor told me three days earlier during my annual physical, where he told me I was fat and needed to work out. Well, more like, "although your BMI is in the normal range, your cholesterol is a bit on the

< 278 >

high for a man of your age, so I would start watching the fried foods and finding time at a gym," and some shit like that.

Parked my bike near Canal Street station and decided to walk the rest of the way, wasn't but a few blocks from the clinic. Why the clinic? Who knows. Hell, I don't even know. Maybe it's my *Interface*, calling me back home, where my new reality was born. Or maybe I just needed a destination and it was the first place that came to mind. Or maybe I had actually wanted to go there, like somehow, somewhere in my day, something somewhere triggered the thought, "you know what I'd like to see? That fucking clinic again."

My choice or the *Interface's*? How would I know, and is there even a difference?

I turned a corner and saw it in the distance.

It wasn't the clinic.

Not the one in the real world that they promised me I'd see after that crazy science experiment called the "User Acceptance Testing." Not the faded buildings, the broken signs in Chinese, the alleyways, the motels, the restaurants, the smells.

No. Glass buildings from the top to the bottom of the block, sliding doors that would float open and close for techies and business-men walking in and out in their suits and dress shirts and badges, unmarked white vans parked out front, a black glass egg shooting into the sky with white lettering plastered onto it.

*Wondervision. Your Better Reality.*

With every step I took, a vessel might've popped in my head. I could barely feel my legs as they moved on autopilot, closer and closer to that strip of buildings that shouldn't exist. So many thoughts ran through my mind as I approached, none of them that I could put into words, just a general feeling when nothing in the world makes sense at the moment and all your thoughts become a billion words creating a cloud of gas.

Soon, I found myself at the entrance standing like a lost child having stumbled into Narnia. There, the minions in white, men and women in lab coats and white pants and black shoes, filed in and out of the building, a shit ton of 'em, way more than I remembered from the first time I was there.

One walked straight into me. He came right out of the sliding doors and as I turned, I was about face to face with him, and I stumbled back and fell on my ass as the people in white just kept pacing on, not one stopping to offer me help.

"Hey, asshole," I started to shout as I turned around just to find him ten steps away, clustered with everyone else, not one turning around.

"Excuse me," I said, tugging on one of the lab coats of an older black gentleman who was talking with a colleague, but he just walked on by.

"Miss," I said to this older Indian lady, waving my hand in front of her face only for her to continue on, like she were under some spell.

I continued, "Sir, miss, sir, hey, asshole, watch it!"

But every time I saw one of 'em face to face, I found myself stunned into silence, like running into an immediate dead end when turning the corner. Like they weren't even avoiding me, my shouting into their faces, my tugging on their shirts, my obnoxious antics that would've gotten the cops called on my ass anywhere else in the city. To them, I just wasn't there.

Soon, the entire plaza was empty, everyone

coming having gone and disappeared and everyone going having nestled into that big fucking egg. I went back to the entrance to peer through the glass just to the side of the door.

There, I saw the lobby. Just the way I remembered it. The plastered white floors, the Zen garden, the statues and displays, the monitors. Almost nobody was in sight but for Dr. Nguyen, the Asian guy, sitting at that crazy receptionist desk that seemed to shoot out of the ground, extending all the way to the back of the room.

I stepped back. Then, a familiar voice.

"You here for appointment?"

And suddenly, everything was gone.

What laid before me now was the inside of that hallway that could very well be the setting of every crime drama ever made in the city; the ceiling tile lights on but barely shining through the filth that covered it, the floors that looked mopped once a year, a dark stairwell at the end. I could barely make it all out through the stained glass of the closed sliding door.

I took a step back and noticed the black metal emergency stairs above me, the worn sidewalk underneath my feet, an empty beer

< 282 >

bottle smashed to bits on the side of the building, the rows and rows of signs of faded caricatures I couldn't read to my left and right, the walls of different shades of red brick from the painting and repainting and touch-ups and patches, the faint smell of garbage. No white vans, no high rises, no people in white coats. In short, the reality I was promised.

"No, wrong building." I waved to the camera.

I tried blinking real hard a couple of times, you know, just to make sure my brain had it all straight. After all, a blink was all the time it took to go between then and now.

Sure enough, my mind had it settled. I was back in Chinatown.

"Those lying motherfuckers," I mumbled to myself a while later, sitting on the curb, not thinking about where to go next. My mind was preoccupied with attempting to make sense of it all, asking over and over again, what the hell have I gotten myself into?

So, what the hell was going on?

Sure, you could tell me it's my *Interface*, how it was the UAT still kicking in full gear and that somewhere in that period while I was there someone had turned it off.

< 283 >

But if it were the UAT server, how would they have known to turn it off? I didn't phone anyone; there isn't exactly a helpline except for these emails I write to Josh, and I know I didn't read the paperwork in full but I definitely recall a section about privacy, you know, of the contents of everything that's in my mind.

Was it the system itself working on auto-pilot? Then why didn't it do anything for the first fifteen minutes or so while I was falling on my butt crack, making an ass out of myself in front of all of those lab people? And what the hell was up with those lab people anyhow? Who were they and why couldn't they see me? Why did they just walk away as I tugged, waved, badgered them in a way that would've gotten me beaten to death on any other street in Manhattan, like I didn't exist to them? Who were they? Were they just products of some software or was it, and you'll think I'm nuts, some other reality altogether?

And if it were a glitch, then somebody tell me, what the hell out of everything that I've come to know since the operation has been real? What have they done to me?

Shit, I tried putting this away in the box like everything else, but this time it just ain't

< 284 >

gonna fit. It's wide open and everything is out there, from the man I saw in the mirror to Rick's double existence and now to this complex and its population of artificial beings in lab coats on Adderall, a reality that may or may not be imaginary. This operation had officially become too weird for my short-sightedness, too much for it to only be about Judy.

Questions, questions, and more questions, the only language that can truly express what happened. Josh and company are gonna have fun when they get around to this. Hope they get to it quick, 'cause every day without answers for an alcoholic is another day he might drink himself to death.

SUBJECT: RE: THE CLINIC
SENT: OCTOBER 1, 2025, 9:31 A.M.
TO: JAYBIGGS1987@HOTMAIL.NET

Hi Jay

I apologize for your experience and do want you to know that we are working actively behind the scenes to determine and remediate the issue.

I had asked the engineering team to validate the UAT server and all of its logs and was able to confirm it was not active, not since your operation. Furthermore, the testing procedure required that the patient be at a certain spot during the onset, that location being inside the clinic itself, so in no scenario would it have activated while you were outside. Lastly, and most importantly, it was certainly not programmed into the system to include random individuals as you described leaving and walking into the building. That would be quite a large yet meaningless effort. Whatever is happening is not an issue with the UAT server.

Since we can only speculate at this point, we will need to create an investigation. We can proceed in two ways.

< 286 >

You give us permission to go through the logs. This will mean we would have visibility into all of what you saw on that given day, should you provide us with the correct time and place of the event, as well as all of the interconnectivities between the various parts of your *Interface* system. This method would allow for us to resolve the issue in a more timely manner. Furthermore, we would be bound to keep all of your information that we may be exposed to secured.

You do not give us permission and we will proceed the established way, which is to say, we would have to replicate your Interface and attach it to an artificial test subject, or to be precise, a physical object with various sensors replicating the human sensory nervous system. From there, we would analyze all the patterns of communication of data between the various touchpoints that make up the product. Furthermore, this would require us bringing the object to multiple various locations to perform the testing and would be highly time-consuming.

Please let us know which path you would prefer in your next email.

< 287 >

In the meantime, I would love to answer your questions, but without having investigated the issue further, it would all be mere speculation. Also, an important thing to note, please refrain from going to the media or other forms of public communication as it would only complicate the issue and hinder your ability to fulfill whatever it was that you were trying to achieve with this product. We believe a timely fix is the best way forward for both parties.

Once again, apologies, and we will get this straightened out.

Josh Rikkard
Relationship Manager
*Wonderlenz* Technologies Inc.

< 288 >

## OCTOBER 1, 2025

These past three days have been trying.

For example, two days ago, it was a nice day out and I sat at a bench near the lake in Central Park with Judy, people watching. I saw a guy walking his dog and I swore after a while that it just disappeared. He kept walking with his hand out, like he was holding a leash, but no dog. But I was pretty far and wasn't able to do a double take, not accurately anyways. Probably just a combination of distance and worsening eyesight from staring at a monitor every day and the brightness and everything.

Then yesterday I was telling Oswaldo, my business manager, what a gorgeous day it was

< 289 >

prior, and he got all confused, asking me if I went out of town or something 'cause he remembered it being real cloudy and gray. I asked around and that seemed to be the consensus, everyone in the warehouse, everyone at Southie's. Only Judy seemed to remember it the way I did. Probably just a clearing in Central Park?

But how would I know? I can't trust anything anymore, not my eyes, not my touch, not any of my other senses, and if you can't trust your senses, then can it even be considered living? Even Helen Keller could rely on three of them, have some sense of objective reality, can at least trust that it's a mouthful of peanut butter and not soil or smell the dog shit on her shoe and be certain she stepped on dog shit, 'cause she couldn't see where she was going and all, or feel her finger burn and know she's standing over a burning stove, know her surroundings, know it with a degree of certainty.

Certainty, I guess you can say it's the building block of our conception of the world. I mean, without it, where the fuck am I? What's left to hold it together? My memory and chance? Know for sure that I'm not gonna trip over one of my sneakers 'cause I'd taken

< 290 >

it off the day before and hope that I was actually wearing it and not only perceiving to? Or anything for that matter? Shit, have I actually been wearing clothes?

Damn, I wish they'd hurry up, 'cause I wanna live in the world again, or at least, live someplace with enough consistency to persuade me it's real.

.    .    .

So, all insecurities aside, I came across Amber's number in my phone this morning (Judy and I have always had this thing where we shared all of our contacts in case of an emergency) and shot her a text to meet.

*Hey, it's Jay, Judy's husband.*

*Sorry to surprise you.*

*Listen, I wanted to talk to you about your Interface, or whatever it was you were talking about last time. Do you have time this month for, like, a 30 minute coffee? I can swing by somewhere close to your place.*

I figured it was time to come clean to somebody. Mostly, I needed to know if all of this was only happening to me, and until there's some reliable virtual community of *Interface* users, she's the only other person I know with the procedure done. Also, I'm pretty sure she and Judy aren't that close anymore, so I think I'm safe.

Actually, she just replied with a date and address. Well shit. You know, with anyone else, you'd think it'd take a bit more convincing given how we've only met once and all.

Hell of a personality.

< 292 >

So, that was enlightening.

Just walked out of the coffee shop and threw away my drink that had gone cold from sitting in front of me for so long untouched. I even ordered a croissant; guess I'd forgotten it was there even after the cleaning guy had offered a box for the half remaining.

Amber had eaten the other half, slowly nibbling away at it while going through two cappuccinos and a tall black coffee to supply her the energy she needed to indulge me, for nearly half an hour, about a fight she and Jaycee had that morning.

< 293 >

"I don't even know what I get out of dating him. I might as well raise a cat."

She was different today. She spoke slowly with a lisp. Her hair was uncombed, her face undecorated, her body no longer decked out in the stilettos, the dress, the earrings, the necklace. Instead, she wore sneakers and a marathon finisher t-shirt over red leggings.

She'd wanted to redo her room that morning again, her bed feeling out of sorts with the window, clashing with her chi or spirit or something. She'd wanted her bed closer to the window and turned, and she needed help with moving the rug underneath as well as re-assorting everything in her room. She said she needed a distraction, and that this was necessary. Before she even mentioned his name, I could hear word for word what would've come out of Jaycee's mouth spoken with fire and brimstone.

"So he told me I was nuts."

Yeah.

"And, like, I told him I was sorry he felt that way and that it was still important to me, but he just kept acting like such a fucking diva the whole time and stuff, giving me this face I could seriously punch. He's got this really punchable face when he gets mad. Like, he doesn't even look intimidating, just really bitchey. God, I'm glad you texted me. Needed an excuse to get away from him before I did anything."

She'd trail off at the end of her sentences and continue unaware of the gap. She talked slowly, slower than what I remember, like in a way where, this time, she was almost easy to follow. Her eyes were swollen with dark circles, her skin pale, a contrast like night and day to the rich coastal tan I remembered from the last time I saw her.

I tried using it to transition.

"You look tired," I mentioned, not waiting for her to finish her story.

"What, is it that obvious?" she replied.

"You look like a raccoon," I responded, pointing to her eyes, "you dying of something?"

"No, just fatigue," she replied, sipping her second cappuccino. "Haven't been able to sleep well."

I found my opportunity. "It's your *Interface,* isn't it?"

"Yeah," she replied slowly, "yeah, it is. Are you just assuming?"

I cut to the chase real quick. "No, I'm not.

As I said in my text message, it's kinda why I wanted to meet."

"Meet about what? Oh, by the way, how's Judy?" she asked.

"She's fantastic. Anyway, I wanted to meet to talk about the procedure, the *Interface Therapy* you were talking about last time."

"Okay," she was hardcore leaning away from me, "what about it?"

I took a deep breath. "What if I told you I've gotten it done?"

She was slowly nodding. "When?"

"A while back."

"For what?"

"Well, you probably shouldn't know this about me," I paused, taking a deep breath for effect, "but I've got a history."

"What kind of history?"

"A violent one. You know, I don't talk about this much to anyone, so please, take that to mean something." She nodded. "So, right before meeting Judy, I'd been arrested. Charged with assault and battery, some club, some schmuck. Had a bit of a history of it too, but as it was the first time coming to the judge's attention, I had the choice between six months in jail or a two-year probation with

< 296 >

mandatory therapy. So I took therapy, and I guess I found it helpful, because after the two years were up, I kept with it."

I wasn't making this part up.

"In fact, I had my last session only about six months back. Didn't go well. I felt like I was rapidly regressing, what with the stresses of work and life and I was drinking myself to death and needed something drastic."

This part I was.

"I had my reasons."

Yes, I lied. Backed out at the last second. I put a lot of work into it too, enough to be compelling but not too much to have to go into details.

"Well, like," she replied, nodding, absorbing the information, unsure of what to do with it, "I'm happy for you, I guess." Then after a brief pause. "But, why didn't you bring it up when I met you guys last?"

"Judy didn't want me to go through it. That's why. I did it without telling her or anyone."

"You told your therapist, right?"

"Oh, yes, of course. I told my therapist."

More awkward silence, she finished her cappuccino in that time.

I continued.

"Amber, can you please tell me what's been keeping you up? I'm telling you, I might be going through the same thing."

She hesitated. "Well, I guess it's only fair if you started by telling me what you flagged me down to talk about."

Fair, but I was only gonna talk about the clinic. Just being cautious. Not sure if she'd connect the dots with anything else 'cause my mouth doesn't do well in navigating the lies I tell. I went into full detail about the buildings, the street, the lobby, the men and women in white practically walking through me. I talked about how they vanished as I approached the door and heard Dr. Nguyen. Hell, I even showed her part of my email exchange with my relationship manager that I'd proofread ahead of time to make sure there was no mention of Judy.

Without talking, she pulled out her phone and showed me an email she got from Derek, her relationship manager, this morning.

It was almost verbatim. Everything starting at the point where she was offered up the two options for debugging. Every sentence, every word, copied and pasted.

So I think we can conclude this isn't some

one-off occurrence happening to me the way they made it out to seem; these bimbos had so many, they've standardized their responses. You can bet your ass I was pissed, if only for a moment, but it was placed in timeout 'cause of everything she told me right after.

"So what's your story?" I asked.

"Same shit, different place," she started. "So like, I work near Sazera, Judy's old store. You knew that. It's how I know Judy and stuff. So I like to go to Sazera a lot, especially after work, not to shop but to browse. Have you ever been?"

"Yes," I said.

"Did you ever notice the sales floor people?"

"Yeah," I replied, "beautiful women, wearing these black and white dresses."

"Yeah, you saw the ones in white too?" She asked, a bit startled.

"Yeah, like I said, black and white, like everything else in the store."

She shook her head, "Wow, well, none of them are supposed to wear white."

"What do you mean by that?" I replied.

She sat back and drew in a deep breath. "So, about a week ago, I'd gotten out earlier and decided to, for whatever reason, check out the store, you know, browse a bit to de-stress and then meet Jaycee near Macy's a little later and decide on dinner. I think it was, like, last Friday or something."

She paused to double fist her cappuccino and her cup of coffee, a sip at a time from each hand.

"I didn't think of it much at first. I guess I assumed they'd changed up the attire or something, which would've been a first. I mean, I've been going to that store for years, you know? I've never seen…well…anyways, I went on shopping like usual, checking out this satin blouse near the entrance that was new and had these ruffles along the shoulders that I really liked, you know. I could probably put it with this pair of slacks I had at home or with this skirt and some boots I got at Anya Ponorovskaya for my birthday two weeks earlier. I made Jaycee buy them for me—"

"Yes, so you were checking out that blouse," I interrupted.

"Yeah, so I was checking out this really cute satin blouse and I wanted to get a price check because, you know, that's how you shop at a store like Sazera. Anyways, I flagged down this sales rep in white, but she just, sorta, walked by. I followed her. I guess I could've just found someone else but I thought it was rude how she just brushed past me and I just couldn't let it slide."

"I was like, calling out and stuff, getting really ticked, but she just kept going. Then, this saleswoman in black walked up in front of me asking if I needed help, and I was really annoyed at this point by the way, and I told her that lady in white behind her was being a bitch."

"*Bitch*, you used that word?" I asked.

"But when I glanced past her shoulder, the lady in white, she just—"

She dropped her pitch to a whisper. "She just vanished."

"Vanished? Like, turned a corner?"

"No, vanished," she closed her eyes, "this sounds crazy, but, like, she was walking and faded away into thin air."

"Like a ghost?" I asked, laughing all confused.

"Yeah. Like a ghost."

The hairs on my arm felt like spikes at that point. "Wow."

"I asked the saleswoman in black, who

was, like, by then looking at me like I was some psycho, if she saw what I saw. She just shook her head and told me there were no saleswomen in white uniforms, not at that location anyways. So I basically grabbed her hand to drag her around the store, looking for others, but.."

She flicked her wrist, "they weren't there. All gone. God, I was babbling like I'd lost my tongue. She must've thought I was nuts."

"That's.." I started, not knowing what else to add. "What'd you do after that?"

"Well, I was only a little freaked at first. I just got out of there as fast as I could. But it was when Jaycee told me he thought it might have something to do with my *Interface*, well, I guess that might've been what stuck with me. Stuck with me and grew."

"I get it," I said, "it made you question your senses."

She only nodded, slowly, muttering. "I haven't been sleeping well the past few days. First few days didn't really leave the house, which was nice, because I could more or less trust what's around me. Well, trust is a word of art. I still forget sometimes that the window's not actually there. But then came Monday and I had to go to work."

< 302 >

She'd been massaging her forehead so hard it'd turned red, every passing memory intensifying her anguish. "Like, that morning I saw this woman right outside my apartment lobby holding her pet dog, and out of the blue, I thought, 'nobody holds their pet dog, who the hell holds their pet dog, why haven't I seen her before, who is she?' I suddenly felt the urge to wave my hand in front of her to see if she'd notice me. Over the course of the next few days, the more I thought about it, the more I wanted to do that to everyone, turn everything around, flip the world upside down to know what's real. My mind kept going back to that day, thinking about the women in white, how they were helping other people, Jay. *Other people!* There were other people walking around that store who they were interacting with. God!"

She fell back into her chair, closing her eyes and taking a few deep breaths to focus.

"You know, I know what you're thinking. I'm overthinking it." She let out a deep exasperated sigh, "it's what Jaycee tells me. It's what he always tells me when he isn't listening."

"Anyways, as the week went on, everything just got worse. The thought of something wrong with my *Interface*, my perception of reality. It just grew in all directions into this insane cluster of doubt. Doubt about if I were actually at work, if that was Jaycee holding my hand, if I was on the right subway, everything! I found myself running back to the store over and over, hoping I could see those saleswomen again, hoping I could decipher some pattern, isolate the incident."

A tear streamed down her left cheek. "It just slowly tore my sense of security to shreds, Jay. I kept trying to calm myself, trying not to think about it, trying not to make it something more than it is, 'cause that's what I do. Can't let things go, can't hold my worst predictions down, wondering whether or not I've made a mistake and what I'd gotten myself into."

By now they fell one after the other, her face flushed as red as that mark on her forehead. Her voice had dropped to something soft and intense, as if speaking to her conscious self from the outside. "I mean, just *one* incident! But if there's something wrong with this thing, how would I know for *certain* that's the only one? And if I don't know what's wrong with it, how can I be certain of anything?"

"I know, I know," I kept repeating as she spoke. I put my hand on hers.

< 304 >

She stared at it for a good minute without pulling back. Then, for a moment, her eyes lit up.

"Wait, if I could feel you, does it mean...?"

"No," I replied, "trust me, it doesn't. But, for what it's worth, I'm talking to you, acknowledging you."

"Yeah," she wiped her face, taking a few deep breaths to calm herself before asking, "but is that all?"

I shrugged, "I don't know. Did your relationship manager say anything?"

"I showed you what he said," she replied, taking her hand away. "He took a whole week to get back to me. God he's so useless. What do they do for us anyways?"

"Well, we're just going to have to be patient with them," I said. "I'm sure the system's big and complicated and who knows how many smart folks it's gonna take to screw this lightbulb back in. But they're gonna get it done. Otherwise, we're just gonna turn our shit in, one by one, and they'll lose all their business."

"You'd do that?" she asked.

No.

"Of course, wouldn't you?"

She was already shaking her head before I asked the question. "I need this."

"So how about this? The media's gonna go shitstorm with them if this gets out, so maybe we at least hold that much power?"

"If it gets out, then what? They'd shut down and I'd still lose it?" She shot back sharply.

"Okay, let's just take a moment, breathe, chill out, and focus on what we can control. We've still gotta live our lives, go to work, live in this world until there's a fix, so why not we concentrate on what we can control? Why not we concentrate on coming up with some way to determine what *is* and what *isn't* real?"

"How?"

"By connecting the dots. Let's start with our two stories. Like, for instance, the saleswomen wearing white dresses. I saw 'em too! I saw 'em when I had that encounter with Rick. Maybe he was also a product of my *Interface*. Actually, no, it makes total sense!"

"You're losing me. What happened with Rick?" she asked.

Oh well, what's the harm?

"Long story short, I was supposed to meet him at the store that day. I did. He told me he wasn't the store manager but a salesman. I thought he was fucking with me until I found out he was at the *other* store that day. Don't ask why I was looking for him. I was trying to help Judy get her job back without her. Dick move, I know. I've grown since. But I *saw* those women in white."

Likely, I was, by now, more or less thinking out loud to myself. "What if, by chance, he wasn't real? Like, he was also just another product of my *Interface*? A product of my *Interface and* aware of me. Maybe that's a place to start?"

Amber wasn't listening, just nodding her head along with that stone-cold gaze, like there wasn't a single cog spinning behind those eyes.

"Amber, did you see Rick Joy? Or at least, did you see any salesmen?"

"Uh, no," she responded. "No, I wasn't paying attention."

By now, she'd gone through her last cup of coffee and was motioning for the check.

"I don't know, Jay," she began. "I don't know where we'd even start. I mean, even sitting here, I couldn't be confident if *you're* real or not."

"What, don't be insane. Of course I'm real!"

< 307 >

She stood up, took her chair, and sat it next to me.

She stared at me straight in the eyes and put her hand on my cheek.

"You're warm. I can feel it."

She put her face close to my shirt.

"Cheap cologne. I can smell it. But it's just information, right? Just data that my *Interface* is feeding me to my senses."

She held her hand up, staring at it like it was covered in blood. "My five senses, five little liars. Even if they fix it, how would I know for sure anything is real anymore? But at the same time, even if they switch it off forever, how would I ever know for sure?"

She looked at me. "If your reality is lying to you, how *could* you know?"

"Amber," I tried to interrupt.

"How could I even know if these five fingers actually exist?"

"Okay, Amber, stop!" I snapped. "You're driving yourself further into the hole. Look, trust me, I know what you're going through. I do. I'm as freaked out as you are but I've got to keep it together. That's what people do. We figure shit out, and right now, I'm certain that there's still a way to recognize what is and what isn't real. For instance."

< 308 >

I waved my hands around the café.

"You've been here, right? You had to, 'cause it was your idea to meet here. You said you know you can trust that you're at home, and if you can establish that, you can trust you walked down the flight of stairs, took a left, and made it all the way to the corner before turning into this store. You've probably done it enough times where you could find this place blindfolded and know you're here for sure. And if you're certain about *this* place, your home, you've got something real to work with! At least until a fix is in place."

The check came. I put a twenty and a ten down for the two of us, leaving the change for a tip. Amber got up as fast as I put the money down.

"Well, thanks for the coffee," she said.

"Can we talk later?" I asked.

She shook her head. "Not now. Just, not now."

"Wait." I needed one last piece of information. "Before you go, I just need to know. What time on Friday did it all happen? The saleswoman in white?"

A moment later, I texted myself a mental note. *Sazera, 5:00 p.m. Friday.*

Like I said, enlightening.

I think I need to chill out a bit. I think Amber does too.

I think we're heading down impossible roads, where every stone must be turned and every atom must be dissected to prove itself.

I think I need a drink to think, a martini. That'll work just fine 'cause the barkeep has Aviation gin in stock and judging by the size of those glasses, it'll probably be a two for one deal.

Yeah that did the trick.

Thank god for Bard and hole in the wall joints like Southie's, where the blue collar come to spend what little they can of their hard day's earnings on themselves, where the bathrooms are for the brave and nobody with any sense brings their wives or girlfriends and others, like me, bring their mother in laws.

Oh and don't bother looking it up on Yelp, ain't looking for any judgment from those elitist shits that infest the rest of Manhattan.

I've been coming to this joint for as far back as I could remember, probably ten years or more. Known Bard that long too. You could spot that fat bastard from a mile away with his

< 310 >

afro and his beard, like a short Quest Love with the perfect Manhattan in his fingers rather than a pair of drumsticks.

I know one thing for certain right now. He's real. This is real.

There's that smell of stale beer spilled all over the floor, where rugs are decaying, where cockroaches hang out free of fear. There's that fake Flushing metro sign over a room full of other fake signs that Bard swears on his dead grandmother's grave are authentic but of course are never stolen 'cause there's a good number of off duty cops who frequent the joint too.

These are all real too. I swear it on Bard's dead grandmother, it all is.

I'm not gonna make an ass of myself and tip over every drink, knock on every wall, or pick up and drop every chair to figure out if they're there or not, wave my hand in front of every brut at the bar to test how real a sock to the face from 'em feels.

I'm gonna trust I'm here, where my soul rests to the sound of nineties rock and watches the Mets lose another playoff game to the Dodgers as the guys whistle and belch to everything that catches their attention. I've filled myself up here every other day and I'm a better man for it. It's been my stabilizing force, my respite, my base, my second home.

I know I'm here. I know this is reality.

So I'm gonna mark it as safe, right here in my phone.

How can I be sure with what's going on with my *Interface*? I can't be, the way I can't be certain that I'm placing my fingers on my touchscreen right now or if it is even there. I'm just gonna have to trust my instincts, 'cause after all, it's been half a year since the operation and somehow, by some miracle, I'm still in one piece.

\* \* \*

I was gonna call a cab after my meeting with Amber; didn't feel like subjecting myself to the whims of my *Interface* by walking the rest of the day up 8th avenue with God knows what would show up. Plus, all I wanted to do was go home and sleep it all off, preferably drunk after a swing in at Southie's or a few of my own famous cocktails of vodka in a tall, empty glass, the only way I could actually sleep anymore it seems.

But I ended up walking. There was no way

< 312 >

I'd be able to think with some cabbie talking on the phone to his wife in some foreign language. And boy did I need to think long and hard.

Hit 34th Street-Penn Station. I remember it because it was the first time I let my head up, probably deciding it'd be nice to see all the people I was about to run into before pissing 'em off. I let my head up so I could face the situation I was in, call it a mental check to make sure The New Yorker Hotel was still in front of me rather than some other building from some other reality like freaking Orbit City surrounding the lab.

That hotel was still there, and so were the McDonalds and Qdoba on the other side of the street (I pride myself on having visited every Qdoba on the island), and so was the sea of people in all their different colored shirts and hair and faces that cluttered the sidewalks like a Van Gogh painting, and so were the streets and all of the yellow cabs and buses and cars from the sporty kinds that ran on diesel to the ones that ran electrically to the ones that shouldn't be running at all, and so were the smells of smoke and middle eastern food, and so was the echo of traffic and millions of people doing a million things, bouncing against the side of the buildings, flooding the void as white noise.

And suddenly, I no longer saw the need to keep my head down.

*　*　*

I thought about it on the way. I thought about what would happen if by some fuck-up-pery of all of my friends at Wondervision I were to lose all of my senses entirely at that moment; my ability to smell the fumes of food and petrol, to feel the shoulder of some big guy who almost knocked me over without noticing (he apologized, so no hate), to see I was crossing into a street full of cars, to hear the honk and tirade following, to taste the salivating combination of fats and salts and sugars and all the spices of the Mediterranean when I bit into that Donner Kabob after having gone a day without eating anything real. Could they do that? Do something so that the processing stops and the emptiness in perception somehow overrides my brain? Could my own brain do that, theoretically?

If that happened, what then? Would reality cease to exist for me? Or would there be something to weigh it down?

I made a quick stop in Central Park after grabbing a pack of cigarettes at some convenience store. I found a bench and began lighting 'em up one at a time, soaking every part of my system with delicious nicotine to calm my nerves down to think. It's been so long, the best drafts are always the ones after a period of abstinence, and I swear, I could feel myself becoming one with that bench.

I promised myself I'd never buy another pack again, but today, at that moment, I needed it more than I ever needed anything in my life, given the circumstances.

I decided to try and write it all down, everything that I knew to be real, reasoning it'd help me cope if I could organize my reality, help me keep my head together, feel more secure.

I pulled out my phone and opened a new spreadsheet. On it, I started jotting down a few fields across the top row; *subject, details, verdict.*

*Subject*, any place or thing. *Details*, all of my memories of the subject and any other things I could add. *Verdict*, a choice between "real" and "questionable".

I wasn't going to list every goddamn thing in front of me, not that squirrel burying a nut,

< 315 >

not that bum sleeping on the third bench down from me, not the ground under my feet, not the cigarette in my mouth. No, that would be overkill.

Instead, I started with Central Park. Details were obvious. I'd been coming here my whole life, seen and know every goddamn inch of it too. *Real.*

Manhattan Island, the place I was born and raised. *Real.*

Every building on the island, every street, every restaurant I frequent, every bar in Harlem. *Real.*

Every Chinese restaurant in Queens. *Real.*

Home, the block around my apartment, every hotdog stand owner on every corner and their Slovakian names, every little grocery store. *Real.*

Highlighted column B, *Details*, and pressed "delete." Unnecessary.

Third cigarette down, I was feeling a lot better.

I got up off the bench and laid the rest of the cigarettes underneath the bum who was knocked out cold. It'll be like Christmas day when he wakes up.

Besides, I didn't need another cigarette. I needed a drink.

< 316 >

## NOVEMBER 1, 2025

I'm sitting outside of Sazera.
I'm in a coffee shop across the street, just a few hours away from four p.m.

Not much else to say, other than the fact that once it hits the hour, I'm going right in with my phone held out, and as soon as I see a woman in white, I'm going to hold my camera up and push record.

Not 'cause I'm being a perv or anything, although they do tend to pick out the finest in the batch at this store for sales reps, but because I want to see if I've figured out a way to distinguish what's real and what isn't. If nothing shows up, then I'm golden. I'll have an extra pair of eyes.

< 317 >

But that's not my main reason for being there. The recording piece was just for Amber.

If there are saleswomen in white, then I know he's probably there; that man from the last time I was there, the old guy standing next to salesman Rick Joy.

And if I see him, I'm going to shout his name at the top of my fucking lungs, make an ass of myself if I need to. I don't give a shit. I'm not leaving until I see him.

And if I do see him, I will know I'm in the right place. I think I've figured it out, all the weird shit I've been seeing, and it starts with this old guy.

Dr. Bosma. The dead founder of Wondervision Inc.

*   *   *

It was by chance I suddenly gave a shit about the company.

I can't explain it. Sometimes as I'm sitting there on a conference call, this time another boring union meeting about my warehouse workers putting in overtime or missing days or whatever, I tend to look up the first thing in my head that would remove me from the room at that moment. Random shit usually,

< 318 >

like the average height of giraffes or how smart a dolphin is or creep on someone's profile I knew from high school who something at that moment reminded me of.

This time, for no reason I could understand, I had the idea to google it.

*Wondervision.*

A contact lense cleaning solution. Tried again.

*Wondervision Inc.*

A Wikipedia page for the company, and holy shit, what I learned from that page.

At the top, under the summary info, a picture of an AISys tower. Specifically, it was the one above *Sazera*. It was an older photograph, taken back in 2025 when the company was first bought out. I did a quick search on the image using this new app (Flickrcrawl, just copy and paste an image and it'll do its own web search on it) and, what luck, found it was *AISys's* original executive building. Apparently, the company set up shop there at its infancy before moving out, with the rest of the executive team, to Brooklyn about a year back. That explain why Judy stopped seeing them around.

But that wasn't the crazy part.

< 319 >

Scrolled to the *History* section and clicked to expand.

First picture that came up? The founder, a smiling older man probably in his late sixties dressed in a pressed white button-down shirt tucked into a pair of tight-fitting jeans with thick white hair covering his mouth and running along his jawline to the sides of his head right above the ears leaving the rest of his head bare. Broad, skinny, and tall, he was standing hunched over a diverse team of a group of scientists who stood to his sides.

Dr. Aldi Bosma. The man himself.

I couldn't help but notice that this man looked identical to the old man next to Rick Joy from the last time I visited Sazera. I know. I could remember faces like staring at a photo.

I clicked on his name and the site took me to his page. My eyes immediately darted to his profile information, his date of birth, then to his date of death.

He'd been gone for nearly three years.

I flipped back to the screen where I had the building info up. I flipped back to the doctor's profile. Back and forth, back and forth, all the while the negotiator lady was sounding more and more pissed.

"Mr. Valentino, it appears you might be busy right now. Should we reschedule?"

No shit.

.   .   .

I've given this a lot of thought since. Honestly, I've taken time off work to wrap my head around everything, which basically means I put a big "on PTO" sign outside my office while I'm sitting there drinking fifty milliliter bottles of scotch right out of the container while posting shit up on my whiteboard like I were on an episode of CSI New York. I'm not going to go into it, but I might've done more thinking this week than for any business decision I've ever made.

Let's pick up from where we left off earlier, with me going between those two images. I've got an idea, well, maybe more like this abstract concept of one with a lot of colors but no lines. Let's pick up from when I was speculating that the old man I saw next to Rick was the good doctor.

So, for it to make sense that it was him at *Sazera*, he would've either have been alive and that Wikipedia was wrong and Josh was bullshitting me a while back, or it'd be something else. Something I seriously cannot describe with words, enough words to have it even make sense to myself.

But let me try.

So let's assume that Rick and the old man were also creations of my *Interface*. I am going to assume that because I couldn't think of any other likely scenario where that whole series of events would unfold. I mean, he could've been putting up a show, but if that were the case, he'd have been a convincing actor.

He would've pulled one hell of a performance 'cause the confusion written all over his face over who Judy was and how he talked about the way management was structured and how he even talked about his position as a sales representative despite his very public Linked-In profile, where anyone could check showing him as the district manager, seemed so damn genuine.

Trust me, I've got a sixth sense for this kinda stuff 'cause I deal with con artists as part of my job. Also, there's the case of my Linked-In chat window, where my conversation with him vanished for that moment in time.

So yeah, let's assume.

< 322 >

And on that note, let's also think about what happened. Both of them noticed me. To me, this probably means they stood out from the others.

But the difference between them is that Rick *does* exist in the real world and he *did* message me afterwards as if completely unaware that I just crossed paths with some other version of him, as if the salesman version just did his thing, unrelated to where he was or what he was doing at that point in time. If the older guy is truly Dr. Bosma, then he *wouldn't* exist in this reality. Not while being dead for three years.

Also, how would Rick explain what I saw at the Chinatown clinic?

I dunno. If these events are somehow related, then, as of now, it'd only make sense to me that the old man is Dr. Bosma.

Hear me out.

Let's talk *Sazera*. It'd make sense to find him there for one, given that the store was once right under where he would've worked. It'd explain why Rick Joy was still a salesman. As you might remember (and I'm checking right now just to be sure) that was his title there three years back. Plus, he was wearing a light-colored outfit as opposed to the black tuxedos salesmen wear today. Hell, the same probably goes for the saleswomen in white. If you think about it, it'd be like going back in time to a place when everything at the store was as it was for how Dr. Bosma would've perceived it when he was still alive.

Then there's the Chinatown clinic, with all of those workers who'd ghosted me in the same way the lady in white did to Amber. Not much I could say at this point about who those people were and what was up with their behavior, but I can say that if that old man truly was Dr. Bosma, being the founder and all, he'd be the only one who can bridge the two places together with both of them being the prime locations of the company. Nothing more I could honestly say as to who those zombie people were.

But if that *were* him, that still doesn't answer the question of how he would've been able to see me vs everyone else. I mean, of all these figures from whatever kooky *Interface* dimension they live in, are they the only two who can?

And importantly, what does any of it have to do with that guy in the mirror I saw at the

< 324 >

hotel that day when I got Judy's mother all wasted?

Damn. Looks like that's where I trailed off. I tell ya, I'm liking the enhanced memory that comes with this *Interface;* it sure as hell made this ordeal a lot easier. But maybe they could upgrade my processing too?

Just kidding, these sons of bitches better not do anything more to my head. Especially after all this.

I'm going to have to extend my time off. I admit, I'm starting to get a kick out of this.

For all I know, this may be the closest humanity has ever gotten to living in a parallel universe.

*       *       *

Anyhow, it's about thirty minutes till , so I'm going to wrap this up.

I'm going to try and analyze these digital apparitions (that's what I'll call 'em) by hunting them down in both locations, *Sazera* and the Chinatown lab. I'm going to find them and analyze them. Namely, I'm just looking for one person.

Dr. Bosma.

I'm going to track the progression of these

< 325 >

apparitions from when they appear to when they disappear and how they do so relative to Dr. Bosma; if he disappears with them, if he remains intact, if he would recognize me if I called out his name.

I'm going to switch between these two places as many times as I can in the next week, see if I get any answers. I've extended my PTO. I can do that as the owner of my business, you know, and I'll still make sure to leave and come back as if I were going to work so Judy doesn't start guessing or what have you.

I get it. It won't answer all my questions, but it's a start, and if it all goes well, maybe I can start building my theory as to whatever's happening before these bozos can.

Also, if the camera doesn't record them, then maybe I've got a way to keep Amber sane until it happens.

Then again, if they tell me in the next fifteen minutes the issue is fixed, I'll turn right around and enjoy a soccer match at Southie's.

< 326 >

## NOVEMBER 9, 2025

I'm getting fed up with these guys at Wondervision. I'm getting fed up with Josh.

It's been more than a month since I last heard from him. A month and nine days. A month and nine days where instead of doing my job, I found myself doing his, trying to figure out what the hell is going on with my *Interface* and the world before my eyes, piecing the dots together, creating a picture, bridging that last five percent of trust to believe *everything* around me rather than what I've *settled* on believing.

A month and nine days of walking around holding up my phone at strangers.

< 327 >

A month and nine days of wasted hours, eight of them a day, my ass alternating between concrete and plastic, my liver sorting out every beverage you can get at a coffee shop, my eyes alternating between my notebook, a computer screen, a book of choice, and whatever the location I was stalking.

And yes, I was staring at my computer screen for work. Guess I didn't need to go on PTO after all. Go figure, huh? I found myself spending most of my eight hours working out of boredom. On a sidenote, mighta provided Oswaldo with some relief. Poor guy. I feel like I've been putting him through overtime while I've been going through all of this shit. But he never complains. I oughta give him a raise or a share of the business or, even better, a bottle of twenty-one year old single malt when this is all over.

A month and nine days of wasted time trying to piece my reality back together.

But this shouldn't be the case, right?

I shouldn't be wasting a week trying to figure out what's wrong with me. Instead, I should've been focusing on rebuilding my life, my relationship with Judy, reeling us in back to normalcy while slowly forgetting this year

< 328 >

ever happened. That's what I should've been doing. It's what was sold to me!

Yet there I was, playing cat and mouse with something that theoretically doesn't even exist, and as far as I could tell, was fixed.

That's right, fixed. Because, like I said, it was a wasted week. Didn't see any of those goddamn apparitions, not in either location.

Not from seven to three at the Chinatown Lab, where I alternated between sitting at the window of a Starbucks at the street crossing directly diagonal from it or on a concrete bench near its entrance, bringing my head up once every ten minutes to see if any of those people in white would show up or if the buildings would change.

Not in the afternoons at Sazera, where I would, promptly at four p.m., make my way to the store entrance and wait to see if those saleswomen in white would show or if salesman Rick would show or, most importantly, the old man.

Not even from Amber's updates. She'd only agreed to help me check out the store during her lunch hour while I was in Chinatown to see if she could see any of the saleswomen in white and try to record them on her

< 329 >

phone if she did. Not sure if she was looking that hard though. She seemed spooked by the idea of laying foot in that store again after what happened.

I guess I could broaden my investigation and find other parts of the city, but what would I find if there isn't even an issue anymore?

So is it fixed? Is the defect gone? To hell if I know. They haven't reached out like they promised, so until then, I can only alternate between my assumptions that I'm just missing him, missing the timeframes for when the apparitions appear, or not missing anything at all.

Jesus, it's like Schrödinger's fuck-up, like the *Interface* is both malfunctioning and functioning at the same time. What the hell am I supposed to do? Wait?

One week.

One week where they've left me on my own, chasing my own fucking tail while they sit with theirs between their legs, doing God knows what with all that information they're collecting from the deepest parts of my memory. Had I made a mistake? Wasn't giving them access to my *Interface* supposed to speed things up?

What do I have to do if they don't get

< 330 >

back to me ever, threaten to cancel the service altogether and demand a refund? Threaten to go to the media?

And here's the shitty thing, I can't do either of those.

I can't even get rid of these fucking little bits of silicon in my brain even if I wanted to. Not now, not after all this time. Not after all this time where I've been able to go down on Judy night after night only to stand with my deflated dick between my legs trying to come up with some reason as to why it doesn't work anymore. Not after all this time where I've been able to bring our marriage back to something I could work with. Not after all the emotion I've put into this ordeal, the time spent outside of work, the toll it's taken on my sanity, the sanity that has been robbed of its most crucial component. Certainty.

Certainty as to whether or not the microchips are even out, if everything I think I see is there or not, if I can ever be the same again, not knowing if something in front of me is objectively real or just another defect.

I don't wanna threaten.

I don't wanna plead.

But I don't know what more alcohol

might do to me. I feel like I'm eroding from the inside out. I just need a reply.

Just a sentence, an emoji, or something to take the edge off.

Something.

< 332 >

## NOVEMBER 17, 2025

So I guess it is still broken after all.

Sazera, four p.m. I'm not sure why the hiatus, but this time, I saw it all. The saleswomen in white, the salesmen in light grey, salesman Rick, a posse of people I've never seen before, Dr. Bosma.

It literally just happened, about an hour ago.

And in that hour, I'd been running, looking for any street vendor who might've been selling phone chargers so I could plug in at any café I could find and write this all down while the adrenaline is still there.

And the adrenaline was definitely there.

Honestly, had I tried processing it all

with that old brain I used to use, I don't think it'd store any of it into memory. It's so out there, like trying to put words to it feelings, like trying to describe a third state between "on" and "off," an experience that isn't anything I was ever conditioned to perceive or make sense of.

So bits and pieces, I'll try to cut and paste every little detail using as much as I can from this pool of a million words that make up every particle of memory of what happened in my head.

Try and make sense of it.

. . .

Today I'd wanted to talk to Eric Joy.

In a last-ditch effort to prove to myself that any of my theory was true, I was going to just simply ask him if he'd ever met Dr. Bosma, when he did, and what his relationship with that man was, and see where our conversation might lead. I guess it's obvious, given that his parallel self seems to be close friends with the late doctor. I was just going to ask that and leave, and I'd messaged him on Linked-In this morning to meet me outside. He told me to be there at around five, but I happened to get there an hour earlier.

< 334 >

I hung out near the entrance for a few minutes, sipping on a chai tea latte while checking my emails, making sure Oswaldo, once again, had a handle on everything while I was out. I hung out until it started to rain and went inside and sat on a bench in the lobby.

Now, I fully expected to wait the whole hour, and from all the good practice from this week, I've gotten good at sitting in one spot doing nothing for periods of time. Guess I didn't need to, 'cause out of the blue, as I was staring straight, I saw someone appear near this figurine wearing a petticoat in the distance. A young woman, brunette, tight, white dress. She just appeared the way things do in badly edited films that leave out all transitions, walking out of thin air.

I got up and began moving in for a closer look.

She had moved towards a trim middle-aged woman dressed in a white polo and black slacks, who was looking through some shit that I couldn't make out.

I moved in closer and closer, eyes never leaving the target, not even after bumping into a saleswoman (in a black dress) who might've quipped something nasty at me as she was getting back up, probably since I didn't bother to

< 335 >

turn around to apologize. I kept moving in until I was within audible distance. I wasn't going to lose this moment.

"Well, we've got a new assortment of skirts from *Madame LeMond*, do check that out, and they go very well with any satin blouse."

The saleswoman in white was holding a tablet PC, flipping and explaining and pointing.

"You think they'd go with one of these tops?"

The older woman was holding a black leather coat, the kind where the bottom half is cut off, where it just sorta keeps the top half of you warm, I guess.

"I'd think so. Would you like to give it a try?"

"Excuse me," I tried to interrupt.

Neither noticed.

I looked closer. The middle-aged woman had on a name badge that swung from her neck, and although I didn't catch her name, I did make out the distinctive logo above her photo; *AISys Inc.* It was there and embroidered onto the left side of her polo too.

"Oh, my, you look really cute with this top," said the saleswoman who was holding a mirror in front of the middle-aged lady who had stepped back two feet to eat herself up.

"Mmm…I dunno…a little too retro with the broad shoulders, don't you think?"

It was a bit unsettling. I was right there between the two. I could hear them talk, smell the perfume from their skin, feel their presence in that strange way I feel anyone's presence when near. I raised my hand to touch the coat the older woman was trying on, felt the little tinge of warmth emanating from below her chin. Every part of my mind was telling me they were there, so much that I could've sworn I felt a tinge of chill, the kind you feel when you are left out of a party, at the way neither were paying me any attention.

"Well, Aldi is waiting for me over there," said the older lady, "but I'll keep my eyes on this. How long will it be up?"

"Another week."

"Perfect. Thanks, Misty."

I stepped back and watched as the saleswoman in white walked away and, in the same way she entered this reality, vanished.

Then it hit my mind.

Aldi. Dr. Bosma.

I turned around and they were gone. I moved to the center lane.

There, in the distance, standing with the

< 337 >

older woman and one other guy with the same uniform, Eric Joy in his gray suit and the old guy, or who by now I was certain was, Dr. Bosma himself.

What struck me, however, was that he wasn't standing directly in the group. Rather, he seemed distant, having taken a few steps back to let the other three converse. He was moving his head around with a puzzled look on his face, turning to every saleswoman in a black dress, and salesman in a black tuxedo, watching them as they continued down the aisle.

His eyes then settled in the direction of the older woman who was chatting with the saleswoman about the coat moments earlier.

I followed his sightline and noticed the figurine with the top was gone. In place of it, was an assortment of designer pants on a round table.

I looked back in the doctor's direction. He had rejoined the group and looked to be trying to leave, eagerly.

Right about then, it hit me that I was supposed to be recording this. I grabbed my phone, opened the camera, and turned it to record.

< 338 >

When I looked back up, his two associates, the older woman and the other man, were walking away while he stayed, whispering something into Rick's ear while delicately holding his hand. He then reached over and gave him a peck on the lips before hurrying to join the other two.

Yeah, I know, turns out they were a little more than friends, an affair of some sort. Stuff was beginning to make sense. But, whatever, I didn't have time to dwell on it. I had to catch up, follow him out of the store, and confront him if possible.

As he went, I noticed stuff vanishing left and right. A saleswoman in white, a man in a gray suit, customers, displays, garments. Soon, all that was left on the salesfloor were the real people, the saleswomen in black dresses, the salesmen in black tuxedos, the few customers who were looking at me like I was some schizophrenic nut as I stumbled over them to make it to the entrance, holding my phone out and waiving it around as I went.

But as soon as I was outside, I literally fell backwards in terror.

The streets and sidewalks were flooded.

< 339 >

Rear ends of taxis sticking out of minivans, trucks on top of cars, the sound of honking double what it was before. People, as many as there would be at the Macy's day parade, walking and running around and *through* each other, as if nobody and nothing was made of solid matter.

I looked up into the sky. It was blue, blue with gallons of water falling and splashing and soaking, and the buildings and the concrete were painted with shades of dark, untouched by the light coming from the sky.

I went to the side of the road and looked down the street, pointing my phone, trying my best to not attract attention. From my point of view, from left to right, it was as if the crowds of people and automobiles were only doubling in size near the entrance to the store, with half of all vehicles and people appearing and disappearing as they moved from left to right, right to left.

Right then, a man in a golf shirt wearing a red baseball cap walked directly into me. I stumbled back into a woman in a raincoat, who pushed me forward, screaming some random shit before moving away.

I looked back and he was gone.

< 340 >

I ducked to get out of the way of a woman with two kids before moving directly into the way of a guy on a bike who peddled on through me like I wasn't there.

I finally found my bearings and made it to the side of the building, which was the only spot I could find out of everyone's way. From there, I could see that Dr. Bosma was faring no differently.

His aides were holding him up. Someone must've walked through him in the same way. They were trying to bring him to his feet, appearing to ask him if everything was alright. He wasn't responding, instead focusing his attention on the chaos that surrounded him, surrounded me, surrounded *us*.

I realized that it was my chance. It was now or never.

I moved towards him, dodging people, assuming everyone could see me, finding a path like a running back through a defensive line from some interdimensional hell, holding my phone up, shouting his name.

"Dr. Bosma!"

He looked up.

He was staring directly at me.

And boy, that look on his face.

< 341 >

I couldn't know for sure, but from what I remember, there was no confusion. Instead, it was the kind of look when you watch your child get hit by a car, when you find your home blown to bits, when you look up and find the world you have so meticulously built collapsing around you and not knowing how to react.

It hit me that maybe he didn't know he was deceased.

It hit me that although his world might be a mere defect to me, mine was an existential reality to him.

It hit me that he must've known. This was all his creation, after all. The *Interface* and everything that has to do with it.

Or maybe not yet.

I realized just then I had to get out of there. I turned to leave.

I continued to feel his glare as I went, turning back every few seconds to see him still there, wondering who the hell I was, and, likely, if I had something to do with all this.

I kept moving, without being run into, might I add, until the sky above was once again gray, and the cars and the people no longer moved through each other, and my reality, *this* reality, was the only one that was left.

*   *   *

I guess I never did get to meet up with the real Rick Joy. I did send him an apology, nonetheless.

I think I've learned a bit from today. More than I ever would've by talking to Rick anyhow.

To begin, I learned that the video idea worked. Didn't record a thing; not Dr. Bosma or anyone from his group, not the overlapping realities, nothing but random people giving me that half pity half disgust look you give to every drugged-out schmuck convulsing next to a subway.

I've learned that the old man was indeed Dr. Bosma, or as I'm thinking, his mirror, *PMS* self. That's a big start right there.

I've learned that, when in close proximity to each other, we can see both of our realities at once.

I've learned that, as he was walking away, those outside of his immediate reality fades away.

I've learned that he likely lives in his own reality, and that it could explain the people in white at the Chinatown Lab, where had I looked for him in that crowd, I might've found him.

I can't confirm that last one, however. Just like I can't confirm if it has anything to do with that guy in the mirror at the hotel. I just don't have enough avenues to explore any more, and honestly, I'm a bit too tired to at this point. I seriously don't know how much more my mind could handle.

But I can confirm that at that time and space, with everything that I saw and felt, the order of events, conversation between the two women, the quick but sweet love between the two men, the agony written on the doctor's face when looking up at the world outside, I couldn't be convinced out of believing that everything was real. That there was the poor doctor, living on somehow in an afterlife, in his own head.

I wonder, if I can't confirm *that* was a reality of some form, what can I confirm *is*?

And if that *was* a reality, then from his perspective, was everything in it objectively true? And if that's the case, was *I* not?

And how the hell can he be so certain about it? That's the part that freaks me out the most. How could he not tell the difference?

Whatever the issue is, I hope to get an update soon.

Hope they can explain this to me gently.

SUBJECT: RE: DR. BOSMA
SENT: NOVEMBER 25, 2025, 9:31 A.M.
TO: JAYBIGGS1987@HOTMAIL.NET


Hi Jay

I do apologize for the delay. I can understand
the frustration, and I do wish I had the liberty
to reply quicker. You were not the only one. All
of us in the professional services organization
were going through quite a trying couple of
weeks as we were figuring out how best to
communicate our status without inflicting more
anxiety.

Let me begin by letting you know that the issue
has been resolved. In no instances in the future
will you perceive anything that you shouldn't
perceive. That we can promise you. In fact,
should you do so, report it, and we will give you
a 20% refund for each defect until you are fully
refunded.

That is our guarantee.

Now, you must be curious as to what the issue
was.

There are two explanations at hand, one
being more technical and the other a tad

< 345 >

more colloquial. Let me lead with the latter explanation.

For the colloquial explanation, you were perceiving both your own perception of reality as well as that of other customers utilizing our product.

If you were sitting with someone who, due to the operation, was looking at a ball sitting in a corner that isn't there, you would see it too. If you and another individual were staring at the same apple and one of you is conditioned to see it blue, you'll see either the apple in the color blue or red depending on a set of tie-breaking factors the system uses in its algorithm. If someone, once again due to the operation, perceives there to be a person standing next to you when there is not, you will perceive that person too. Others would be able to see Judy's face in the way you would like them to see it, and you would be able to see things like your friend's window.

As to the technical explanation, there are things you must understand.

You must understand the system, and to understand the system, you must understand reality.

You must understand that reality is less of what is around you and more the output of all the systems within you, an output of process.

You must understand that for you and me, reality is just data. It is data synthesized into information and displayed to you somewhere in your head.

Your five senses pick up signals from objective reality, transforms it, stores it, displays it, then stores it just to be displayed whenever called upon.

Also know that when I describe reality, I speak of your immediate surrounding world, the color of the sky, the smell of a rose, the taste of peppermint gum, or the sound of the birds chirping in some invisible distance. I speak of your concrete reality.

The way the system was designed is so that all the data, all aspects of your consciousness, your memories short and long term, are stored in the cloud, a system that maintains a mirror of all these things. It is done so to ensure that the alterations are executed to absolute perfection, as it depends on recognition of the target object to alter as so much of recognition relies on every part of your consciousness. I will only

< 347 >

be explaining, however, your concrete reality, as that is the focus of the product and, as you know, the issue.

The way the system was designed was to copy and add to the existing systems your brain uses to view reality; intake the senses, process them into information, store them in memory to form a big picture and, from there, display to you what you need to see.

The intake comes from the sensory data you accrue, sent right to the cloud as it is being sent to different parts of your brain for processing.

The intake then transforms the data, with your memory long and short, and the alterations you desire. At this point, while your brain is sending the processed information to working memory, the system sends it to a storage area, called the consolidated reality (CR) server, just the same, to collect all the transformed data and create a reality. From there, the system picks out the data to send back to you, in a package called your *Interface*.

At this point, you must be wondering if the CR is your own server or storage that hosts all of this reality that you draw from. It is not, this reality is not hosted in a personal location. Rather, the CR is a shared server, presumable from the name consolidated reality, intaking transformed sensory data from every customer.

This means that at a specific point in time and space, should you share it with another, all of your sensory information, including all of its alterations, and all of theirs, will be available. Both of the conceptions of your concrete realities will be on full display for that point in time and space in the CR and all duplicate information will be consolidated, creating a *flattened* one.

For example, the tree you see and the tree I see becomes the tree *we* see. Should any of us have had an alteration done for something within our flattened reality, a squirrel could be of two different colors at the same time, and there could be a man standing in a spot where there isn't.

From this flattened reality in the CR, the system picks out the package that becomes your *Interface*, selecting only the data relevant to your needs, or, your *optimal reality* while discarding the altered realities of others. It is then stored locally and sent back to you to perceive in whatever way you intend to.

< 343 >

This process happens like a conveyor belt, operating at speeds neither you nor I can comprehend.

Your reality, your better reality, is all an output of this process.

This architecture was coined by Dr. Bosma as *Layered Realities*. It is the idea that multiple realities could share the same space, so long as there is a system in place to ensure each person perceives only one of them; the one that is optimal for survival and all the additional pieces they define the term to mean.

Like "normalcy.".

It was built for the purposes of efficient storage and scalability, or, reducing the amount of memory needed for a service so large, more than it was built to affect customer experience. And as you could probably see, should this work correctly, the customer wouldn't be able to tell the difference.

But it didn't work correctly.

The problem stemmed from an error in the parser that was supposed to pick out the correct optimal reality to send to each user, specifically the added component in charge of filtering out the altered realities of others. This left two dilemmas as to what should end up in each user's Interface.

The first example would be if I perceive an object and you don't, our consolidated display would render the object for both of us. This explains why you and Amber seemed to be able to perceive the saleswomen in white, although the specifics of this we will discuss later.

The second example, and a more complicated one, would be if there are competing objects in a space, where we both see an object but differently. Both versions of the display would be sent back, with an algorithm based on the length of time the version of the object was perceived (who saw the display first) and the sequence of events to determine what either of us would end up perceiving through our Interfaces. This explains the inconsistencies you were experiencing with respect to our Chinatown Clinic.

That is the full extent that I can speak to, unfortunately. I do hope this makes sense to you.

Lastly, you must be wondering about Dr.

< 351 >

Bosma, if he's still alive somewhere in his own reality.

I inquired myself but was given little information on it. This might be something you would have to acquire through deposition, likely with individuals all the way up the chain.

I have verified, however, that the *Interface* infrastructure could sustain a consciousness without the physical individual present. As I have stated in an earlier email, it is why we have the parallel memory synchronization (PMS) procedure, so that both individuals can continue living in sync with one another. Otherwise, we may end up with a situation where the user receives a completely different view of reality, completely divergent from the one he or she is currently living in, putting the individual's safety at risk. It would be a situation where the consciousness crafted by the *Interface Therapy* would live on its own, its reality driven completely by memory.

Further, I know you might want to know if the face in the mirror is related or if the incident at Sazera or the clinic is as well. Unfortunately, I cannot go into specifics due to customer confidentiality.

< 352 >

I apologize if that all sounded confusing, but as of now, it should all be fixed and you should only be able to perceive what *you* need to perceive; *your* reality, *your* truth.

Again, apologies for the delay in getting back to you. There was a period of deliberation as to how we should approach this sensitive correspondence with our customers. We are thankful for your patience and understanding.

Take Care.

Josh Rikkard
Relationship Manager
*Wonderlenz* Technologies Inc.

## NOVEMBER 25, 2025

Don't know if I'm going to keep calling him Doc. Feels like my mind has been more and more broken since I've taken his pill.

Wasn't sure how to take that last email. On one hand, I'm glad the issue's been resolved, but on the other, I'm trying to stomach the resolution.

I can't say I'm certain I believe these guys all know what they're doing, or what they've gotten themselves into, this business of messing with other peoples' realities for profit without much consideration for dignity. Like my consciousness, the embodiment of who I am, and my world, thrown into a blender

< 354 >

with everyone else's so they could save money. How much money saved, might I ask, is worth stripping people of their humanity? Stripped and saved as software objects? And what is my physical self then, a dumb terminal to this interface? And my mind shares everyone else's conception? Am I everyone else or am I myself? Who am I?

I can't say I'm certain I can see reality the way it is, or how I would be able to tell. I've been around a lot of fellas over the year up until this thing was fixed, not at work but around the city, where money comes to few but in quantities where an operation like this could be treated as another day with a cosmetic surgeon. How many of them had the operation? How many different realities overlapped mine, and why wasn't I able to tell?

Also, you'd probably figure I'd been wondering about Michael in the mirror and if that fucking woman went through with it like I did. Or pondering about Amber looking Judy dead in the face and told her she looked fine and if she was telling the truth. And of course, the saga of Dr. Bosma, that dead man who never sleeps.

You'd be right, but only for a day.

Only for a day did I have enough brain cells left to care, the energy to seek out information, the willingness to dwell on this any longer. Only for a day, and then I finished a six pack and passed out.

And you know what I'm going to do with all of these questions going forward?

That's right, absolutely nothing.

That box, I have it right out of storage. I'm going to take all of these questions and fold them up nicely and stick them in and seal it shut. Actually, I'm just going to shove 'em in, 'cause fuck it if I'll ever need to open this box again. Not if everything returns to normal.

Oh normalcy, you sweet sound of love. Always growing, changing, making me wish for when it was a year younger. If I ever can get it back to that time, I'm never going to think again. I swear. I'm just going to carry on with a fat, retarded smile, even when I've got a flat or even if my business goes belly under. Normalcy, *that* normalcy, it's worth being lobotomized for the rest of my life if I could lie on my bed staring at Judy massaging my chest with her breasts.

Jesus, it's been a while. I've replaced making love with squeezing my dick between my legs while I try to calm myself with a Vicodin or a joint or, of course, any alcoholic beverage you can conceive of.

But even that normalcy, the one where I'm happily married, the one where, out of everything, I've been able to keep steady up until now, was never mine to begin with; just borrowed and due to time.

So fuck me.

But of course, I'm glad there was a resolution.

*   *   *

I've noticed that I haven't spoken about Judy much, and you might be wondering how she is and how we're doing.

And she was well.

We were well.

Our marriage was doing very well, thank you, or maybe it was doing well, 'cause even with a robotic memory, I don't seem to remember things straight.

Let me begin by saying that I've started noticing some things, small things buried underneath our livelihood together that have started to show, like when you notice imbalance in your floor for the first time after your pen wouldn't stop rolling.

I've noticed how she doesn't care anymore. I've noticed how I could come home at midnight drunk to her waking up without asking a thing about it. I've noticed how I could throw my clothes all on her side of the bed and how she'd just crash on top of them as if they weren't there.

"This t-shirt stinks."

I've noticed how time seems to have stopped for her, or maybe it's accelerating all around, or maybe it's both, 'cause as the wrinkles pile on and the hair starts to fall out and the circles around my eyes fill and my shits get harder to take and my stomach starts to extend, she stays right where she is.

Yeah, I know what you're going to say. It's the *Interface*.

But it's more than just the face.

Hell, I don't even have a belly, well, not *that* large of one. It just feels that way. It just feels like all the shit in my head has poured into my body, flooding the shoulders, the back, the gut, the legs, a weight gain you can't measure with a scale but heavier than any number it could give you. Like gravity had upped a notch for everyone, everyone except for Judy, who breezes from the bed to the couch to the dinner table to the three blocks around our building for a run for a run and back in time to read a book or watch a movie without a moment of boredom. Like we live in the same room but on different planets with different laws of physics, an omnipresent deity being a dick and playing favorites.

Maybe that's what happens when you stop caring. Like when something so traumatic happens to you, all you can think about for your sanity is today, the stresses of what was and what's to come lifted like unshouldering a pack of rocks, like you stumble into this bottomless pit where you only fall up.

Or maybe she was always this way, and I've been too far up my own ass to notice.

Or maybe this is something else to do with the *Interface*?

Oh fuck, of course not.

< 353 >

Shit just hit the fan, and it's everywhere.

We were watching a local news stream a morning ago when this segment came up.

"Plastic surgery or face transplant? Can you tell the difference?"

I sat up. That woman on television. Wanda. The plastic surgeon. The lady who stitched my head back into one piece after the operation.

"Dr. Wanda Jennings will be joining us in a bit to discuss a series of miraculous transformations she's performed that have been making waves across social media. But before we do, let's take a look at a few."

I felt Judy at my shoulder. She was also at

< 360 >

full attention, staring at the screen as if she'd just seen her own face on the television.

The first set of pictures was of burn victims, three of them, faces charred beyond recognition, some of 'em without hair and others without half of their lips. The first one, a guy from a barbeque gone wrong, the fire hit him on the right side of his face; the second one, a veteran who'd lost her face in an explosion out on some patrol; the third, a man who worked in a lab of some sort who got exposed to some gas. They all looked in pain, staring into the camera the way Judy looked at me every day after the accident until she left, trying to smile when it hurt to, mentally and physically.

Then, the second set, the "before" pictures I presumed.

Except that they weren't.

I swear, not a fucking blemish. One of the guys looked a bit red, but that was the extent of it. It was like Dr. Wanda had gone back in time to find their pre-accident selves, murdered them, and ripped off their faces to bring them back to present day. Just apply some glue.

And they looked so happy. Their smiles were so goddamn big, liberated from the face that held them back for years, like it didn't

< 361 >

matter if they looked good or not. Just so long as they can show you how happy they were.

The interview went on for about ten minutes or so. She went through the details about some brand new face-transplant process she's been cooking up with *AI-Sys*.

The title of the company? *Beautiful-U, your optimal you.*

And it doesn't end there. The operation would begin with a written introduction, followed by an assessment, followed by a follow-up visit, followed by the operation. The operation itself would be brief, she said something like half an hour or so, and of course, you'd walk out without ever remembering having gone under.

In and out, face as good as new, probably even without any of the acne's or wrinkles or dead skin you would've worn before your accident.

"Well, that's the thing, Donna," Wanda was saying, "this isn't just for individuals who have burnt faces or any other medical issues that would 'cause them to seek a face transplant."

"Oh really?" replied Donna, "like who else?"

"Well, we've recently expanded our

product offering to any line of cosmetic surgery. This includes a new nose job, scar tissue
removal, acne removal. Our technology is
durable."

"So I could walk out looking like Beyoncé
if I wanted to?" asked Donna.

"Yes you can," she replied, "might cost you
a little bit more, but yes, absolutely."

"What's that supposed to mean?"

"Oh no, I didn't mean it like that!"

While they were cracking up, the host,
Alan, who'd been sitting quietly the whole
time, chimed in with the dreaded question.

"And how much, may I ask, will this cost?"

"Ah!" Wanda replied. "Well, that's the best
part of it. The price will range anywhere from
a thousand for minor alterations to around
seventy thousand for our high-end services
like facial transplants, and for life-saving or
health-related alterations."

Fuck.

"Jay?" Judy was nudging my arm already
with her elbow. "Look."

"And our patients will have the benefit
of a relationship consultant who will be in
touch with them, make sure everything feels

< 363 >

okay, walk them through the steps, that sort of thing," Wanda continued.

"Jay?" Judy was nudging harder.

"Yeah, babe?"

"Are you seeing this?"

"Seventy thousand for a full facial transplant?" Alan exclaimed.

"Yup! Seventy thousand," replied Wanda.

"I mean, that's not cheap," he continued, "but compared to how much?"

"It's almost half a million nowadays to get a full facial transplant," she replied.

"Jay…I" Judy could barely get the words out. "I think we can afford this."

We couldn't. I mean, we could've if I hadn't blown about thirty grand of our savings at the beginning of the year on this fucking experiment.

"Yeah, yeah, Judy. I'll work out the numbers."

I wish I hadn't said that. I wish I had just slumped back into the couch, told her how beautiful she looked already, how she didn't need it. I wish I had given her a kiss, dumped the rest of the bowl in my mouth, wiped the milk off with my arm, and went to put some pants on or brush my teeth or do some push-ups or whatever I do to get ready for the day, anything to keep my trap shut.

"Yeah, yeah, Judy. I'll work out the numbers."

God, I'm a fucking idiot. Work out the numbers? What numbers? I'd spent thirty grand on this surgery at the beginning of this year and by now I've only recovered that much. You know how hard it is to save even a thousand living in Manhattan? It's a goddamn miracle I could net back at zero. Do you know what the utilities cost here? The mortgage? The fucking parking spot I get that's equivalent to a month's rent in some places in Jersey? The gas, the food, the booze that goes with meal-time? The booze that goes with all the times in between?

"Yeah, yeah, Judy. I'll work out the numbers."

I swear, if you'd seen her face.

It was the first time I'd seen her like it in over a year, hell, a decade, even before the night of the accident. There's a certain look to someone who's more excited than her face can show, where every muscle fiber wants to smile but all she could do is sit hunched forward, arms propped up against the knees with the fingers pressed against the top of the head, lips puckering, eyes wider than they've ever been, like she was holding up the weight of what will happen with all the most exaggerated emotions she could summon at that moment while still trying to keep herself together.

It was a spark of light in the distance, a reason to care, a moment when hope returns.

"You've gotta," she murmured.

"What?"

"You've gotta work out those numbers, Jay."

"Well, babe, that's what I'm gonna do. I'm gonna work out those numbers."

"Now."

"Now? Judy, babe, I've gotta go to work."

She looked up. A tear had found its way out of her left eye socket and was making its way down her cheek. She was looking at me with hope, the way religious people do looking up at the altar. Knee shaking, her body rocking back and forth, like she was trying to absorb the shock of what she'd just seen.

"Now," she said.

"I promise, I'll do it at work, babe." I paused. "Besides, what if this is some kind of scam? You don't know what's behind the curtain of these techno-miracles nowadays."

"It's backed by *AISys,* Jay," Judy was glaring. "Everything they do goes under the microscope; I don't think it's a scam."

"Well," I started.

"Don't you remember our conversation with Amber?" she asked. "About *Wondervision*, or whatever that technology was?"

"Yeah," I started, "I mean, of course I do. What about it?"

"Well, Amber's doing fine, right?"

Thankfully, I caught myself from exposing our coffee date.

"How should I know, babe? You talk to her?"

"Just from the way she was carrying herself," she replied, nearly whispering. "She seemed to be fine."

"Yeah, well, like you said, she always seems to be fine."

I was looking for an exit, but she just wasn't letting me go. Had I left right then and there, I was going to come home and find her having gone to one of the clinics herself, researching, planning, and God forbid, checking our joint account to see if we had enough. No, I had to stay and find a way for her to trust me somehow, one way or another.

"But I think you look beautiful."

She paused, her facial expression far from one of appreciation.

"What the fuck is wrong with you?" she asked.

"What do you mean what's wrong with me?"

She pointed to her right cheek. "Did you forget that half of my face is burned off? Do you *really* not see it anymore?"

Jesus, I was doggy paddling in the deep end of the pool.

"Of course," I stammered. "Of course I see it, but I don't care. It's not important to me. It hasn't been important. Christ, we've been living together for more than half a year now and it's *still* not important. Why can't you..."

"Okay, okay, fine," she interrupted. "Sorry, I get it. You don't care."

A temporary save. She looked like she was buying it. Maybe it was my chance.

"I care," she was choking up. "I really care. It's," she took a deep breath, "I really care."

The emotional storm came, and it was so fierce she couldn't get the words out. Instead, they came out like static between deep sobbing inhales and exhales. "This year...has been... hell. I want it to stop!"

I sat down and put my arm around her, repeating the only thing that came to mind

< 368 >

without pissing her off even more. "I know, I know, I know."

"I think I still have some money," she continued. "We could pool it. But babe, *please* make this happen!"

"Of course babe, of course, of course." I just kept repeating it. Kept repeating it while I rubbed her back and gave her a kiss.

"Of course, of course," while I got up and made my way to get my coat.

"Of course, of course," all the way out the door.

"I'll make it happen, babe. I'll make it happen. Swear to God!"

*   *   *

Don't get me wrong, it wasn't that there was a bit of relief, and if I somehow had the money to pull this off, it would be a God given gift.

But thirty thousand dollars doesn't come out of thin air, not unless I pull a heist with the mob or sell my balls for science.

There was, of course, my company. Like I said, because of Oswaldo, things were going relatively well. I mean, we were expanding

< 373 >

across New England and getting calls for business left and right. Hell, give it a few years and it could be a multi-million dollar company. But not right now.

We made profit, but most of that was squat shit. It all just went back to renting out or building other warehouses and expanding business operations. Every penny was tied to something; the overhead, the variable cost of every piece of junk we received and delivered, the salaries of every man and woman sweating their balls or breasts (or whatever it is for women) off on the dry-goods floor or freezing their asses off in the cold storage.

Yeah, it's my company. But even a hundred dollar loan from our cash balance to myself would be enough to get Oswaldo to quit, knowing how seriously he took his job. And after everything he's done for the place, everything everyone's done, it just wouldn't be right. Sure, I might be a shitty husband, but I'm a damn good businessman.

And I guess the only other way I was going to get thirty grand out of the business was if I sold it. First off, I'd be throwing everybody who'd busted their asses for me all these years under the bus 'cause no big company would purchase these places without firing everyone first and automating everything. Secondly, I'd be out of a job. Sure, after taxes, my windfall might be enough to get me through another decade, but I'd lose my reputation amongst everybody I know or have any connection to, doesn't matter what industry. Thirdly, it'd still shake up suspicion from Judy. Like, why am I selling the business if I had the thirty grand in my savings?

What else? Take out a loan? Who'd give me a loan for something like this? Plus, Judy's name would have to be on it, given that we're married and all.

Donations from strangers? Set up a *GoFundMe* account or something of that sort? Would I be able to stipulate that I need all the money *today* so that my wife wouldn't be suspicious of something that I don't wanna explain? It's like, screw that guy with cancer who wants enough money to send his kid to college, or that girl who's in need of a life-saving surgery soon or else she'll die. No, give it to that guy who wants cosmetic surgery done on his wife so she can look hot again.

What else, what else, what else?

A refund? Can I call it quits and get my money back? What's the return policy?

What else, what else, what else?

Maybe I could rob a bank, or take on a hit job, something that's liable to get me killed in the process if I'm lucky.

What else, what else, what else?

Wait? Explain it all to Judy and wait a while until we have the money again? Maybe she wouldn't be too angry with me? Maybe she'd understand if I explained it to her nicely?

What else, what else, what else?

I guess that's it, what the fuck else?

< 372 >

Hello Jay,

As noted in the agreement you signed before the operation, we can only offer refunds for reasons specific to defects in the product itself. The basis for it would have to be in a written email, which we would then review and process.

Since this last email clearly has your intent spelled out that your only purpose for this refund is something completely unrelated to the actual performance of the Interface, or anything else related to its technical aspects, it would be a very difficult sell to grant any refunds.

I apologize, and I wish you the best of luck in getting this sorted out with Judy.

Josh Rikkard
Relationship Manager
*Wonderlenz* Technologies Inc.

< 373 >

I guess this is where my infatuation with Dr. Wanda Jennings comes to a close.

Disappointing. I didn't think of her as the type to go hunting for that pot of gold her parent company promises.

*Beautiful-U.*

Probably some name that came out of a boardroom meeting, the same place they must've set the prices, her salary, the hours of operation, the growth strategy. The same place where they must've sewn those invisible strings into her delicate little fingers and legs and toes, extracted her soul, her independent brilliance, standardized her and everything she's ever built into the same line of prof-it-puppets that fills its corporate party chests.

Damn shame. It'll happen to all brilliant people nowadays; their marks in history replaced by dollar signs, their potential always just inches beneath a glass ceiling that they'll keep shifting upwards, their ethics filled by corporate training videos rather than the little voices in their heads.

Ethics like giving me a goddamn discount.

"Sir, you're over the line. Leave or I'll call the cops."

I guess she didn't like this speech, not the way I delivered it, not the time or place; in her lobby, middle of the day, in front of all of her new customers.

I guess I could've said something nicer, leveled with her, re-explained my predicament in detail.

I guess I also could've been a little more controlled, held my desperation at bay, reverted to all of those techniques I've accrued over the years since my arrest (long story), all of those invaluable therapy sessions paid by you and all the American taxpayers.

"But, Doc! It's just *half* her face! $35,000! I promise it's all it'll take!"

< 375 >

"Sir," she was almost seething through her teeth, "Like I said, all face transplants, regardless of whether half her face or her entire face, cost between $60,000 and $70,000. These are set!"

"Got it, corporate daddy's orders, but hear me out," I took a breath to gather myself to explain. "I'm out of options. I'm out of all other options to save my marriage and *you*, only you, could give me this *one*. We'll push friends and family over. I tell ya, I've got this mother in law who'd pay you enough to make up for *twice* the amount I'm asking for! Just let me talk to your sugar daddy!"

Regretted that last part; regretted it as soon as it left my mouth.

"Okay, sir, I'm calling the cops."

"Please, Wanda, Dr. Jennings, whatever your bosses say you are."

"Actually, Brian, Steve, you guys mind helping me with this guy?"

Two big guys in white lab coats, plus a big guy in the lobby, appeared from my left.

I threatened to invert their testicles up their butt cheeks.

"I swear, come any closer, and I'll kick your balls up your...hey!"

In a second, I was completely off the ground, the big guy with a lock on my top half, the two others with my legs.

"Wait, Doc! I'm sorry, just give me a minute!" I shouted, barely audible as I couldn't really breathe with the big guy's arm around my neck.

"What the fuck is wrong with him?" Not sure who said that, but it was the last and only full sentence I managed to make out over the adrenaline in my skull, as everything else had just become background noise beneath my panting and begging, the last thing I heard before I was shoved onto the pavement outside.

"Come anywhere near this building and we're calling the fucking cops!" said one of the guys. Don't remember who.

I guess I'm lucky she kicked me out rather than having called the police, 'cause there might be a charge out there you could file against threatening battery while scaring the shit out of everyone else in the lobby.

"Yeah, kick me out. She's the one who'll be sucking corporate tits for the rest of her life!" I screamed.

At least I had the last word.

*  *  *

I guess this is the part where I admit all my wrongs.

I can't get a discount, can't find the cash, can't hide from the inevitable.

Guess I was pretty dumb. Dumb to think things can just go back to normal on a lie, that I've got complete control over all the things that could expose me. Dumb to think that Judy would be dumb enough to go on for years and years without realizing. Like, somehow, had I only gotten everything back to normalcy, it'd all work out.

Normalcy.

Whatever it could be; the days before the accident to just spending each day with her, both of us working and raising a family to sitting in hanging limbo with each other, wondering if things will ever get better.

Normalcy. I'll take any definition of it now, any definition that includes getting through this, anything that includes her somehow finding it in herself to understand why I did what I did, that it was truly out of a good place, a place that included both of us rather than just one, that was meant as a last resort so that she could feel a sense of home with me.

I figured that even though what I did was shitty, whether it be getting the operation without talking with her or going on for a year without telling her, it bridged the gap in our relationship up until now. And if we wait just a little longer, like a year or so, I'll have the money to pay for the *Beautiful-U* operation. Heck, it might even be cheaper then.

I figured that she could at least see, from my angle, that everything will work out, if not for us, for her. Actually, it might even give her a reason to go back to work, something for us to work together on to save for, a better and brighter tomorrow, rising amidst the backdrop of this year in hell.

I even figured that maybe she'd appreciate the honesty. Maybe if I lie to her that I could've purchased the surgery by cashing out of my company, or something like that, she'd understand that I'm finally trying to do the right thing.

It makes sense, right? That maybe in times of crisis, little lies like this could serve a purpose? You think she'd buy that? Or am I just

< 383 >

getting a little ahead of myself? These sweet thoughts, tempting me like cinnamon rolls, sweet thoughts that this next hour is going to be anything but the drama I've feared since getting the operation. And worse, I don't have a clue as to how bad it will get or how I am to begin explaining or if even *I* will accept what comes out of my mouth. 'Cause I'll be honest, figure this or figure that, I'm just making most of it up right now as I go; just throwing darts at the board to see which one'll make me hate myself a little less when I stand before judgement.

If I'm square with myself, it's almost like the burglar giving back the watch when he's already in cuffs; that the only true reason I ended up figuring was that I had nowhere else to go.

And she's going to be home any minute. I can almost feel her presence entering the building downstairs.

I'm sitting at the kitchen table, upright, typing this as if talking to my one and only friend. I can't move any other muscle; I think I've hit a new zone of nervousness where all twitching stops and everything just freezes. All sensations, all feeling, my *Interface* receiving nothing to process. Nothing but all of my thoughts spelled out on this screen, each new piece of my angst popping up one word after the next.

I think I'm going to need a drink.

Shit, fresh out. Not even box wine I use for cooking. In my panic, I managed to forget to pick up what would amount to my only lifeline during times like this.

I think I'm going to need a smoke.

Fresh out of that too.

For once in my life, I'm going to have to rely on my sober mind to get me through. It's been a while, don't know if he's still there or if it's just adrenaline dressed up as cohesive thought.

Breathe in, breathe out.

And there's the rattle of the knob. I'm not even going to start a new rant; I'm just going to stop here and continue later, hopefully with good news.

.   .   .

It never made sense to me how to explain something when it's consumed me whole in such a way that I couldn't understand it looking in from out.

Like I want to talk about how it all ended

as badly as I want to talk about where it all started as badly as I want to talk about where it went, every piece of the last hour weighing my head down like bricks.

"Where does it hurt?" you'd ask. "Everywhere," I'd respond.

So maybe I'll start at the beginning. I'll start where there was hope, 'cause there's always hope at the beginning.

And in the beginning, she'd come home from her run, and from the red that painted her shriveled face, she'd been running for a while.

I didn't go right in, choosing to drag it out a little longer, looking to set the stage of discourse with some protective padding.

"Shit, it's crazy hot out. Isn't it, like, November?" she asked.

"It can be hot in November," I replied without looking up, pretending to be hard at work when all that was on my screen was my desktop wallpaper. "It's only sixty degrees, right?"

"In November?"

"Sure, why not?"

"'Cause it's, like, almost winter...you know what, whatever," she replied, stripping

< 382 >

while making her way to the shower. "It's hot enough to make me disgusting. Be right out, babe."

Babe, she called me babe. I almost couldn't remember the last time she's called me anything endearing, not since the beginning of this year. And honestly, I was almost tempted into letting this banter continue, squeezing every ounce of it as if to forget about what was to come, cherishing the mindless little things you and your partner can talk about for hours on end when everything is all and well. Maybe, I wondered, we could let it go on long enough to where she'd forget the conversation we had this morning. On second thought, what else could be fueling this sudden shift in personality from this morning until now?

"So, did you work out the money issue?"

I looked up. She'd barely gotten dressed, her upper body wrapped in a towel and her hair still dripping wet.

"I…" I could only shrug with my mouth hanging open in a half smile, tongue flapping while I could only shake my head. I guess I might've overestimated the size of my testicles coming into this, overestimated my capabilities to come clean when the mass of everything that was to come dangled right above my head like fate holding me at gunpoint.

"Jay?" she asked, her newfound demeanor disappearing by the second, "you said you'd work the books."

"Yeah," I managed to get out, "yeah, I did say that."

"So can I schedule an appointment now?"

Again, all I could respond with was that gaping mouth, like I was in a vegetated state.

"Jay? I asked you to..."

"I know, Judy, I know. We don't have enough."

"What?" She started before taking a deep breath. "What do you mean we don't have enough? How much are we off by?"

"About thirty grand."

She sat down, water from her hair dripping onto the table.

"Thirty grand," she repeated to herself.

"Yeah, we're short thirty thousand dollars. The surgery is seventy thousand, and I've got around thirty thousand from a good year of business and ten from January."

"We started this year off with at least forty thousand saved up, Jay," she said quietly. "Forty thousand between us."

< 384 >

I nodded.

"Where did that thirty thousand go?"

"Judy, babe," I said, getting up and moving to the seat closer to her. "I don't expect you to react like an adult to what I'm about to say, and I wouldn't blame ya. But can you at least try?"

"What the fuck? What are you getting at?"

"Remember the operation Amber was talking about?"

"Yeah," she replied with a shrug, "yeah, the one about having some kind of operation so you could see things."

"See, feel, touch, smell, taste, all of them," I replied. "So that in her reality, there's a panoramic window overlooking the city in her second-story apartment bedroom in place of the only real window that faces a brick wall."

"Right." Her brows had started to scrunch. "That one. What about it?"

"I had it done."

Shoot, I didn't even catch myself before it rolled off the tongue, like the words had been sitting there all this time, all fucking year, waiting in anticipation.

I'm not sure how she reacted, 'cause at that moment I couldn't look her in the face. My head felt heavy, and my back had locked into a hunch. My neck strained. It felt like my head could fall off at any moment, and honest to God, I almost wished it had happened.

I didn't hear her move. Not even a shuffle of her legs or her arms. All I could hear were her deep breaths in and out.

"When?" she asked.

"April," I responded. "After you left for your parents' place."

She stared straight ahead. Her eyes weren't blinking. Her nose didn't twitch. I almost wondered if there was some issue with my *Interface*, if time had somehow stopped and this was all some sci-fi revelation that everything was some kind of simulation.

God. If only.

"*After* I left for my parents' house," she muttered.

"Yeah."

She didn't ask what I got it done for; she appeared a step past that. Her eyes were squeezed shut, tightly, and her head just kept bobbing down and up as if listening and trying to absorb everything I wasn't saying.

"And what'd you get the operation for?" she asked after an eternity.

< 386 >

"Remember what Amber was joking about?" I said.

"Wasn't a joke, was it?" she asked.

"No. I mean, she was. But poetically? No." I replied.

"And you aren't either. Are you?"

"No. No I'm not. I've got the receipt to prove it." I turned my app on and handed her my phone. "It's all in there."

She took it and flipped through the screen, tapping and swiping, swiping harder each time, like any moment she was going to trash my phone against the wall. Instead, she closed it, and set it down gently.

"So," she started before taking a deep breath. Her voice so thin, it was practically a dog whistle. "My face. What do you see."

"You, Judy," I responded. "I see you."

"No fucking shit," she hissed. "*What* do you see, Jay?"

"I see your beautiful face," I stammered.

"My cheeks?"

"Rosy, red, like a peach."

"My eyes?"

"Like fucking marbles."

"My lips?"

"Perfect," I had to compose myself. "Perfect, babe, like I wanna kiss them now."

She was nodding faster, drowning out my crap.

"And, my scar tissues. You don't..."

"No. No I don't. I don't see any of it."

I looked away.

"I don't *feel* it either. To me, it's..."

"It's perfect," she finished. "Because you..."

"Because I had the operation done to alter your face. The thing, well, it took an image of what I wanted to see."

"Oh my God Jay, oh my God, do you think I give a shit how it was done?"

"Well, babe, I thought I'd be open."

She was trying really hard to keep it together, her grip on her right wrist was so tight it was turning red.

"You're being serious." She started to say before getting up.

"No, this is some sick joke," she kept repeating, shaking her head into her palm, talking under her breath. "This isn't you, Jay. Not you. You wouldn't do this, not to me. You wouldn't."

I didn't say anything, just kept rubbing my forehead like I was trying to tear it off.

< 388 >

"Jay. Look at me. Look at me!"

I looked up.

"Can you...Can you *really* not see how fucked up this is?" She was pointing to her face while grabbing and pulling her cheek, her hair, her lips. "You're not seeing *any* of this?"

I shook my head. She collapsed back into her seat.

"Oh my God. Since April! This has been going on since April. This whole time."

She made this face, like she was watching a dog eat its own shit.

"*You* kept telling me how beautiful I was. You kept telling me how all of *this* didn't *matter*! You *fucked* me, over and over and over, kissing me, licking my *neck*. You kept making me feel like *I* was the one overthinking everything, like *I* was the one crazy for being self-conscious about how I looked."

Then she was glaring at me with those eyes, and let me tell ya, I'll never forget those eyes. It was the kind of glare you make at the man who murdered your child, that con man who swindled you of your savings, the husband who'd been fucking your best friend for a year. It was a glare full of hate, pointed, targeted, eyes full and red, and honest to God, even after having lived a life in New York, I've never seen something so terrifying.

"*You* are so sick."

"Hold up, babe, hold up," I replied real fast, reaching over to touch her wrist.

"Don't you touch me!"

"Okay, okay, sorry, I'm not touching ya," I stammered. "Look, babe, Judy. I'm sorry. I'm really fucking sorry for not telling you earlier or coming to you."

"Coming to me? Telling me earlier?" she interrupted with mocking laughter. "*That's* what would've made this all better? Like all you needed was my permission?"

She grabbed my hand and slapped it against her cheek. "God damnit!" she shrieked before throwing it off.

"Okay, let's just calm down," I tried to say.

"I couldn't smile. I still can't fucking smile," she said between breaths, broken down sobbing by this point. "I couldn't move a god-damn muscle in my face. Out of the hospital, I couldn't eat, couldn't sleep on my side, couldn't meet another human being, couldn't work. It's been almost a year and I still can't stare at myself in a fucking mirror! I was going to live the rest of my life like this."

"And you, this is the only thing you could think of. You." she said, the words going through her teeth like steam out of a pressure cooker. "You just needed something to *fuck* again!"

"Okay, Judy, that's crossing the line!" I snapped back. "*I* was willing to take a flamethrower to my *face*! I would've done it too if it weren't for my chance encounter with… with that random guy at the bar! I was the one trying *everything* to make it work! I was *trying* to take care of you, be *there* for you, *cook* for you!"

"Wow, it's like you take inventory of every nice thing you've ever done for me."

"I *never* take inventory. I'm just trying to make a point! How could you have thought that I was being selfish, huh? What did I do after your operation, *before this* surgery, up until you fucking left me, what did I do that was selfish huh? What? How did I fuck up? Because I couldn't get my dick hard? Sorry, but if I had a face just *half* as bad as yours, you wouldn't have fucked me either!"

"Oh go fuck yourself!"

"Well, sweetie, kindly, I couldn't even do that. Oh shit, no, I'm kidding, babe listen!"

< 391 >

I grabbed her wrist as she was getting up to leave.

"Babe, no, look, sit down. I'm sorry."

She shook free and bolted to our room. I followed right behind.

"Judy, what are you doing? Will you listen? Are we adults or children? Come on!"

She grabbed her suitcase out of the closet. She started throwing her clothes, her purses, her shoes, her entire half of the closet onto the bed. And I just stood there, helpless, watching as it all started happening again like some time loop we couldn't escape.

"Oh, wonderful," I said, "you just go ahead and do that. Easy. No need to think or talk things through. You could just walk your ass right back to momma."

Jewelry from her table, her computer, her books, her facemask.

"You know, I could've left you," I started. "I could've. It would've been that easy. Most guys I know would've done it. Heck, the entire crew at Southie's told me they would've done it!"

"Good to know," she muttered while rolling up her purple leggings. "I'll make sure to avoid you and every one of those sad fucks with your DNA."

< 392 >

"But that's my point, babe, I *didn't*," I was almost begging. "I didn't and I'm still here. I'm still here, trying to make it all work. It's what I've been doing this whole fucking year. Hell, it's what I was doing when I had that operation!"

She stopped and looked up. "You thought *that* was making our marriage work?"

"Yes!" I couldn't hold it in. "I did. What do you want me to say, babe? Huh? What did you want me to do? You were the one lying on the ground half-naked drooling outta your mouth with a bottle of vodka, bitching at me for not being able to get it on with you."

"Sex?" She was laughing. "So that's what you thought it was all about? Sex?"

She put her clothes down and came closer. "You couldn't even look at your own wife in the *face*."

"I tried, Judy! I tried! And I felt like shit, but what could I do? Change the way my brain functions? Look at something and think it's attractive by sheer force of will? I know it sounds harsh, babe, but it's the truth! I wasn't attracted to your face! There! I said it!"

"Thank you." She went back to packing.

"But it doesn't mean I didn't love you!" I

< 393 >

quickly added. "Simple attraction isn't love! Looking at you in the face isn't love! Taking care of you *is* love! Sticking it out with you through your agony is love! *Loyalty* is love!"

"Oh, so you think you were loyal?"

"Yeah, Judy, I thought I was being pretty loyal."

"To *whom*, Jay?" she raised her hands to her face. "To whom were you loyal? *This*?"

"What are you talking about?"

She grabbed a chunk of her cheeks and pulled. "*This* or that monster you *don't* want to see? Who were you loyal to, Jay? Which woman?"

"Hold up," I backed up. "Are you seriously insinuating that I was cheating on you some-how? Are you listening to yourself?"

"Yeah! I am! I'm listening to every god-damn word coming out of my mouth, and they sound just the way I wanted them to! Who were you loyal to, Jay? Who were you fucking all this time?"

"Judy, you're fucking insane! Who was I fucking all this time? *You* or you?"

"I'm the one who's insane," she laughed, "and you're the one who's calling me two dif-ferent people. Me or me, you fucking idiot.

*I* had half of my face blown off, Jay! I can barely see out of my right eye because the flaps stitched over squeeze it shut. I've only got half a head of hair. My lips sag because of the extra skin! *This* is who I am. So who the hell have you been fantasizing I was this whole time? Who the hell have you been with?"

One last time, the tears started falling. Once again, her voice started to crack.

"*Me*, or this twisted, idolized version of your perfect woman?"

I shook my head. "Wow, you're overthinking this to the point of delusion."

"Oh my God," she whispered as she continued packing. "And all you thought I wanted was a dick in my vagina. I mean, who did I marry?"

"You know," I had enough by this point. "Go. Get out of here. Go find that righteous human being who could somehow magically see past what's right in front of them. And let me tell ya something. If you're going back to your mother's place, tell her everything. Tell her about the operation, about what a sick asshole I am. Then watch if she takes out her phone and deletes something. Yeah, that's right. She's a customer too. Super-imposed your ex-boyfriend's face over mine. Michael, right? Black hair, thin jaw line, pretty face, Disney boy band?"

She paused and stared ahead before taking a breath to continue, as if she felt a pang of interest before remembering that she was pissed off.

"Wake up babe. *Everyone's* doing it. And look at me, am I pissed?"

She looked up.

"Do you think I gave a shit when it all made sense to me? Hell, I can actually have a decent relationship with your mother now. We had drinks, I took her to her hotel room, I might even be able to come over for coffee or brunch now! So who the fuck cares who she's *really* looking at?"

For a while, she didn't respond. Instead, she shut her suitcase, and zipped up her book-bag. Half of her shit still lay scattered over the bed, but she didn't look back as she darted to the front door.

"Babe," I said, trying to throw anything out there to slow her down. "Judy, stop, come on! What, you're just not gonna address that?"

She paused at the door, took a deep breath, wiped off her tears, and looked back one last time.

"That's because my mother loathes you. But she can look at me straight in the face with a smile. And you know what? Really, that's all I wanted from you."

*   *   *

No, I didn't follow her out.

I just sat back down in my chair at the dinner table. I sat back down and covered my face with my hands, rubbing it hard to where it hurt, trying to induce enough physical pain to divert from the torture of sitting still and letting her go.

Letting her go. I wasn't sure if I was doing it out of hopelessness or anger. And if it were anger, I didn't know if it was directed at her or myself. In a cruel, fucked up way, it almost felt like I was holding myself back as she slammed that door, refusing any pain killers, letting myself feel the emptiness writhe and the agony of inaction become the agony of guilt.

Some part of me was telling me I deserved this. Some part of me was telling me I should let her go for good and die alone for what I did.

Was this something they did to me?

A rewiring of my conscience? Some lesson in ethics they're trying to put me through?

Or was it all me, some part of me, a piece of me, who'd been sitting in the back of my head this whole time, seething with disapproval? A feeling I've managed to block out as I bathed in this reality I needed so desperately with every kiss to her cheek to every moment I caught her gaze to every time I shoved my dick into her like I was digging for oil.

When I couldn't stare her in the eyes when she took off her mask for the first time, when I couldn't keep it up before my operation and when I was able to after, every moment we've been together since that accident that seemed like an eternity ago, that little voice in my head wondering quietly in the background.

*Can I do better than this?*

Maybe that little guy finally grew a pair to be loud enough so I could hear.

Or maybe I was too tired to fight anymore, knowing that she left with the kind of fury that only time could quell. That there was still some hope that if I just let her go, she'd chill out and find her way back so we could talk with cooler heads.

Maybe then she'll understand my position better.

And maybe by then, I could understand

what on God's green earth she was talking about towards the end of that spat.

It's been a day now. I'm sitting once again, alone.

I've managed to secure a fifth of vodka that I'm sipping out of the bottle. I get the stigma, but the bottle tells me a lot more about how the world works than any friend or therapist. Always has and always will. It'll have to be my company until Judy returns, this or my conscience, and I'd rather hang myself from the ceiling fan than spend a month with that ass.

I'll try not to think about it anymore; put it all away in that little box that's about to burst open with all the shit I've stored in it.

I'll just go to work, count the money we're making, think about the next day, and swallow chemicals to deal with all of these inconvenient, unpleasant feelings that keep surfacing until Judy comes back.

Before I do, however, I'm going to send her a quick email, 'cause God knows she's probably blocked me by now.

I'm going to send her every piece of correspondence I've had with Josh so that she'd understand the whole truth, call it a little light reading. Everything she'd want to know about why I did what I did, all in there.

I'm not hopeful, but maybe from the earlier emails, she'll at least see where I'm coming from.

Then again, maybe I'd rather her not.

< 400 >

## JANUARY 15, 2026

Things have changed a bit in the short amount of time since that spat.

You're probably wondering if she ever came back. If somehow she came to her senses and turned that car around, if we'd finally made peace with what I did.

I imagined it myself. It comes to me whenever I have a moment alone. Us in the café downstairs, heads cooled, talking about what she meant or what I meant and how I'm a bastard for what I did and how sorry I am and how I'll go to therapy over it or something before capping it off into what we'd gone

< 401 >

through this last year, and most importantly, where we'd go from here.

The worst part is knowing that had I just waited a year more, there'd been hope. If I just knew everything this fucking company was cooking up in its books, none of this would've happened. There was an ending to all of this, a happy one. It was so fucking close, just a year more and we would've had enough for that face transplant, and man, I would've gotten, at last, normalcy, that goddamn normalcy.

But I guess it wasn't meant to be.

It was evening, ten p.m., just a few days after our fight.

I received a text from building security. Someone was downstairs looking for me.

When I got downstairs, I saw that it was two police officers, both with their hands clasped over their wrists in front of them.

One of em, the younger one, couldn't help but look down or to the side, trying real hard to not look into my eyes.

It must've been his first time.

.  .  .

She wasn't wearing anything but a white sheet that covered her from her shoulders to her legs.

Her face was pale from the loss of blood, and her eyes were shut as if she was having a bad dream.

Her skin was still smooth. The moisture hadn't left since it all happened just a couple of hours earlier. Her hair was a mess, like she hadn't shampooed for a year.

And here's the weird part. Her cheeks, her lashes, her perfectly rounded nose, her paint stroke eyebrows, those perfect fucking lips, every part of her face, was gone. Gone and replaced with what I was always meant to see, the agonizing face of a woman scorched in hell and lived to suffer it. Except right then, she looked a little more at peace.

I guess the *Interface* stops working when the subject is deceased.

And I don't know if it was the room or not, but I felt a cold that I've never felt before, like my heart had stopped pumping blood or something. If you asked me how I felt at the time, all I could've told you was nothing; like my mind couldn't handle any more and ordered all functions, save the life-sustaining ones, to stop.

All I could do was move on impulse, answer questions without knowing what was

< 403 >

coming out of my mouth, and stare ahead into the void, half-conscious of my surroundings.

The coroner stood to the side, waiting for me to finish, like I was examining some art exhibit and not the remains of the one thing I had in my life worth living for. Actually, that isn't fair to him. I might've been there a full hour, alternating between standing up and sitting on a chair they pulled up, and he didn't say a thing the whole time.

And it'd taken me the full hour to finally ask.

"What happened?"

"Well, the police reports suggest."

"Yeah, I know," I interrupted, "I've gotten the spiel from the cops. Car accident, running at full speed into the trees or something."

He nodded, "well, that's the full extent of what I know."

He pulled out his tablet PC.

"The toxicology reports showed her BAC at .18. If that'll give you any more answers."

Probably a bottle of vodka, naked, and now lifeless.

"It doesn't," I answered.

"Well," he replied while closing out his tablet, "whatever happened, it happened. Don't know what to tell ya. I guess I can only pray you find your answers."

"No, Doc, please," I honestly didn't know where I was getting at either, "I just need to understand what happened."

"Son, I told you, I don't know."

"Well if you don't know the fucking answers then what are you doing here?"

I caught myself a bit too late. "Sorry, Doc."

He didn't seem at all fazed. "Well, I've got to put her back. Still have another showing to do in half an hour. You, uh, can come back tomorrow or anytime next week if you like."

I just shook my head. An hour and a half north, I didn't know if I could do another drive all the way out here just to see Judy like this. Didn't know if I could make the drive back with this image of her in my head either, whether or not everything would hit while I'm at the wheel and I'd end up on a metal cart next to her.

And you know what? Even now, that doesn't sound too bad.

And yeah, maybe it's melodramatic, but even as I express this, I haven't been able to cry or yell or fall to the ground the way I

< 405 >

thought I would. This whole time I haven't been able to feel. Not even the anxiety of when it hits, when everything falls into place in my mind and reveals it's face from hell, when I wake up from the motions and find myself all alone somewhere I've never been, when I'll either surrender or fight or run to no avail.

And shit, it's been a whole week.

"Well, son," he said, "I'm sorry to put you on the spot, given what you're going through right now."

"No, I'm good," I said. "I'm good to go."

.    .    .

There wasn't much on the police report.

Witnesses saw her flying down the highway at almost double the speed limit of fifty-five, threading between cars, high beams on, honking, swerving. At some point, she flew off the road and into the trees.

She was found ten feet in front of the crash site where her car lay turned on its side, its nose inverted into the front two seats, bits of flames scattered along what was left of the frame.

She was labeled unresponsive by the time the first responder arrived and deceased by the time the paramedics got her to the emergency department.

Her toxicology report had her blood alcohol level at .18.

Her phone was on.

It was around midnight.

That was it.

It's too bad. I felt like a person's final moments deserved a little more color than a few badly written sentences.

"It's just protocol, friend," said the officer as I sat there at his desk, skimming through the document over and over, trying to lick up every little detail I might've missed.

I asked if her parents were informed, to which he shook his head.

"They were able to track you down from what was recorded in the system. Luckily, it looks like she landed in a hospital in the same network as the last one she was in a year back."

"Yeah," I replied, head still buried in the paperwork, "lucky her."

"Oh, I didn't mean—"

"Nah, don't worry about it," I said. "I doubt she'd mind now."

He did this half-smile, half-chuckle, as if

< 407 >

unsure if it were rude or supportive to laugh at that.

"Well, lastly, we've got some of her things in the back, don't know if you wanna bring it home with you or what. Either way, I've got someone bringing it out now."

A moment later, a lady officer came out with a plastic bag and dumped its contents on the desk.

"That's it?" I asked.

Her cell phone, her wallet, some random sheets of paper, a jumper cable, some wires, a GPS.

"That's everything," said the lady cop.

"What was she wearing?" I asked.

"All thrown out," she responded. "It was soaked."

"Uh, we *don't* need to go there." The officer sitting across from me gave her a nudge to leave.

"Blood?" I finished after she was gone. "That's fine. You can tell me it was soaked in blood. I mean, she's dead, isn't she? This thing here says she went through the windshield with her car hitting a tree at a hundred miles an hour. She's probably gonna be soaked in blood. Her face was probably ripped to shreds too."

"Well, you saw her, didn't you?" he asked.

"I did," I said, nodding. "I saw her. She looked none of that."

"I see," he continued, handing me some brochures. "I guess we all have our ways of dealing with loss. Not my place to question. But here, take these. Some support groups and numbers you can call, just in case you're open to some other voices to help you through."

"Thanks," I said, taking 'em and shoving them in my pockets so I could find 'em easier to throw away later. "Is that it?"

"That's it."

"Case shut?"

He shrugged. "It was a car accident. She was heavily intoxicated, there was no evidence of foul play. We get about a dozen of these a month."

"Where she was coming from? Where she was headed to? Where was the rest of her shit?"

He just shook his head. "We can only tell you she was driving south. That and what happened."

He looked like he wanted to shake my hand, likely a gentle hint that I was overstaying his sympathy.

I didn't give a shit. I just kept my ass on that seat, sorting through Judy's stuff, toying with her phone, her wallet, not paying attention to what he might've said afterwards or who he was calling to escort me out.

Twenty bucks and a driver's license.

A screen at 10% battery asking for a passcode I didn't know.

Useless.

.　.　.

I've lost people before.

I lost my mother and father right after I got married, both in one month. I think I dealt with it well. Nobody at work knew, kept the business running like a well-oiled machine. Judy could barely tell the difference, took her on our honeymoon to the keys that very fall, and we had great booze and great sex for five days straight. Don't remember how I got through with it, if I was feeling the way I am now, feeling the same numbness, the same state of suspended animation, like everything around me was nothing but a stage. Maybe I was, and the thought of life with my new wife kept it just inches underneath the surface at all times until it disappeared.

Now there's nobody.

I wonder if all the booze I drank over the years had dried me out so much, I didn't have anything left in my aqueducts for moments like this.

I wonder if, rather than breaking down in grief like a normal human being would, I'll spend the rest of my life living in a shell of my soul.

I wonder if my mind isn't even going to try to heal, its only source of happiness gone forever. No need to waste any energy on grief.

Most importantly, I wonder if this is some punishment from God or the universe or whatever higher power there might be for what I did.

Yeah, maybe this is my fault, but I swear, I could have played it out a million times in my head and not once would it have ended up like this. Not once. Relationships are hard, couples fight, but how many of them end up dead in a drunken road rage?

Or was it just a drunken road rage?

Okay, I'm not even going to entertain that,

not here, not now. She overreacted. She's an adult capable of making her own decisions. We screw up, we learn to deal, we seek help, we talk things out. We don't get into a car piss drunk and put people's lives in danger. She made that choice, not me! I wanted to work things out. I tried to keep her from leaving. I was explaining myself, she was the one who didn't want to listen!

We were just a year away from having enough money to put all of this behind us. She's the one who wouldn't fucking reason with me about any of this! How the hell is this my fault?

I asked her to talk about it like an adult. I tried to reason.

I spent all year being the perfect husband, cleaning after her, cooking for her, providing her space, time, whatever she needed so that we could move on, and I don't give a fuck *what* she said, I didn't even so much as *look* at another woman! I tell ya, this woman is something; she's got issues. I didn't deserve this, nobody deserves this. What the hell was wrong with that *bitch*!

Putting the blame on me for *her* mess; that's all our marriage ever was!

Okay, I need a drink.

That's better.

You know what, this isn't my fault. I'm not going to take it from her, let her get to me beyond the grave, make my life a living hell in the form of being the scapegoat to her family circus of missed expectations. Yeah, you know the drill. Take a wild guess who her parents are gonna pin this on. Hell, I'd be surprised if they didn't press some bullshit murder charge on me just to see me in handcuffs!

But it wouldn't go anywhere, 'cause I'm not at fault.

Not my fault.

Not my fault.

Not my fault.

Maybe if I repeat it over and over, it'll become truth.

Maybe if that becomes truth, it'll be something I can hang onto.

Hello Jay

My deepest condolences for your loss.

I suppose the only way forward from here is to address your concern in the last portion of your last email.

You now have a choice. You may either leave the hardware on or get it removed.

If you do choose to remove, there is a fee of $1000 unless if you can prove there was a valid defect with your product that was causing you physical harm. If you do believe your reason to be valid, there is a form that you can fill out that would begin the petitioning process, which would take seven business days to review. This can be coordinated through the app I can send you the directions should you choose to go down this path. Otherwise, if you only choose to remove, you just need to let me know and I can set up an appointment for you.

Whatever you choose, however, do give

< 414 >

yourself some time before jumping into anything right now.

It was a pleasure working with you, and, again, my deepest condolences for your loss and all the best wishes for you in finding yourself through this tragedy.

Please reach back out to me when you do make a decision.

Take care, Jay.

PS: I did check and confirmed that your *Interface* has not yet been turned off.

Josh Rikkard
Relationship Manager
*Wonderlenz* Technologies Inc.

Judy just came home.

I'm gonna let that linger for a bit.

Judy just came home.

I got back from the liquor store, and she was on the couch.

Passed out. TV turned on. Random things of blankets and pillows and shit all over the floor.

Same leggings, same athletic T, same face—unscarred, perfect.

What the actual fuck. What the fuck. God, it helps to say that, so I'm going to do it a few more times. What the fuck. What the fuck. What the actual fuck.

< 416 >

'Cause I swear to God, didn't I just see her lying on a stretcher underneath a white sheet?

I know what you're wondering. You're wondering if I'm hallucinating or if it's all the stress or some shit like that, and yeah, I figured it was too.

I had to run out and drink out of the bottle of bourbon from my book bag. Downed it like cold water. Had to take a few chugs before I could go back.

She was still there.

Had to sit in the hallway for a minute, letting the alcohol fill up where testosterone wasn't. Tried again.

Still there, almost as crystal clear as everything else.

Okay, so I dropped everything and continued to her.

She woke up.

"Jay?" she said.

Next to the couch was her bookbag and suitcase that she'd left with, both unzipped.

"Jay? Everything alright?" she paused mid-stretch. "What, is there something on me?"

"You're," I started. "You're," I continued. "You're, you're, you're," I gulped, stammered, sighed.

"I'm...?"

Here's what's crazy. I could feel her as I got closer. Four of my five senses. One by one, picking up every bit and piece. That blend of lemon and cinnamon and strawberry breeze shampoo, the warmth coming out of her body, her arm so smooth and bony, light breathing.

There was that face, those big fucking eyes all wide and circular. Those pupils, deep and dark. Those paint stroke brows, scrunched towards that little spot where they meet the nose. Those rosy cheeks, those pink spongey lips, that black hair so straight it glitters even in the dark.

Judy.

This was Judy.

"Okay, Jay, stop. You're seriously freaking me out," she pulled her arm back and began scooting away. "What the hell are you doing?"

I didn't respond. Ignoring my senses, my intuition was telling me to keep quiet.

I got up and went to her suitcase. There was noticeable weight to it, and I could feel the worn rubber handle pressing against my palm. I put it down on my foot and felt the pressure on my toes.

Like a maniac, ignoring all the pleading

and questioning coming from her as she sat up and watched. I started doing the same for her bookbag, the blankets, the remote, flipping the television on and off.

"Jay, babe, stop. Jay, c'mon, talk to me. Look at me. Jay!"

When I had nothing else to fuck with, my intuition lost its footing, and I blurted out my first words of the night under my breath.

"What the fuck are you?"

"What do you mean *what* the fuck am I?" She put her hand on my arm. "Jay, I'm your.. Jay, I'm *back*!"

"You're back," I managed to say, "how the hell are you back?"

"*Time*, Jay. I had time and space to think." She put her other hand on my back. I felt that tingling sensation I always get when she touches me there.

"I was hurt, okay? What you did, the way you covered it up, the way you lied to me all this time, it was," she paused to exhale. "Hard. I needed someplace quiet and alone, so I booked a hotel and just stayed there to think and collect myself. It was then I saw your email."

"At first I couldn't make it through the first few paragraphs but as the anger disappeared it got easier and easier. Jay, look, I'm sorry for expecting so much out of you. What you did was seriously messed up, but I realize, and I get that, none of this was any easier for you, and you stayed with me, and I've been such an ass."

She paused. The tears were coming down again.

"Just a year," she said. "Just a year and we'll have enough for that face transplant. That's fine. That's fine. Just promise me a year and we can put this all behind us."

Shit, okay, I admit it, at that moment, I almost nodded. I almost put my arms back around her, told her that it was all okay, that we'd have enough, that it'd only be a year, that none of it mattered and that we were going to make it.

I almost brought her back to the room for some of the craziest make-up sex that'd eclipse anything you'd find on the internet.

Normalcy, that sick siren. Always singing, always luring me in, always tempting me, and if I hadn't just gotten back from seeing her corpse, the police report, the remnants of her things, I might've walked into that light.

But it was all still fresh. The images from the coroner's space replacing anything I wanted

< 420 >

to see. Judy, pale, sapped of all the blood in her veins. Judy, standing and embracing me in my living room. Judy dead, Judy alive.

"Jay?" she kept asking. "Yo! What the fuck is up with you? Did you listen to anything I just said?"

Instead of responding, I just sprinted to the elevator, pushing, stabbing the lobby button, stumbling half-drunk down the cold city streets, not a clue as to where I was going, hoping the rest of my senses would catch up to me in time before I do something stupid.

.　　.　　.

So here I am now, in some wine bar that serves merlot that costs a day's salary but tastes like it came out of a box.

And I'm looking at the last string of texts I've ever gotten from Judy, eyes fixated on the second to last thing she wrote.

*Just letting you know I'm getting out of here in five days. Have a good day.*

Have a good fucking day.

Guess I should've noticed she never specified coming home.

Jay, I opened your message as soon as it came in and I'd immediately sent out a request to our technical team to look into it.

Thankfully, they got back to me the next day, and although it pains me to say this, we were able to confirm that the Judy in your room was your alteration; her face, her body, her entire self.

Her entire body is the reality projected to your sensory system, not only her face as you believed all along. We believed this as well, but mainly based on our conversations with you regarding your requirements and through our discourse on the operation thereafter.

From where I stand, here's what might have happened.

When you came in for your pre-operation interview, which if you can recall, was your second visit, you were tasked with communicating to the system the part of your reality that you wanted changed and to what you want it changed to.

Here is what you explained verbatim, and of course, all of this was done with your understanding that we were able to access this information due to the consent you had provided some time back.

"I want to *perceive* my wife the way she was before the accident."

As you know, during the interview, for each time you answered, the system was actively scanning your thoughts so to interpret what your requirements were, including what you needed to alter, for what purpose, and for what objective.

In summary, it looked to figure out what your *optimal reality* would be.

Based on what you stated, as well as your screening and your introductory email to us, we had assumed you only wanted Judy's face augmented. But based on how the system interpreted all three, however, it must've come out as something else.

You wanted a reality where you could continue

< 423 >

living with Judy the way you were before the accident. This was the system's interpretation, and based on this, it created your existing algorithm for processing your surroundings to honor it. In other words, it rebuilt your *optimal reality* to accommodate a world where you can live with your preferred conception of your wife.

We aren't certain *how* it built your new reality, including what objects it made available for you to perceive in how many ways and what objects it suppressed, as there isn't any way we can actually interpret the algorithm in charge of intaking and processing your sensory data (the system that produces and alters this algorithm is automated as per NBISS privacy requirements and your algorithm updates to adapt to new situations). Therefore, we cannot ascertain what was objectively real and what wasn't.

Knowing that Judy is deceased, however, we can immediately deactivate your connection to your *Interface*, should that be what you would want us to do. From there, I can schedule you a removal of your hardware and look to getting the fee waived as it is clear your system had produced something you didn't intend on being privy to.

It sounds bad, but we can most likely label this a system issue in your favor because had your *Interface* been working properly, you wouldn't have been able to perceive anything related to Judy's passing.

Let me know what you would like to do.

Josh Rikkard
Relationship Manager
*Wonderlenz* Technologies Inc.

< 425 >

## JANUARY 25, 2026

Just got home. Looks like Judy is gone.

So are her suitcases, her blankets, her leggings, all traces.

Gone.

The room is quiet. Like a different degree
of it, knowing that she's out of my life forever.

Very quiet, too fucking quiet. The kind of
quiet that has a force to it, like it slowly pulls
away at all of your hopes, your dreams, your
motivation for life.

Life.

Honest to God, I was ready to pick up and
begin rebuilding what little I could make of it
to be. Drown myself in my business, continue

< 426 >

my pseudo-therapy with someone else, quit drinking after drinking to the brink of death thinking about Judy.

In short, I was ready to begin mourning.

Then I saw it. Right there on the carpet, in front of the couch.

A stain. Hundred percent sure a stain of red wine.

And now I can't help but wonder.

They disabled my *Interface*.

But how can I know for certain?

< 427 >

I'm in a small reading room inside a behavioral health facility.

No, not a psych ward. Apparently those went out of favor decades ago. It's just a small oceanside facility in Delaware for crazy people like me to check in and check out as I see fit; all covered under insurance too.

Been here for almost three months too, and I think I'm starting to make progress. Lots of meditation, psychotherapy, coaching, and time spent alone without access to anything that I could use to hurt myself.

My room is right next to the ocean as well. They moved me here after they realized

< 428 >

the salty breeze helps calm me whenever I am going through episodes, and so for most of the day, I have my windows open.

I guess even if I don't believe something is real, if it brings me enough peace, somehow I stop caring as much.

And this, I guess, makes for a good segway to why I'm here.

I'm still unable to believe that my *Interface* is out, even after having it surgically removed. I still don't know if my reality is true, still don't trust my mind to be able to tell the difference. Still not certain if the surgery was real or not.

Half a year. Half a year I spent deceived by my own senses. No gatekeeper, no parser of what is real or isn't real. How my mind could've invented an entire reality around a person who wasn't there for an entire year and how I couldn't have been able to tell, I don't think I will ever get over.

Can't get over if this bed isn't still my room, or if I've ever lived in a room in NYC to begin with, or...

Okay, I need to stop.

Breathe in the ocean air, relax, suppress these thoughts. Let myself continue to be led by this lie that is my conception of reality.

Wait, not a lie. Not a lie. Not a lie.

Something happened just now that gave me this unexplainable feeling. Gave me this feeling that I didn't want some shrink to dissect, ruining it with objectivity or some medical prognosis. I just wanted to tell someone without that someone telling me anything about it so that the feeling could linger.

This morning, I got my phone back. Only for a while, as I have to turn it back in at the end of the day.

Judy's mother had texted me this really long message two months back.

First, she had let me know that she knew what I did. Of course, completely tone deaf to her own hypocrisy, she just went on and on about what a shit I am, nothing worth reading so I just skimmed it through.

I did, however, catch the part where they found where Judy was living the whole year after she left her parents' home in Long Island. Apparently, she'd put herself up at their family home in the Catskills. Guess she figured her parents were just holding onto it as an investment property. Place must've been a fucking pigsty when they opened it.

But again, that's not what got me.

< 430 >

No, it was a photo she left at the end from Judy's funeral, open casket, her half-burnt face on full display.

A full close up of Judy's face, lying in wake, all because of me. Her mother's final act of spite.

So here was her face, half of it a lump of skin squeezing her right eye shut, a line for where her lips would've been, a bulge for where her jawline would've been, single strands of hair sticking out of her scalp.

And I expanded it, zoomed in, and kissed the screen.

And suddenly it felt real.

The circle at the center of the spiral.

Bare and alone.

< 431 >

Made in the USA
Monee, IL
25 July 2022